CINDY PATTERSON

Chasing PARADISE

A PARADISE NOVEL

Springbrook Press

In Loving Memory

Irene Turco
September 12, 1925–August 4, 2014

You never had the chance to read my work
but you are always in my heart as I write each story.

❧   I   ❧

R achel Adams shoved the last suitcase into the trunk knowing things would never be the same. Palm leaves rustled against the wind as if waving goodbye. The familiar sound had never been important.

Until today.

There would be no palm trees where they were headed. Paradise, Pennsylvania, over a thousand miles away. Right in the middle of Amish Country. Population 1,269. She disguised her anger with a wounded laugh. Something she had mastered in the last year.

Briny air swept through the window and across her face. She'd expected today to be hard, but the heavy feeling in her chest was suffocating. How could they be going through with this? There would be nothing there for them.

The reason they had to go.

After traveling hundreds of miles, Rachel pulled her tangled hair into a messy knot and turned to her mom. "I can't believe someone else is moving into our house—into my room."

"I know it's hard. Your dad ..." Her mom paused, her voice no less forlorn and tight than it had been for months. "We shared thousands of memories in that house.

Rachel bit back words desperate for escape. She wanted to stay in Florida with her friends—her daddy.

Trees blurred as Florida grew farther from reach.

Mom placed a hand on Rachel's leg. "We'll go back soon for a visit."

When she glanced at Mom's tear-streaked face, remorse crept over her like thousands of piercing needles. Mom had no choice. Beverly Adams could no longer survive in Pensacola, Florida. Not without *him*.

It didn't matter that Rachel had cried for weeks. Somehow, some-way, she had to accept it. "It feels cooler already."

Rachel expected a simple upturn of Mom's lips, but instead, full-blown laughter burst through the tense silence. "It does. Things will be different. Better." She patted Rachel's leg. "Oh, I completely forgot. I found a novel you might enjoy reading. It's in my bag behind you."

Rachel reached for the book in the tote. The black buggy on the cover stared mockingly at her. The title, *Shunned*.

Yeah right, Mom.

Rachel ran her fingers over the title, silent fears choking her. What if the girls at the new school shunned her? What if she spent her entire senior year miserable and alone? What if being this far away from her daddy made her forget him?

Paul Fischer milked Molly while his uncle removed a layer of sodden hay from the stall.

They worked in amiable silence until Uncle Abram propped an arm against his rake. "This is a favorite time of year for planting, but also the busiest, ain't so?"

Paul removed the vacuum from the cow. "I suppose you're right."

"We could use your help more around here." His uncle tugged on his tangled beard. "How's the business coming along?"

"*Gut.*"

Paul couldn't be completely honest. His uncle didn't care for his choice of work or the fact that he worked long hours among the Englischers.

"Eighteen years old and still not planning for the future. It's a waste of time dibble dabbling with this wood building nonsense. You might as well farm here with me and Troy." Uncle Abram heaved a frustrated breath and trudged from the barn.

There was nothing Paul could say. His uncle had never cared for his choices.

Paul finished milking Molly, filled the stalls with fresh hay, then walked to the front porch. He sat on the swing and gave it a hard shove to set it in motion.

Deep down he knew what could happen if things didn't change—losing his construction business.

For weeks, work had been slower than usual.

His youngest cousin wandered out the front door and took a seat on the swing next to him, her lips puckered in a frown. "Did Daed get on you about farming again?"

He didn't feel like talking about it, but it wouldn't hurt to have her pray. The words to one of his favorite Bible verses filled his mind. *Where two or more are gathered together in my name, there I am also.*

"Ach, it isn't his fault. Things have been slow in the business, and I'm worried. You could pray about it too, ain't so?"

"Jah, of course, I will."

His cousin weaved her arm beneath his. "Everything will work out fine. God is good, jah? Come on, let's eat. Mamm made fried chicken." Mary had always been more like a sister than a cousin, and an even better friend. With a playful smile, she jumped off the swing, throwing him in a lurch. She was right, of course. Everything would work out.

Paul lifted his heart to God right there on the swing under the cloudless blue sky. He would trust God whether He decided to close his business or not.

&a;

Rachel opened the novel and read the first few lines.

When Mom pulled off the interstate, Rachel glanced at the clock on the dashboard. Two hours had passed, and she was already on chapter ten. Mom pulled into a restaurant parking lot, and Rachel's stomach rumbled in anticipation. Grabbing her bookmark, she placed it between the pages and climbed from the car.

Rachel slid into a booth across from her mom and ordered lunch, her mind still on the story. The diversion had replaced some of her hopelessness and kept her thoughts occupied.

Rachel dipped a fry in her ketchup. "Do the Amish really live as though the world's not changing all around them?"

"It's been a while since I've visited, but from what I remember they're just as the author describes." Mom buttered a biscuit. "I wish we would've visited more before ..."

A heavy silence hung between them as they finished their meal, each lost in her own thoughts.

After four more hours of driving the next morning, the sign came into view. *Welcome to Paradise.*

"Where do they come up with these names?" Nothing about this move would ever feel like paradise. Acres of farmland, acres of nothing.

"There's also Reading and Intercourse in the area."

A weak smile settled on Rachel's lips. *And I thought Bird in Hand was weird.*

Fields of corn spread in every direction covered the vast landscape. Large houses with no shutters stood solitary in squares of white picket fences. Miles separated the homes. Sheep and cattle grazed, and horse-drawn buggies trotted along the narrow lane. A man with a thin, straggly beard drove one of them. He smiled and lifted his hand as they passed.

Rachel returned the gesture moments too late. "He waved. Did you see him?"

Her mom nodded, keeping her eyes trained on the road.

Did outsiders grow frustrated with the plain people? She couldn't imagine a horse-drawn buggy making it in Florida. They slowed as they approached another. Two children sat in the back, their legs swinging, their bonnet strings flapping in the wind. Rachel waved, and the girls raised their hands before dropping them quickly.

Only moments later, Mom drove the car down a long path leading to a large farmhouse. Mom stopped, stretched out her arms, her hands in a tight grip on the steering wheel. "Here we are."

Deep green grass covered part of the front yard, but the bushes were scrawny. They would be first to go. Evergreens dotting the land gave the house plenty of privacy. The house and two barns needed a coat of paint. A fixer upper. Exactly what Mom needed.

They climbed from the car, and Mom moved in the space next to her. "What do you think?"

"It has possibilities. It'll be a good project for you." Rachel glanced toward the woods.

"Something for you to investigate."

Rachel leaned against the car. "Yeah, after I get the blood flowing through my legs again."

Mom took Rachel's hand and pulled her forward. "Let's check out the inside. It'll take some getting used to, but I can just feel it ... we're going to be happy here."

The older home was something she'd never find in their neighborhood in Pensacola. A huge swing sat on the concrete porch. It would be the perfect spot for reading. Negative feelings stabbed through the barrier, fighting to escape. *There's probably nothing else to do here.*

Mom unlocked the door, and they roamed the first few rooms. "I know it's completely different, but it'll be fun bringing this beautiful home back to life."

Rachel ran her palm across the fireplace mantel, dark brown paint chipping around the corners. With a quick sweep across her shorts, she wiped the dirt from her fingers, but the grimy feeling of emptiness remained. "I'm going upstairs."

"All right." Mom's voice carried from the hallway. "I'll meet you up there in a few minutes.

Once on the second floor, Rachel entered a larger bathroom than she'd been expecting to find. The wallpaper's orange and yellow pattern brightened the room but clashed with the green tub and toilet. Rachel cringed, picturing Mom's reaction.

She wandered into the first bedroom on the right, an oversized room with a small closet. Her furniture was positioned exactly as it had been at home, thanks to the relocation crew. But this was nothing like her house. She sat on the bed, her gaze drifting across the dusty wood floor. How would she ever get used to this? Fighting back tears, she ran downstairs and out the front door. As soon as she grabbed her water bottle from the car, a buggy rolled by, the horse's hooves clicking against the pavement. The sinking feeling bottomed. This was really happening.

Rachel walked around to the backyard and stepped into the barn through its open double doors. The same doors that weren't open when they arrived. The scent of stale hay and old manure seeped from the closed space. An aged wooden rail wrapped around the interior. "Mom?"

"Rachel, you have to see this." Mom leaned over the loft's rail. "This can be your space to do schoolwork, read, or to just get away from me." Mom laughed.

Rachel climbed the ladder. "This is kind of cool."

"I have some ideas to make it perfect for you, honey."

Mom seemed happier already, but a barn loft wasn't exactly Rachel's idea of a great addition to the house.

"When we go into town tomorrow, I'll see if I can find a handyman to help me with some renovations."

Rachel snatched her water bottle open and drew it to her lips, giving herself a moment to minimize the sting. "Already? We just got here. Besides, you decided to keep things simple, remember?" Rachel climbed down the ladder one step at a time, her gaze lingering on the upper mucky window until it was no longer in view. Everything needed a good cleaning. They didn't need a handyman. They needed Daddy.

"I promise I won't overdo it."

Rachel frowned. "It's impossible for you to *under* do anything."

"You can't take away all my fun."

"Sure, Mom, whatever you say. This place will definitely stand out when you're done." Maybe it would be easier to sell.

They stepped back inside the house, and Rachel ran upstairs to unpack, but there was no need to pull everything out yet. Her room needed to be painted first, and she would make sure she did that herself.

She pushed a box of winter clothes into the corner of the closet.

There were only a few garments in there anyway. There hadn't been much need for winter clothes in Florida. Plopping onto her unmade bed the movers had put together, she thought of something else.

It may actually snow.

Later that evening, Rachel helped her mom wipe down the kitchen appliances and scrub the floors, then she settled on the couch with *Shunned*. She read until her eyes grew heavy and the words on the page blurred together. "It's getting late. I'm going to bed."

"Good night, baby." Her mom yawned. "I'm turning in too. We have a big day tomorrow."

Rachel climbed the stairs, the wood floor cool against her bare feet. She settled into bed and snuggled under her lightweight comforter. This would be the first Saturday she wouldn't be able to visit his grave. *Daddy, please forgive me. I didn't want to leave you. Mom just couldn't handle it anymore. I miss you so much.*

She grabbed her leather Bible from the night stand and clutched it to her chest, desperate for consolation. The gold lettering of her name had started to fade. She flipped to a random page and landed on Romans 15:13. *May the God of hope fill you with joy and peace as you trust in him, so that you may overflow with hope by the power of the Holy Spirit.* She searched the passage for a sense of connection, a feeling of hope, peace. There was nothing. After reading through the verse several times, she gave up.

What was she doing wrong?

Tears filled her eyes, and she draped the pillow across her chest to stifle the harsh cries seizing her until her energy waned.

Rachel shifted her face from the damp pillowcase and wiped away her tears. Her daddy would be so ashamed. Mama needed her support now more than ever. And Rachel had done nothing but fill her head and heart with negative thoughts from the time she found out they were moving. The least she could do was give the place a fair chance. After all, it would only be for one year. Her senior year wasn't all that important anyway.

She kept her Bible tucked close. Though it didn't satisfy her yearning to be back home in Florida, its nearness brought a much needed comfort. She meditated on that verse throughout the night and as the first light of dawn seeped into her room, her attitude softened.

Rachel dropped two pieces of bread in the toaster, and her mom handed her a bottle of unopened jelly.

"I guess we should've stopped for a few groceries yesterday."

"This is fine. We'll get a good lunch." Rachel ripped the seal off the top. "There has to be a McDonald's in this vast land of nothing."

"You're kidding, right? I was looking forward to something else. Anything else."

"I would love a juicy Quarter Pounder."

"Yeah, well you can eat all the hamburgers you want. Those days are over for me."

"No, they're not."

Dad's voice was as clear as if he were standing there. *Beverly, are you ever going to start aging?* Rachel's memories spun from one to another and wrapped her in pain-filled comfort as she swallowed the buttered toast with strawberry spread.

The taste of agony bittered the sweetness.

Rachel studied the houses of their neighbors as her mom drove into town. Fields of corn, soybeans, and wheat adorned miles and miles of property. The wilted gold swayed with the breeze like rows of thin, tired soldiers.

In one field, a horse-drawn gadget was being led by an Amish man. He turned just as they drew closer, revealing a full beard. Young girls played in the front yard of another home, their dresses spinning as they chased each other. An older lady crouched low over a vegetable garden.

Samantha would gasp in horror at the thought of digging in dirt. It made the prospect of starting a garden tempting, knowing how shocked her best friend would be.

If there was any hope of contentment, it was up to her to make that happen. Finding a job had to be top priority. She paused as they stepped onto the sidewalk in town. "I'm going to look around, do you mind?"

Mom gave a lopsided grin. "I guess it's safe enough."

"It's Amish Country. What could possibly happen to me here?"

"Plenty." Mom searched the nearby stores. "Stay in this area. Let's meet here at noon, and we'll get lunch."

"Okay."

As Rachel darted across the street, one thing became very clear. Regardless of the name, this would never be paradise.

There wasn't a cloud in the sky, but Paul's feeling of oppression lingered. It wore him down a little more each day. All his friends were already married, or just about to be. The only people he was courting were his customers. But lately even that wasn't enough. He needed more work.

Paul drove his buggy into town and tried to push his unpleasant thoughts away. *Quit wasting time worrying about something you have no control over.*

He arrived moments later at his small office. It was located in the middle of town, squeezed between a coffee shop and bakery. Only a one-room office, but big enough to get paperwork done and store a few things.

The office would be the easiest to let go. It felt stuffy when he wanted to be outside doing physical labor. But he couldn't imagine working with his uncle standing over his shoulder constantly. Paul had just about decided to talk to Aunt Leah, to let her know of his plan to move on. It would be hard to leave her and his cousins, but he could always visit. Besides, both his cousins would be getting married soon. How long could Paul expect to stay with them?

Mid-morning, Paul stood and stretched. He glanced down at the wadded paper on the edge of his desk. Aunt Leah's list. A perfect excuse to get out of the office.

He reached the fabric shop and moved toward the counter to ask a question but stopped and waited by the button display as Emma Zook helped a customer. The customer's short, dirty-blond hair fell to her shoulders, and she stood a foot taller than Emma.

She couldn't be from around here. Not with that strong accent. It didn't surprise him. Tourists visited this part of the country often. He just never understood why.

Hearing his name, he shuffled a step closer.

"Paul, I was just talking about you." Emma motioned for him to join them. "She's looking for a handyman."

He tamed his eager smile into a polite nod. "I'm Paul Fischer. It's nice meeting you."

The woman took his outstretched hand. Her handshake was as strong as her accent. "I'm Beverly Adams. Nice to meet you, too."

"I don't want to embarrass him, but Paul's the best handyman around here." Emma continued. "If he doesn't have the time, I'm sure he could find someone willing to help you."

"What type of work are you needing?" Could this be an answer to his prayer already?

"My daughter and I have moved to the area, and I need major renovations done to the farmhouse I purchased."

Paul's head spun with anticipation. "When would you like to start?"

She stood tall with her shoulders back, her smile confident but warm. "As soon as possible. I wanted to put off most of the unpacking until after the walls are painted."

"I can come first thing in the morning to discuss your plans in more detail."

"That would be wonderful. The address is sixty-four Old Leacock Road. It's a big white house on the right."

She pointed with her hand in the opposite direction, and he couldn't restrain a delighted laugh. "Jah, I know exactly which one you're referring to. It's two houses down from mine."

"Great. I'll see you in the morning then?"

Thank you. You truly are a God of miracles. He stared into the wooden slats of the ceiling as Beverly Adams turned her attention back to Emma. Finishing her transaction, Emma thanked the lady and welcomed her to Paradise.

The woman turned to face him once more before opening the door. "See you tomorrow, Mr. Fischer. Thank you so much."

He wanted to tell her the offer was an answer to prayer, but he simply nodded.

Emma waited until the lady left before turning her attention back to Paul. "Did you hear her accent? I wonder where she's from. A very pretty lady, wouldn't you say? She looked familiar to me for some reason. And she has a daughter ... Hmmm." Her eyes glazed over with thought.

Why had the woman mentioned a daughter, but no husband? Especially since she was wearing a wedding band. It was awkward but none of his business. She was offering a job, and that's all he needed to know. He pictured a little girl with pig-tails, pulling on his pants and asking lots of questions.

Emma took an exaggerated breath. "I can't remember, oh well. You'll be working for her. How wonderful for you! Now what can I help you with, young man?"

"I need a set of needles and a spool of dark blue thread."

Paul thought about all he needed to do. He'd have to catch up on some things before starting this new job. Make sure there were no loose ends with the other ongoing projects. He anticipated the day he could hire more men, instead of paying subcontractors for the majority of the work.

A genuine, thankful smile reached all the way to his gut as he closed the shop door. Maybe that day would come after all.

❧ 3 ❧

Amish women and children strolled along the sidewalk. Their long, plain dresses hung just below their calves. Little girls held onto their mother's hands, their white caps tied under their chins.

One wide-eyed child stood with her mother across the street and Rachel waved. The little girl lifted her hand filled with wildflowers just as her mother turned to see what had caught her daughter's attention. The mother lifted her fingers and extended a warm smile.

With a genuine smile, Rachel entered the bookstore. Shelves were filled with rows of colored spines of different widths and heights. The familiar woodsy, dry scent of paper filled the small space. She planned to visit often but would never get enough hours here. Sighing, she brushed her fingers across the new selection of Young Adult Romance.

She stepped from the store, and the fresh scent of cinnamon and spice from the bakery next door beckoned her forward. Icing on the sweets in the front window glistened. One man stood behind the counter taking orders. A bakery would probably require professional baking experience. But she'd check back if she had no other luck. She wandered a few shops down.

A cool breeze swept her hair against her face, and a hint of sadness nudged her awareness. Florida had never been this cool in June. Not ever.

Shaking the thought free, she spotted a restaurant called *Plain and Fancy*. After allowing a buggy and two cars to pass, she hurried across the street. A sign in the front window read, Open for Breakfast, Lunch, and Dinner. And right next to it. Help Wanted.

She pulled the heavy wooden door open, and a bell jingled announcing her presence. The fragrance of bacon and coffee brewing permeated the dining room. Two rows of booths were lined against the walls. Tables covered with white linen scattered throughout the remaining floor space. A few families were enjoying an early lunch or late breakfast. There were even a few Amish among the guests. All the tables were taken, except one.

Rachel had been standing near the front counter only a few seconds when an older woman approached from the kitchen. A tendril of gray hair curled out beneath her tight bun. Rachel glanced at the blue jeans and white blouse she chose to wear this morning.

"May I help you?" The lady's plump cheeks lifted into a full smile, her accent sophisticated yet charming.

She swallowed hard, tucking a strand of hair behind her ear. "Yes ma'am. My mom and I just moved to the area. I'm looking for a job and saw your sign in the window."

"What's your name, young lady?"

"Rachel ... Rachel Adams."

"Well, as a matter of fact, Miss Rachel, we are in need of a waitress. Have you ever waited tables before?"

"No, ma'am. But I can learn." She twisted her hands together. Maybe she should've talked to Mom first.

"That sounds like the kind of waitress I'm looking for. One with determination."

Rachel bit her lip to hide her smile. Turning from the woman's steady gaze, she met those of a young Amish man sitting in the corner booth.

"Could you come in the morning to fill out the paperwork and start training?"

What? Paperwork? Training? I'm getting a job. Her gaze darted around the restaurant to the customers she would be serving. She reminded herself to breathe. "Tomorrow? Yes, ma'am."

The woman's eyes softened. "You can call me Mrs. Mavis. Be here by nine, and we'll get you hired on."

She hoped Mom agreed. She should've asked first. "Yes, ma'am, uh, Mrs. Mavis. Thank you. I'll see you tomorrow at nine."

Rachel never expected to find a job this soon. The sudden burst of excitement made it impossible to do anything but smile, even though she hoped Mom would change her mind and want to return home. To Daddy.

&

Paul was eating lunch at a table near the back of the restaurant when the beautiful young woman entered. Her long hair, curled at the ends, hung loose down her back. Her white blouse intensified her golden brown skin. As she spoke to Mrs. Mavis, she glanced at him and smiled. Had she caught him staring?

The table in front of him was empty and something in his gut tightened like a bolt. Maybe she would sit there. *Eefeldich!* Ridiculous! Would he talk to her if she did? Of course not! That would be asking for trouble. The kind of trouble his uncle had drilled into him since he was a boy—the kind of trouble too many Amish youngsters were flirting with these days.

Before leaving the restaurant, the young woman glanced in his direction again. He looked away. She wouldn't catch him staring. Not this time.

He slouched against the bench, bored with the estimates spread out in front of him. She had been a pleasant distraction, but perhaps it was better she moved on. He needed this task completed before he started the new job.

Paul's attention returned to the folder until a sudden movement disrupted his concentration. The same Englisch girl sat on the bench outside his window and propped an elbow on her knee.

She twirled her brown hair between her fingers. A hint of sadness mixed with admiration stretched across her features as she observed the community.

"Hi, Paul."

He jerked back, bumping his head on the wooden booth. "Ach, Anna. *Weighets?*"

"*Wunderbaar-gut.*"

He studied the girl's demeanor standing before him. She was everything his uncle would approve. Energetic, helpful, and hard working.

She'd been trying to steal his attention for several years, but he didn't share her feelings. It wasn't her fault, he just didn't. And he knew better than to give her false hope.

Moments passed as he tried to think of something else to say. When he failed, he looked back through the window. The Englisch girl had disappeared, and it felt as if he'd been stung.

&a.

Two bumblebees were circling a row of wildflowers when Rachel's mom called to her from across the street. Cantering hooves echoed against the pavement as she hurried toward her.

"How do you like the town?" Mom carried two bags, and Rachel grabbed one.

The delight of being offered a job helped. "It's okay." She hesitated. "Maybe we should start a garden."

"A garden? What a great idea, Rachel! Fresh vegetables from our own garden. I found an Amish man interested in doing the renovations."

"An Amish man. Really?" *Wow, we're both having good luck today.* There would be a real Amish man working at the house. Then she remembered the man in the field with a full beard and funny hat. "I wanted to talk to you about something." Rachel took a deep breath. "I thought I could get a job for the summer."

"A job?"

Expecting that reaction, she pressed on. "I might meet some kids I'll be going to school with and it won't be so hard the first day."

The approach of laughter and chattering voices caused them to step closer to the edge of the sidewalk to get out of the way.

"I think you getting a job is a wonderful idea."

"You do?" Rachel grabbed her hand. "Guess what? I've already found one. The lady wants me to start training tomorrow."

Mom's brows crinkled. "What in the world? I left you alone for thirty minutes and you found a job?"

Rachel pointed across the street. "It's the restaurant on the corner."

"A restaurant? What would your father think about this?" Mom's lips parted. "Once you commit to this job, you're going to have to stick it out. Waiting tables is hard work."

"I'm sure I'll like it." *Anything's better than being bored out of my mind.* Rachel wrapped her arms around her mom.

Mom pulled her closer. "My goodness, you are excited. I know I'm busy. And I think it will be good for you."

"Maybe your handyman could till a spot for the garden."

"He seems like a nice young man. He's coming first thing in the morning, so we can ask him then."

"Hey, why don't we buy the seeds today, so I can start planting? But we could have lunch at the restaurant first so you can meet Mrs. Mavis, the owner?"

"That's a great idea, and I'll be able to ask questions about this job she gave my baby without my permission." Mom's eyes narrowed.

Rachel was surprised when her laughter came. It felt good.

❧

Anna stood next to the empty seat across from Paul, her hands placed firmly on her hips. "Why were you staring at that girl?"

Had he been staring? He hadn't even realized it. Not this time, anyway. Heat burned Paul's neck, and he grabbed a napkin to cover his mouth. "I don't know what you mean. Besides, why are you spying on me?" Paul focused on one of the worksheets when she didn't move.

"I just happened to see you sitting here." Anna's voice softened and didn't carry the same accusation. "I wasn't spying."

"Ach, I wasn't staring at anyone. I'm starting a new job and trying to get some last minute paperwork finished." He tried to sound convincing.

"Where's the job? Is it paying or is this another one of your charities?"

Where had that come from? No matter. He knew better than to fall for that. Anna wasn't interested in his job. She was only interested in hanging around him.

He would never tell her. It would give her a reason to show up at the work site like the last time. She had brought him a shoofly pie proclaiming her mom had made an extra one just for him. The fellows jabbed him the entire afternoon about her being his girlfriend.

Anna leaned against the table. Paul didn't want to give her the wrong impression by inviting her to sit down.

Then the bell jingled again, and the same Englisch girl reentered with Beverly Adams, the woman he'd just agreed to work for. His mind raced. That couldn't be her daughter. She should be a little girl. Someone to annoy him with questions. "Sit down, Anna." Her standing there would only draw attention.

Anna didn't seem to notice the way he said it, only thrilled that he'd asked. A couple now sat in the empty booth. The only other table available was near the front, but still only two tables down from his. To the tune of Anna's endless chattering, Paul's gaze ran over the estimates without really seeing the numbers. But Anna wasn't the only one distracting him. It was the Englisch woman's daughter, new to Lancaster County.

The daughter who didn't have blond pig-tails after all.

❧   4   ❧

Paul propped his chin against his fist. He would be stuck sitting here until Beverly Adams and her daughter left.

"At the singing Sunday, I'm planning to bring sticky buns. I know they're your favorite. I'm sure Susie Mae will bring them too." Anna rolled her eyes. "She always copies me."

He couldn't let Mrs. Adams recognize him, not now with Anna sitting here. He'd have to introduce her, and she'd ask too many questions.

Tomorrow would be better. He'd be more prepared. Shifting in his seat, he tried again to focus on the column of numbers in front of him with no luck. His thoughts centered on the young woman sitting across from his new employer. She glanced in his direction, and he shifted his gaze quickly and crossed his arms.

Anna sighed. "I might want to leave the singing early. I'm eighteen now. I'd rather do housekeeping chores, and I'd much rather be in the kitchen cooking. Mamm says I'm a natural."

Slumping in his seat, he entertained the idea of leaving anyway. If only this restaurant had another door, that's exactly what he'd do.

Every few seconds, his gaze veered toward the young woman with

Mrs. Adams. Her hair, pulled to one side, hung loose around her shoulders.

"Mamm says we can make a few extra sticky buns in case you wanted to take some home."

Miss Adams' lips curved into a full smile and spread across her whole face. Her eyes gleamed when they flickered in his direction again, but her smile faded when she caught him staring. Her gaze fell to her lap, her brows arched with a deep crease.

"Paul, are you listening to me?" Anna turned in her seat.

"Jah, of course. How's your brother getting along now that he's finished school?"

He had to be more careful. Anna seemed unaware that the Englisch girl had come back into the restaurant, and he wanted to keep it that way. He didn't need Anna finding out that he'd be working for this woman ... or her daughter.

An hour later, the two ladies finally stood to leave. As soon as they were out of sight, Paul stood. "I better go. See you around."

"I'll see you Sunday." Anna called after him.

Paul kept walking and left her with a wave of his hand.

The two ladies were turning the corner at the next block. Paul waited until it was safe to cross the street without being seen.

Why was he acting so foolish? He should've introduced himself. There was no reason to be worried about Mrs. Adams' daughter. It didn't matter that she was the loveliest creature he'd ever seen. She was an Englisch woman, and she was forbidden.

He would think nothing else of it.

Rachel rolled over in bed and pulled the pillow over her eyes to shield the morning sun. She reached for her watch on the night stand and groaned.

Slipping on her flip-flops, she took quick steps down the stairs, then tripped over a box as she turned the corner. She pulled herself up, her knee burning.

The scent of muffins flooded the kitchen. She grabbed one, took a small bite, then hurried through the back door.

Rachel strode into the barn hoping to find the box with her running shorts still buried inside.

A young Amish man, his look aimed over his shoulder, stepped across the threshold and nearly ran into her. She staggered to miss the collision.

Reaching out, he grabbed her arm and kept her from tumbling down the two steps. It wasn't until he pulled her away from his firm, broad chest that their eyes met.

It was him.

The guy from the restaurant yesterday.

She stepped back when he released his grip and cleared his throat.

"Ach, are you all right?"

"Yes, I'm so sorry. Thank you."

Mom hadn't noticed their near catastrophe, her eyes trained on a brochure. "Oh, Rachel, this is Paul, the handyman I told you about."

It couldn't be. She caught him staring at her with the same look she'd seen in his eyes yesterday. Under his scrutiny, heat rose to her neck. "Hey." The simple response leaked out between stumbling lips. Holding her head high, though it only reached the bottom of his chin, she trudged past him.

"Hullo." The word sounded forced, unfriendly.

She stopped and cast another glance in his direction. His dark eyes fluttered to hers, but he looked away, more quickly than she could.

Rachel was still wearing her pajamas, the oldest, most comfortable plaid pajama shorts she had. Her snug fitting, faded T-shirt looked even worse. Her hair was pulled back in a knotty pony tail, but had probably fallen after flipping across the hall over that box. Biting her lip to keep her humiliation in check, she dropped her gaze to the ground.

I must look ridiculous.

"Mom, I'll be back. I'm going for a run." Rachel's gaze flashed his way, but his expression was still uninterested. "After I change."

Great. She'd insulted him. She wished the ground beneath her feet

would swallow her whole. She was sure the Amish had some rule about dressing fully before coming outside.

"Okay. Be careful, sweetheart."

Rachel hurried to the house. How could she have forgotten about the handyman coming this morning? And of all the Amish men, why did it have to be the same one who'd glared at her yesterday with something close to revulsion. The same one with the deepest blue eyes she'd ever seen trapping her in their gaze. She'd anticipated meeting a real Amish person. But now, had second thoughts.

Rachel ran upstairs. She brushed through her hair, pulled it into a neater pony tail, and slipped on her running top and shorts.

She took off in a fast-paced walk up the path. Maybe she shouldn't attempt running today. She had already fallen one time this morning and now had a funny feeling in her chest. She brushed it off as some crazy reaction to her embarrassment and the defiant stare the handyman had given her in the restaurant. The first chance she had at meeting a real Amish man and she'd ruined it. She would be prepared the next time. And fully dressed. Was that the reason he looked so angry? What did she care?

He certainly wasn't an older man with a bushy beard and funny hat like she'd imagined. Not even close.

❧

Paul's temperature increased the moment he reached for the girl, the warmth burning his neck, his face. Her hair was strewn all over her head, but he had never seen anything more beautiful.

And now he couldn't help but stare as Rachel walked on the path heading toward the road and disappeared around the corner. Where could she be going? Surely she wasn't planning to run on the road. Careless drivers in Paradise were innumerable.

He tried really hard to concentrate on Mrs. Adams, but his brain wouldn't cooperate. Paul kept checking the path and had to stop himself from asking Mrs. Adams if she worried about her daughter, too.

Mrs. Adams spoke, breaking his thoughts. "I definitely want to remove the carpet downstairs and replace it with hardwood floors."

"I'll bring some books tomorrow, and you can pick out the style and color."

"That sounds great."

"I know we've talked about painting the inside, but what about the outside?"

"Do you have any experience with vinyl siding?"

The more Beverly Adams talked, the better things looked for him. "Jah. Do you want to replace the wood siding?"

"I was hoping to."

"That shouldn't be a problem."

It would be enough work for him and his few guys, considering the other jobs he'd already gained. They would stay busy through the whole summer. He would do most of this work himself.

Was that a mistake? He was confident about the work, just not about the daughter.

They headed inside to discuss what needed to be painted. A beige, leather sectional sofa sat against the front windows. Glass tables stood on each end and a redwood bookcase stood against the opposite wall.

Mrs. Adams handed him a paint swatch with "living room" printed on the back. "I'll start with this color for this room."

Paul couldn't wait to see the finished product. Living so plainly, no brightly colored paint or pictures, he enjoyed being a part of the Englisch world in this aspect. He didn't care to have material things, but it was nice to see the way things were made beautiful with a coat of paint or fancy trim work.

"How old is your daughter?" His gaze fell to the table. How could he have asked her that? Why had he? He had broken his own rule. A rule one of his best friends taught him. A friend who had been burned. Revealing interest in Englischers, especially the females, would only lead to trouble. Especially a beautiful, young woman like Beverly Adams' daughter.

"Rachel's seventeen. How old are you, Paul?"

"I'm eighteen. I had a birthday a few weeks ago."

"Happy birthday. She'll be eighteen in just a few more weeks. I thought you might be about the same age. Oh, I almost forgot. She wants to start a garden. Would you happen to have a tiller?"

"Jah, I have one at my uncle's house." He couldn't picture Rachel working a garden. But he was certainly having trouble keeping the mental picture of the beautiful young woman out of his mind.

"Would you mind tilling a spot so she can start planting? She's so excited."

"Of course not. I'll go home at lunch and load it." He cleared his throat, fixing his gaze on the color samples.

"Great, I'll let her show you where she wants it." Mrs. Adams smiled.

She'll show me? It felt as if a vice tightened across his middle. He hadn't expected to have to work directly for her.

Once outside, Paul searched the road again for the strange, beautiful girl. They were inspecting the wood siding that would have to be removed when Rachel finally came down the path. Beverly Adams didn't notice his uneasiness or even that her daughter had returned. Halfway to the house Rachel paused. With a lingering stretch, she lifted her right arm across her body, and then her left. A layer of sweat shimmered against her skin. He should warn her to find a different route for running. But it wasn't his place. He'd already overstepped his bounds.

About half an hour later, slouched over the table set up outside the barn, he wrote a list of things he'd need to get started. Speaking to Rachel about the garden blurred his concentration. But moments later, she drove away without a glimpse in his direction. That vice tightened again. Where was she going? And why was he disappointed?

% 5 %

Rachel stepped into the strong aroma of bacon, sausage, and sweet pancake syrup. She pressed her hand against her stomach before moving forward. *I should've grabbed another muffin.*

"Rachel." Mrs. Mavis's animated voice rang out from behind the counter. "I'm so glad to see you."

She took a slow step forward and wet her dry lips. "Good morning."

"Kelli? Can you come out here please?" Mrs. Mavis turned toward the kitchen. "My daughter will be training you today."

A pretty blonde approached from the kitchen and stood facing them. "Hi, I'm Kelli."

Mrs. Mavis left the girls to their private introductions.

A huge smile filled Kelli's face, but there seemed to be a deeper understanding shining through her blue eyes and a sense of calm settled over Rachel. "I'm so excited to have someone my age working here. Mom says you're new to town. Are you still in school?"

Mrs. Mavis returned, but Kelli had captivated Rachel's attention. "Yes, I'm a senior."

"No way! Me too."

Mrs. Mavis handed Rachel a folder. "I'll need you to fill these out, and then you'll follow Kelli and help her today. I'll get you on the schedule for Monday and have you train everyday next week." Rachel took the papers from her outstretched hand. "You can sit in the back booth. If you have any questions just ask."

"Yes, ma'am." She took the seat, the same one Mom's new handyman occupied yesterday. A light dance skittered across her chest.

"We'll talk later." Kelli moved away with a bounce in her step.

After completing the application, Rachel spent the morning assisting Kelli with the breakfast and lunch crowds, helping take and fill orders.

It had just been over an hour, but already Rachel had fallen in love with the prospect of the job.

"Do you have a boyfriend back home?"

"No." The question caught her off guard. "There wasn't much time for dating. My whole life was consumed with school and softball, until my daddy died." The last of her words poured out before she could stop them.

"I'm so sorry. About your dad."

How should she respond? With the truth? *I want him back.* Most people didn't want to hear the real truth. They just want you to know they're sympathizing with you. "Thank you. You're the first person here I've met my age." Other than the gorgeous Amish man. Was he her age? She couldn't be sure. There was something about him, something youthful hiding behind all that strength. So, maybe. "I think I'll like working here."

Kelli's face lit up. "I have a feeling we're going to be great friends. But right now, we better get back to work."

After memorizing many of the menu choices, filling and refilling drinks, carrying entree's to the last few guests, and even taking an order or two, Rachel was feeling accomplished. She wiped tables and swept part of their section at the end of the shift. Mrs. Mavis praised her for a job well done and let her go for the day.

Arriving home, Rachel pulled onto the long drive, but the old-fashioned wagon wasn't in the yard. She took a deep breath. Good. Rachel was in no mood to be around the Amish man with eyes of steel. What if Mom decided not to hire him after all?

She'd waited in anticipation today as every Amish person came into the restaurant, worried how they'd treat her. Only friendly smiles of welcome and greeting. Confusion set uneasily within her. What was it about her that he didn't like? Why should she care what he thought?

She climbed from her car anxious to change from her grease-filled shirt and could hardly wait to collapse on the couch. Never had she worked so hard.

Mom was seated in the recliner, reading, when Rachel walked inside. "How was the restaurant?"

"Great. Mrs. Mavis has a daughter that will be going to school with me. She's actually training me."

"Really?" Mom lowered her reading glasses. "That's wonderful."

"How was your day?"

"Paul's aunt stopped by to welcome us and brought a loaf of bread and pot of soup. She joined me for lunch, and we had a really nice visit."

Paul, so that's his name. Where is he?

The fumes of paint gave the old house a new, fresh scent. "You've already started painting?"

"Yes, and Paul headed home to get the tiller while the primer dries."

So he would be back today. Unexpected relief swelled through her middle. Rachel ran upstairs, dropped her keys on the dresser, and changed from her dingy outfit into something more comfortable, something cuter.

Taking special care in her appearance, she brushed through her knotty layers, bringing back the silky shine. Her hair spilled around her shoulders, but she flipped it back up into a pony-tail. She didn't want to overdo it, but had to look decent, better. For him. Especially after the impression she'd left on him this morning. Staring into the mirror, she shook her head. It felt like inches of grease layered her skin. It would be impossible to remove the grime without a shower. But there was no time for that.

Rachel returned to the living room and sat in the plastic-covered chair and closed her heavy eyelids. Drowsiness worked its way through her, and she slipped into a daydream.

"Can you show Paul where you want the garden?"

She sat up straight. "He's here?"

"Not yet. I meant when he gets back. It surprised him when I told him it's your garden. He thought you were young to be into that sort of thing."

"He said that?" What was that supposed to mean?

Mom smiled. "Not exactly, but I told him you did all the cooking, which surprised him as well."

Did he draw that conclusion from their brief, unpleasant meeting this morning? *Mom! How embarrassing.*

Rachel crossed her legs. The plastic fused to her skin and crinkled with each movement. She tightened her lips and exhaled hard. It would be better to keep her mouth shut. Mom seemed pleased to have him working here, and she didn't want to ruin it. She had already ruined everything else. It wasn't Mom's fault. She had offended the handyman by staring at him in the restaurant and wearing pajamas in the yard. Of course he'd think her incapable of simple tasks.

"You're close in age. He's only eighteen. I'm sure you'll become friends."

"I doubt that. He's Amish. He'll probably think I'm weird."

You've already given him a head start. Rachel leaned her head into her hands. Why did he have to be so gorgeous? She already struggled with gawking at the Amish.

"He's a nice young man." Rachel didn't miss the warning in Mom's voice. "He's doing all the painting, except for your room which needs to be done so I can get the carpet put in upstairs."

"I can start on it today. Ms. Mavis put me on the schedule every day to train. But I can finish this weekend." She didn't want Paul in her room, sneering at her personal things.

"Paul could get it done in one afternoon, honey."

"No, I really want to do it. I'll start this afternoon."

"We're putting in all hardwoods on the first floor ..." She paused at the sound of his buggy. "Here he comes. Can you run out there and show him where you want the garden?"

Me? She wants me to talk to him. Rachel stood to put on her shoes, feeling the slightest hint of butterflies. Why did she feel so nervous? She'd waited on Amish people all day. Why did this particular one get to her like this?

"I'm so excited. A garden was a wonderful idea, Rachel. Be nice. He's going to be a real help to me around here."

Rachel slipped through the back door and sauntered around an apple tree, hiding behind its early blooms. She hadn't noticed it standing there until now.

Paul proceeded around the buggy and stepped onto the back of the wagon. His hat tilted to one side when he leaned over. He reached for it and placed it on the rail, shaking his head, his wavy dark hair flipping in an uneven manner. Her smile came naturally.

He hadn't noticed her yet. Not wanting to get in his way, she moved closer but stood to the side and waited for him to finish.

He pushed his sleeves further up his arms and pulled at the steel protruding from the wagon. His muscles bulged with each tug. Seconds later, he turned toward her and as their gaze met his eyes widened. He reached for his hat and slammed it on his head. In one fluid motion, he jumped from the wagon. Lifting the tiller in his arms, he moved past her without saying a word. Did it irritate him that she was adding to his workload? She combed her fingers through her hair.

He probably thinks I'm wasting his time.

"Hi." Rachel forced the word from her mouth. "I appreciate you going home to get this for me." She lifted her chin. "I mean for my mom."

Rachel searched his face for any expression that would give her a clue as to what he thought. She didn't worry about staring at him. He wouldn't even look in her direction.

"Jah." He looked across the yard and then peeked at her before taking a few steps.

She knew the tiller must be heavy, so she headed in the direction she'd decided on. He followed.

"This is my first time doing something like this, so I'm not really sure where to put it." It wasn't a question, but she expected a reply.

None came. Not immediately. Rachel glanced in his direction. His bleak expression irritated her.

It's like he's already decided.

Had he treated Mom this way? No. Beverly Adams would never allow that. Rachel almost told him to just forget it. She wanted to walk away and leave him standing there.

"I'll be glad to till wherever you would like, Miss Adams." He placed the tiller on the ground, locking his gaze with hers. The corners of his lips lifted into a slight smile, shattering the unfriendliness that was there just moments before.

Her defenses crumbled and she tried to smile, but her mind whirled in a confusing spiral. She blinked. "You can call me Rachel."

He propped his foot onto the machine, his broad shoulders pressing against the white shirt straining the first few buttons. "Okay, Rachel. Where would you like me to start?" He gave her another smile, this time it was stronger and mixed with confusion and determination.

She stared into his eyes and his rudeness was forgotten. "I thought about putting it by the barn."

She paused to make sure he wouldn't disagree. He would definitely know more about this than she would. But he said nothing.

Rachel advanced toward the barn and pointed to the area she'd already chosen. "Can you make it about this wide and this long?" She walked off the small twenty-by-fifteen foot garden, feeling awkward with each step. It had felt like the perfect spot earlier, but now she wasn't so sure.

In his presence, she was sure of nothing.

❧   6   ❧

Careful not to look directly at her, Paul set the tool on the edge where he'd planned to start. How long would she care for the garden? She said herself she'd never had one. It would only be a matter of time before the weeds overtook it. And all of this would be for nothing.

The tiller eased into the soil, gas fumes elevating from the machine. It worked into the ground effortlessly. She'd chosen the exact spot where a garden had been before. Had she known that? It wouldn't take long at all.

He must have seemed extremely rude earlier. This wasn't the first time he'd worked around Englisch families with teenage daughters his age. It had never mattered. Not like this. She could be no different than any other spoiled Englisch girl. After all, he'd only met her this morning. Of course she would put on a front for a first impression. And he knew better. It was an Englisch girl who'd destroyed his best friend's life.

When she spoke, Paul had expected to see her shallow side, but that hadn't happened. She seemed nervous. Like him.

Then she did the unthinkable. She stood right there.

"Can I help?" She spoke but over the machine, he had trouble hearing her. His gaze drifted to her mouth with every intent to read her lips. That was a big mistake.

She shouldn't be here with her long tan legs, waves of sunlight dancing through her thick, brown hair. Far too pretty. Far too distracting. If he wasn't careful, he would enjoy her company. "Nein. I can manage."

Taking a few steps back, he thought she would change her mind and head toward the house, but she stopped—in his direct view.

When her brown eyes attached to him, a jolt shot through his chest, causing a lump to lodge in his throat. He directed his gaze toward the tines, locking his focus on something else. With each thrust of the tiller, he gained a portion of control he'd lost since the beginning of this unlikely meeting with Rachel.

A film of dust covered her black shorts and top. "You're getting covered. Maybe you should wait over there."

"Oh." She swiped at her bare leg and a layer of sand scattered in the wind. "A little dirt never hurt anything. I might as well get used to it if I'm going to be out here every week working in it."

"You're different than any Englischer I've been around. That's for certain sure."

A smile that was downright breathtaking slid over her lips. "What did you say? That sounded just like ..."

"Like what?" He wanted to see that smile again.

She didn't give him what he wanted, but the color in her cheeks deepened. "Nothing. I love your accent. Maybe it *will* be better if I get out of your way."

"I'll have this ready for you in a couple of hours." Paul strained to keep his focus on the tiller, when all his impulses urged him to look at her. No, it was too dangerous. Those deep brown eyes with specks of gold that were impossible to read would grab a hold of him for sure. And he wasn't all that certain, he would be able to resist it again.

"I really appreciate this. I hope I'll be able to grow something."

Regardless, he had to be friendly to her. It wouldn't be right to treat her different than he would other Englischers. "Jah. I'm sure you will."

After thirty minutes, he wiped the sweat from his brow, stretched out his arms behind his head, and gave into his yearning to look in her direction. Kicking the swing back and forth with her foot, the young woman concentrated on the book in her hands. The leather bound book could only be one thing. Her Bible.

He yanked his hat farther onto his head.

Watching Paul work was nothing like watching the man in the field earlier. The comparison wasn't even close. His shirt sleeves were rolled up over his muscular forearms, the first few buttons unfastened below his collar. Rocking to the rhythm of the steady hum of his big metal tool, a warm breeze swept across her face. She forced herself not to stare as he worked, yet her eyes were disobedient and flickered again and again in his direction. She'd finished her devotional reading for the day, the Bible still lying open across her lap. She couldn't move from the spot though. Not with Paul working in her perfect view.

A few minutes later, he loaded the tiller onto his wagon. Rachel looped a few strands of hair around her finger and hurried to grab her new gardening tools and seeds. With awkward steps, she wandered out to the garden, holding a basket filled with supplies. His work was beautiful, but he had disappeared. Rachel studied the perfect rows and hated to touch it. He'd even raked and swept the outside corners.

She shouldn't have asked her mom to have Paul do this. If she'd met him first she definitely wouldn't have. *That's for certain sure.* She laughed out loud at the common phrase she'd read in the Amish novel—the phrase that Paul had just used. Thank goodness she hadn't blurted it out. She would've ruined everything.

Staring at the flawless rows of soil was getting her nowhere. She should've bought a garden manual. The vision of Paul doubled over in laughter, expecting her to fail, spun circles in her mind. He believed her to be weak. Unable to care for a garden. She saw it in his eyes. And she had to do whatever it took to prove him wrong.

Rachel opened a small pack of squash and read the directions before she buried them in the first section. After only a few minutes, she had all the packets of seeds dispersed. Her back ached and her hands were filthy. She pulled the water hose attached to the barn, unraveling it with each step, praying that she'd spread the seeds out far enough, buried them deep enough, and now hoped she watered them enough.

Sweat beaded on the back of her neck and gathered around the inside corners of her sunglasses. With a swipe of her hand, she brushed the sweat away, leaving a trail of burning in its wake. She placed the glasses on her head, then returned the hose, rolling each heavy loop across the bar before heading inside.

Her mom leaned against the door. "This isn't going to work."

Paul stood on a ladder in the living room. He was shaking his head and looking down, but then his gaze shifted and in the briefest of moments met hers.

Rachel hurried upstairs. She should thank him, but that could wait.

She entered her room and closed the door behind her. Why was her heart pounding through her chest?

Two gallons of paint and utensils were already set against the wall. With each stroke of lime green, she thought of Florida and how different everything would be now. What was Samantha doing today? What would she say about planting a garden?

And she thought of something else she wanted to share with her best friend right this very minute. There was no doubt in her mind, Samantha would flip if she saw Paul.

An hour later, Rachel ran downstairs to fix something to drink. Paul was still painting, so she poked her head into the living room.

Rachel waited, trying to find the nerve to speak when he turned toward her. "I wanted to tell you thank you." Her words came on a rushed inhale.

"You're welcome." He gave her the same smile as before, but this time she fought against it.

"Would you like something to drink? We have lemonade or sweet tea." How stupid she must sound. Of course her mom had already offered him something.

He took one step down and faced her. "Jah, *danki* ... yes, thank you. Lemonade sounds *gut*." He cleared his throat. "Good."

Rachel turned quickly toward the kitchen, her legs were moving in a quirky way, her gait unusual.

"You've been painting too," he spoke, sounding closer than she expected him to be.

A surge of blood heated her cheeks as she spun around and found him standing in the kitchen doorway. "Oh." Streaks of green paint stained her arm. "I'm painting my room."

"Jah, your mom told me you would be."

Rachel managed to get the glasses filled without spilling any of the yellow liquid. Paul took his lemonade from the counter, sloshing the lemon around his glass, the ice clinking against the sides. She waited by the sink for him to leave, but he stayed until he emptied his glass.

"Danki ... um, thank you." He rubbed the back of his neck before meeting her gaze. "That was refreshing. Did you make it yourself?"

"Yes, the lemons I bought ... I mean, I bought the lemons yesterday." Rachel tried to keep eye contact with him without losing her concentration. It was impossible. She took a sip and a cool rush soared through her body, but she wasn't convinced it had anything to do with the drink.

"It tasted delicious. Some of the best lemonade I've ever had." He placed his empty glass on the counter next to her. "Thanks again."

With a brief smile, he walked away, and she raced up the stairs trying to escape the strange flutter filling her stomach.

❦ 7 ❦

Rachel drew in an invigorating breath and braced herself for another day in the restaurant. The shine of a new job was wearing thin, and though it gave her some purpose, it did little to ease the persistent ache. As always her gaze roamed the tables, searching for that same Amish man she'd seen the first day. The man who was working at her house, right now, while she was here, avoiding the steely eyes of one of the guests.

Kelli nudged Rachel when she stepped through the kitchen door. "That guy sitting in the corner booth keeps staring at you."

Rachel cringed. "I know. What's his problem?"

"I don't know, but he's got it bad for you, girl. Didn't he come in yesterday?"

"Yeah, I remember seeing him." It wasn't unusual for guests to visit several times a week. "Do you know him?"

"Not really. He doesn't live around here. I heard he visits his aunt every year."

Rachel sighed. It was a little creepy. "Maybe he's leaving. Today."

Kelli's laughter rang through the kitchen. "You're crazy, girl. He's gorgeous."

Rachel gave a half hearted laugh before walking through the double doors leading to the dining room.

The second time she passed by, he grabbed her wrist. His gaze roamed her with an appreciative grin. "I'm Jason. Let me take you out tonight."

He released her, letting his fingers trail down the length of her arm. She snatched away from the intimate touch.

"Sorry, but I'm busy tonight."

He sat there for over an hour and she wanted to scream in frustration. Her anger had tripled since the time he'd made his advance. What was he looking at anyway? She wore the sourest looking face she could muster every time she passed him and never, not once, did she glance in his direction. Why, she had a mind to march over there and—

He stood to leave. Finally. She released a deep, satisfying breath.

Please don't come back tomorrow.

Paul entered Rachel's room and stared at the walls. She'd done a great job. Her color choices were feminine yet bold. The lime green was striking against the white crown molding. Her room stood empty of any furniture. He had hoped to learn something about this girl he'd tried so hard to ignore, other than she wasn't too bad at painting and didn't mind getting dirty.

Light colored fibers clung to Paul's dark pants as his two helpers stretched the beige carpet. It would look like a brand new house by the time they finished.

An hour later, he strolled downstairs to find Mrs. Adams sitting in her office. She continued to type unaware of his presence. "I'm sorry to bother you, but we've finished the carpet in Rachel's room."

Deep creases filled her forehead as she stared at the computer. "Okay, that's great."

"I wanted to move her furniture back in for her."

She leaned back. "No, that's okay. She wants to do that herself."

"I don't mind. And I have plenty of help."

"That's nice of you, but I'll help her. You go ahead and finish the rest of the upstairs. Except of course for the room where her things are stored." She left no room for further argument. "You should be able to get in there by tomorrow."

Mrs. Adams focused again on her computer.

Paul stepped outside and, like most days, glanced at the road as a car drove by, expecting it to be Rachel. But it never was.

If only he could listen to headphones with music like all the other guys, maybe he'd quit daydreaming so much. But he shouldn't listen to their worldly songs, no more than he already did when his crew listened to music on the job. He already sang the lyrics in his head. He had enough trouble with his uncle.

Where could Rachel be spending so much time? They just moved here. He'd been working here for a week and a half, but had only seen her a couple of times. It was probably best their paths hadn't crossed much. A slight smile roused his lips as the nudging in his gut took flight. He longed to see her, but just as suddenly as the notion appeared, it dissipated.

He didn't want to think about the Lord purposefully bringing her into his life. Not the way that Englisch woman secured her hooks on his friend, only to leave him months later. His friend loved her, gave up everything for her. He was devastated when she left.

No, God had nothing to do with this. It was selfish desires creeping into his life. And he knew better. It was against their rules to court and marry Englischers. And *that* was the reason why.

Paul arrived at the Adams' at his usual time on Friday morning. His cousin needed to borrow the buggy, so she dropped Paul off at the road.

Something was different this morning, something very different than every other day this week. Rachel's car was parked in the yard, but her mom's car was missing.

Once Paul reached the other side of the barn, he pulled the first piece of wood across the table and carved the design into the crown molding by hand. It took more time, but Mrs. Adams requested a design not found in stores. When she painted a picture with words describing what she was looking for, he drew the design and she agreed to pay him well for the extra work.

The sun rose to its highest peak at noon, and Paul moved his supplies inside the barn adjacent to the big shade tree. He carved through another piece of wood, desperate to empty his mind of chestnut-brown eyes, that eloquent accent, and carefree smile. Long, tanned legs covered in a layer of dust.

He rearranged his tools along the table. Not even his most passionate desire, his construction company, could free him from the images.

A tiny chuckle halted his action. The object of his distraction was standing next to her garden.

Ach! How was he supposed to stop daydreaming about her now?

Though she seemed unaware, he worked only yards from her. He stayed seated inside the barn near the door where he could catch the breeze but still linger in the deep shadows. She lifted a hoe and whacked a row of weeds, then bent to retrieve them and threw them into a pile. Why was she using that hoe? She could easily pull the few blades of grass by hand.

He shouldn't keep glancing.

Paul quietly whittled and skinny, curled tendrils of wood gave way beneath his carving tool. He tried to give his full attention to the detail, but couldn't help the occasional glance in her direction.

Time after time, she readjusted her gloves. That simple action distracted him, amused him, made her even more appealing.

Before moving to the next row, she propped an arm against the hoe and wiped her face with a towel. Her hair had been pulled back in a ponytail, but a few dark strands had fallen loose around her face.

This was his territory. She shouldn't be out here. The sun blazed and the temperature rose quickly.

Her eyes were weary, her face beet red. She wore a pair of ragged edged jean shorts with an oversized T-shirt.

She dropped her hoe and grabbed the tail of her shirt. He cleared his throat to expose his presence, but she didn't hear him. She tugged the shirt over her head and threw it. He looked away, but back again quickly, his eyes widening.

Why was she undressing in the yard? She wore a white tank top that fit so snuggly it unveiled every curve of her body. It wasn't appropriate, but he couldn't steer his eyes away. She lifted her hoe and started swinging again, oblivious to the fact that he was there.

Apparently, she saw nothing wrong with working outside in her underwear. He would hate himself for it later, but he wanted to memorize every inch. Her long slender arms bulged slightly when she lifted the hoe. Everything about her was beautiful. Paul followed the length of her body until his gaze came to rest on her feet, and the squirming object behind them. Terror stricken, he bolted from the barn.

$$\text{❧} \quad 8 \quad \text{❧}$$

It had been fourteen days since her conversation with Paul in the garden. Fourteen days since she'd seen that smile that smothered her skin with goose bumps. Fourteen days of admiring his handiwork and longing for Friday. The day she'd be home to see him again.

It had finally arrived, but he wasn't here.

Maybe that wasn't a bad thing. Her nerves were like frenzied tentacles coiling through every vein when she found herself anywhere near the man. Serving wrong orders would've been a sure way to lose her job her first two weeks of work.

Feeling faint from the heat, Rachel stopped to rest and admired the first few rows free of weeds. Would Paul approve?

Where is he?

The sun burned her shoulders, and her parched throat ached. She had already taken her shirt off, but that produced little relief.

"Rachel, don't move."

Dizziness swept through her at the sound of Paul's captivating voice behind her.

She searched for his buggy, but didn't see it. Where had he come from?

Oh no, her shirt.

She began to turn for where it lay on the ground.

"*Nein!* Stay very still."

Startled, she obeyed, her torso in a half-twist, bringing them face to face.

He was staring at the ground near her feet. "Give me your hoe. Slowly."

She handed it to him, terrified of his concentrated look.

After he gave one brutal chop into the earth, she turned to look behind her. Not one stride distant lay a separated copperhead, it's body still squirming. She gasped. The sky darkened and foggy white bursts of dots flashed before her eyes as she faded into a world of nothingness.

Opening her eyes, she found herself lying flat on the porch. Paul sat on the balls of his feet leaning slightly over her to her right and uttering her name. He held her gaze, never blinking. She pulled forward, her head pounding at the sudden shift. Regretting the decision to sit up, she leaned back. "What happened?"

Instead of meeting his gaze, she zeroed in on his chest. "You fainted."

"I'm terrified of snakes."

He laughed and the deep-throated sound was unexpected and soothing and compelling all at once. "Are you still lightheaded?"

"A little, yes ..."

He leaned so close she could feel his breath. A fresh clean scent mixed with damp earth clung to him. "You should take it easy until you feel better. Do you want me to help you inside?"

"No." She swallowed hard. "But thank you." Her head continued to pound, and she stretched her fingers across her forehead. "How did I get up here?"

His deep laugh broke through the moment, relieving the tension. "I carried you. Your mom isn't here, and I couldn't lay you down in the sun." The color in his cheeks deepened, and his eyes sparkled.

She had fallen into him? "I'm so sorry."

He pushed himself up with both hands, his muscles bulging from the effort. "I'm just glad you're okay. Let me help you stand." He took her hand and helped her up, then led her to the swing. "I'll be right back."

Her mind raced. How long had he been here? Images of Paul carrying her in his arms assailed her. His footsteps sounded on the porch. Rachel straightened her tank top, leaving a trail of dirt across the white fabric.

He offered her a tall glass of lemonade. "Here, drink this slowly. It should make you feel better."

Rachel brought it to her dry lips. The juice dribbled down her chin and onto her shirt. Paul reached out his hand as though to wipe it, but stopped.

A frisson of awareness trailed through the air between them.

"Thank you. I'm okay now. I don't want to keep you from your work."

"I haven't taken my lunch break yet. I'm in no hurry."

Rachel wanted him to leave. But didn't. Would he stay? What was wrong with her?

"Paul ... I didn't know you were here. I would've never ..." her words caught in her throat.

A small frown appeared. One she couldn't interpret. "It's okay." He left the porch and within minutes came back and handed her the neatly folded shirt.

"I should've let you know I was there." He gave her a smile that sank through her skin all the way to her bones.

She blushed as she slipped the shirt over her head. *He was watching me.* "Thank you."

He hypnotized her with his gentle gaze as he slid a chair across the porch and positioned it facing her. It was nothing like the first few times he'd looked at her.

His smile faded, allowing nothing but compassion to linger in his gaze. "Drink as much as you can, but slowly."

Rachel took small sips, avoiding his eyes. They fell on his lips instead, and she instantly wanted to bury her head in her arms.

"You shouldn't weed in the heat of the day." He glanced at her feet.

"And it would be better to wear ... different shoes." She was struck by the alarm in his features, by the determination in his voice. It was as if he feared something dire would happen to her.

Rachel felt it again, the way her feminine instincts awakened in his presence. She lowered her chin to hide her smile. "I'll be sure to start in the morning from now on. And I promise to wear different shoes."

"Gut." He reached toward her, pulled off the glove still attached to her left hand, and placed it on his lap. She stared blankly at her bare hands hoping he didn't notice the heat in her cheeks. "You shouldn't need these for awhile."

She spread her hand across her shorts, wiping away the sweat gathered on her palm. "I forgot I was wearing that."

"It's gut to see the color's finally coming back to your face."

He *did* notice. And she couldn't even look away. The magnetic pull he had on her was stronger than any embarrassment demanding her attention.

"You had me worried there for a minute." His tone remained sincere.

"I should've known better."

He raised his brow. "You've worked a garden before?"

She loved this, sitting across from him. Much as she wanted to laugh, she looked across the yard, binding the giddiness easing to the surface. "No. I've never even thought about it."

"I've spent a lot of time around other Englisch teenagers, but never have I met one who *wanted* to plant a garden."

"Yeah. I sort of jumped in headfirst. I had no idea what I was doing. But I wanted to try something productive." Anything to give her something to do. She skipped that part. There was no reason to complain. Especially not here, not now.

"I'm impressed." The look in his eyes took her breath. It was as if he wanted to stretch their time together as badly as she did. "That's for certain sure."

Losing the battle against his gaze, she blinked several times. "Thank you. That means a lot coming from you, an experienced Amish farmer."

For several seconds, he only stared at her. Again giving the impression he didn't want to leave yet. "I grew up on a farm, and still do my chores, but I'm no farmer. I'm much more at ease with wood," he said, his blue eyes gleaming.

She wanted to say his work was impressive, that she couldn't believe the difference in only one full week, but her mouth and brain didn't cooperate.

"Your mom wants me to pull up all the bushes in front."

"I knew she would. I'm hoping she'll plant a flower garden." Her gaze followed the bushes lined below the porch. "The smell of fresh flowers, and all the colors would be ..." healing ..."nice. Especially this time of year."

"You're into flowers?" He gave her a lazy smile as he stretched out his legs. They were long, and she could tell they were strong. The way he had pulled her to her feet, like she was light as air. There was nothing about this man that appeared weak. She shouldn't keep staring. "I am too."

She laughed. "No, you are not."

"Are you saying just because a man isn't a farmer, he's no good with flowers?" His head tilted to the side. "I'm no good at corn or alfalfa, but with flowers, I have the greenest of thumbs." He held out his fingers and she wanted to touch them.

She pushed her hands beneath her legs. Something about being with him lifted her spirit. Her laughter was once again real.

"Are you feeling better?"

"Yes, thank you." She shifted awkwardly. "I'm so glad you were there. And so glad I didn't see that snake before you. I would've tried to climb on your head."

He laughed. It was an easy sound. All those hesitancies she once thought she perceived seemed forgotten. "I'm glad I was there and glad you're feeling better." He stood, keeping his gaze locked with hers. "I should probably get back to work."

She didn't want the moment to end. But she had no choice but to let him go.

"I'll be right over there." He turned and started down the steps. "Call out if you need me."

"Thank you." She waited until he disappeared around the corner before she swayed toward the door, still feeling woozy.

Was the feeling from earlier or the way their gaze lingered? She would die of embarrassment if she passed out again.

She thought of how he'd carried her before ... and how, unfortunately, she'd missed the whole thing.

❧ *9* ❧

Rain beating against Rachel's bedroom window woke her on Monday morning. She snuggled tighter under the sheets as memories of Friday crept into her thoughts. Pulling the comforter to her face, she couldn't stop dreaming.

He was amazingly easy to talk to, this Amish man who'd entered her life. Every encounter she had with Paul made the scales tip in favor of staying in this small town—of even being happy about it.

After making her bed, she stepped into the bathroom. She grimaced, remembering Mom's face when she'd first seen the shower and toilet. Puke green, she'd called it.

The changes Paul made were incomparable. She no longer recognized this room. His work was brilliant. He had a gift. There was no doubt. New tile, new shower, new vanity ... new life.

A life without her daddy.

If only her own private world could be as trimmed and polished. Staring at her reflection, she quoted a verse. "Create in me a clean heart, O God, and renew a steadfast spirit within me. Psalm 5:10."

After watching reruns for over an hour, she pulled her sweatshirt hood over her head and ran from the back porch to the barn. She climbed the ladder and settled into her favorite, plush softball blanket on the corner bench in the loft. Rain trickled against the tin roof, the sound soothing. Opening her book, she started where she left off, hoping to lose herself in the world of the Amish.

The damp air soaked through her skin, so she tucked the blanket under her chin.

Thirty minutes later, the barn door opened and slammed shut. Rachel's heart leapt to her throat. *God is your refuge and strength* ... She pressed her palm to her chest and exhaled. *Mom.*

"I'm up here." Her feet scrambled in the hay as she moved to the railing and peeked over the edge. She stiffened when Paul lifted his head at the sound of her voice.

"Hullo, Rachel."

"I thought you were ... I didn't realize you were working today." The thought of another close proximity with him threw her into action. She moved toward the ladder. "I can go back inside."

Paul shook his head. "Nein, you don't have to leave. I'm just grabbing my wrench." His smooth, tranquil voice sharpened her senses. "What are you doing up there?" The brim of his hat shaded his eyes, hiding the gleam that surely matched the tease in his voice.

"Reading," she said, thankful her voice didn't reveal that horrible quiver identical to the one bouncing all over her stomach as she settled back onto the bench. She reopened the book, but it would be impossible to concentrate with Paul below.

"What're you reading?"

Not expecting that question, she lurched to her feet. She would die if he knew she was reading an Amish romance. "A ... uh, it's fiction." She stared at the book, like she would a stick of dynamite waiting to explode.

"Do you read a lot?"

"Yep, ... I uh ... when I have time." The clumsy words fell out, and she squeezed her eyes shut. Something about being alone with Paul again made her jumpy. "I thought I'd have more time here, but haven't had much at all. Surprisingly." *Please leave.* Her pulse quickened at the shuffle of his footsteps climbing the ladder. And then suddenly, he was standing at the top. His gaze held hers, as he diminished the distance between them.

As she took a step back, her blanket tangled around her legs. The book slipped from her grasp and landed on the hay bordering his feet.

"Nice reading place you have here." He removed his hat, rain dripping onto the wooden floor then he grabbed the book. He started to hand it back to her, but hesitated. "Shunned." He read the title in a whisper. His gaze reclaimed hers, his expression blank, his silence deafening. He handed the book to her.

Heat burned her neck and seared all the way up to her head.

Finally he met her gaze. "You're reading an Amish book?"

"It's just a silly story."

Turning, he raked his fingers through his hair before replacing his hat. "I found my wrench and thought I'd say hullo." He fumbled with it and hurried down the ladder without saying another word.

Rachel followed him. She didn't know how with her knees quaking beneath the heaviness settling on her. Or why. She just needed to.

He had already reached the yard when she caught up to him and grabbed his arm. "Paul, wait." A sudden stream of rain drenched her within seconds.

He shifted his focus toward the house. "You should go inside." His voice sounded rusty, his mouth drawn tight.

She raised her voice, the rain drowning out their words. "I want to talk to you."

"What's so important you would come out here and get soaking wet?"

She didn't reply, but drew in a deep breath willing her stomach's foolish fluttering to dissipate.

"Let's at least go back inside the barn." Paul gestured with a jerk of his head.

"Are you upset with me?" Rachel asked, ignoring his advice to follow him. The rain beat against her face, stinging her cheek.

"Nein. Please go inside, you're getting soaked. You'll be sick."

Her shoulders slumped slightly under his gaze. "You don't have to worry about me."

The rain changed direction and beat against his face.

"*Eefeldich*. This is ridiculous. There's no reason we should be discussing this. I work for your mamm. You're Englisch and I'm Amish." His voice remained calm, though the rain continued to pour.

"What does that matter?" The rain fell into her mouth as she spoke. Mascara was burning the back of her lids, and she could barely keep her eyes open.

"Our lives our different. We have nothing in common." He stopped and the rain slowed for several seconds.

She heard his words, yet couldn't believe what he was saying. Especially after the way he had protected her Friday, the way he looked at her. "I thought we could be ... friends."

"Rachel, you will make many friends here, but you and I? It wouldn't be a good idea." His voice may have been controlled, but his words pounded against her like bricks.

"Okay." She paused, giving him a chance to change his mind. To tell her he didn't mean it. But he said nothing. He just stared at her with confused interest, proving her foolish for ever having thought otherwise.

She lifted her hands, but then let them fall. Her stark laughter matched the emotions zigzagging through her. Surprise. Anger. Humiliation. "I'm sorry for bothering you." She took off, running for the house. When she was safe inside, her breath caught and couldn't reach her lungs.

She hadn't been able to take a full breath since that horrible day over a year ago. It felt as though a knot pressed between her chest and heart and suffocated her. Slowly, each day. More and more, until she thought she would give completely out of air.

How could she have let herself believe things would get better here? Or that he would want to be friends? She climbed the stairs to her room, and found her warmest pajamas, the ones she never had to wear in Florida.

It rained all afternoon, and she stared through the window, the tightening in her chest strengthening with each hour. Paul stayed in the barn. She had kept him from working too.

After hours of feeling sorry for herself, she finally trudged downstairs to start dinner. She opened a cookbook and pulled out the ingredients for chicken tetrazzini, hoping it would keep her mind off him.

As the noodles were cooking, Rachel sautéed chopped mushrooms, onions, and peppers. She remembered every word Paul said. Why did it matter that they had nothing in common?

She drained the water from the noodles. After mixing the cream of mushroom soup and sour cream with the cooked noodles, she added the vegetables, and placed everything in a glass dish. Why would it be better if they weren't friends?

She shredded a cup of sharp cheddar cheese. Despair rolled in her stomach as the meaning of his words settled in. He didn't want to give her the wrong impression, so he didn't even want to be friends, because he had no interest in her at all.

She sprinkled cheese on the prepared casserole and placed it into the oven. Of course he wouldn't be interested in her. He was Amish. How ridiculous she must have seemed! Like a lovesick puppy.

This recipe wasn't keeping her mind off him, it was making it worse.

Why couldn't she go back to Florida, move in with Samantha, and finish high school with her friends? She would never have to face him again. But the thought of never seeing him again stung.

She moved to the living room and, still shivering, curled up with her thickest blanket on the couch.

Her eyelids were heavy, and she had nearly dozed off when the rattle of Paul's buggy leaving the yard woke her vaguely.

She stood and rushed to the front door. She wanted to apologize, but he was already gone.

The book lay in the swing. Panic twisted in her stomach. She had left the novel in the barn. What if he had read some of it? What would he think of her?

Rain fell in a drizzle and the sky formed dark, gray clouds. A perfect setting for the way she felt.

The scent of cooked peppers and onions flooded the kitchen. When the timer chimed, she pulled out the tetrazzini and placed it on the counter to cool.

Pain throbbed through Rachel's temples as she fumbled through the medicine cabinet for Tylenol. They were out. She took a long, hot shower hoping the steam would diminish the tightening through her chest.

After grabbing her blanket from the couch, she shuffled upstairs and crawled into bed, feeling more alone than she had in a long time.

＊ 10 ＊

A twenty-minute wagon ride into town for supplies and another twenty minutes on the ride back, gave Paul plenty of time to ponder. Even now as he steered his horse into the Adams's drive, he seriously reconsidered his earlier actions. He needed to talk to Rachel. He'd run numerous scenarios through his head on how to explain.

His first thought was to tell her the truth. But the truth was he had no clue why he'd reacted that way. Except for the fact that not too long ago he'd watched another Englischer woman pursue his friend, as if it was some kind of game. Once she'd won his heart, she no longer wanted him. But none of that had anything to do with Rachel.

So he conceded to do the next best thing.

Apologize.

Disappointed Mrs. Adams hadn't returned, he waited in the barn. It would be improper to go inside with Rachel's mother not present. Especially with the feel of Rachel's fingers still tickling his flesh. And he certainly didn't want her out in the rain anymore.

The question kept nagging at him. Why would she be reading about his people? And why had he overreacted?

When Mrs. Adams returned, he stepped onto the porch and glanced at the swing, the book no longer there.

He inhaled the aroma of onions and peppers as he entered the house, but there was no sign of Rachel. Thankfully, Mrs. Adam's idle chatter didn't require much more than an occasional *jah*. It wasn't exactly the best time to discuss important matters concerning any project changes. Not when all his attention was centered on his employer's daughter and her whereabouts. He removed the linoleum floor from the hallway, checking and rechecking the stairs, but Rachel never came down.

That should've been a good thing. He hadn't realized that he would endure this particular difficulty when he took the job. But he needed this income for his business to survive. If he was going to continue to work here, he had to set some boundaries. He was already walking a fine line with his uncle. His construction business was top priority. He didn't need this distraction. The best way to keep that distraction at bay would be to stay as far away from Rachel Adams as possible.

After finishing the preparation for the hardwood floors to be installed in the morning, Paul left the their house and led Nelly down the country lane. Once in the stable, he set out piles of hay, filled the water trough, and packed the feed barrels.

Uncle Abram entered the barn. "Dinner's ready. Your aunt's waiting on you." His voice was gruff as usual.

Paul kept his head lowered. "Danki." He followed his uncle inside and spoke to no one as he took his seat.

Uncle Abram grunted. "I knew nothing good would come from you working with Englischers on a daily basis. If you're going to let it change your attitude, you're not cut out for it. Especially when I could use you here on the farm. I've given you a roof over your head and taken care of you as one of my own since you were a boy. But I will not allow you to come into this house with the sour attitude you've developed in these past few weeks."

Both his cousins avoided eye contact as if they were banned from speaking to him. His arm muscles tensed as he refrained from arguing. Instead, he met his uncle's gaze and kept his mouth shut to the things he wanted to say. "I apologize, Uncle Abram."

After the blessing was given, Paul took a bite of moist cornbread and barbeque chops. The subtle hint of celery, mixed within the red sauce, reminded him of his own thoughts. Jumbled and confused. He knew better. He'd been taught to be polite, but not to get into deep conversations with the Englischers. It was better to distance themselves. Yet, he'd broken every rule. And he was paying a very high price for his selfish desires.

At the end of the meal, he left through the backdoor and went to the barn to hitch his favorite horse. He stroked her mane. "What's wrong with me, Nelly? Why am I letting this girl get to me?"

Paul drove with no destination in mind. It was time to leave his uncle's house. He wasn't a farmer, and he would never live up to his uncle's expectations. That was for certain sure. He approached Rachel's house and slowed his horse. He wanted to stop, to apologize for being such a *dummkup*, an idiot. A light burned in the upstairs bedroom. Rachel's silhouette moved against the window.

It took every fiber of his being to lead his horse past the house and not turn on the familiar path, knock on the door, and ask to speak to her. What good would that do anyway? He rode for over an hour as the sky darkened, yet shapes of light filtered through his thoughts of her. He returned home long after his uncle was sound asleep.

His determination to move on—to forget her—shattered.

❧　I I　❧

P aul was standing at his buggy gathering supplies to install the hardwood floors when Mrs. Adams approached him.

"Paul, I need your help. Rachel's sick. I have to go to the store. She's burning up with fever, and I have nothing to give her." She turned, not waiting for his answer.

Sweat beaded across his forehead. He trotted to keep up with her long hurried strides. The woman was terribly worried. Should he be too? "What's wrong?"

"I don't know. A virus, maybe."

He ran his hand across his freshly shaven chin. A symbol that he was unmarried, unengaged. "I'll be glad to go to the store for you."

"My car will be faster. I was hoping you'd sit with her? It shouldn't take me long."

It felt as if an air compressor filled his chest as they climbed the stairs. What would he say to Rachel after the way he'd treated her yesterday?

Mrs. Adams entered Rachel's bedroom, but he hesitated outside the door.

"She's sleeping," she whispered. "You can come in."

He pressed a fist to his stomach before moving forward. Rachel lay facing away, beneath a bright green bedspread. Pink curtains with lime green polka dots fell to the window's edge.

Mrs. Adams pressed a cold wet cloth into his hand. "If you'll keep this cool and on her forehead, it might help with the fever."

Not expecting to see her lying so still, he inched closer to get a better look. She was sound asleep. "How long has she been this way?"

"When I came in from my meeting yesterday, she stayed in her room and never came down last night. I checked on her before turning in and she told me she wasn't feeling well." She kept her gaze on Rachel, her voice edged with peace. "It's very common for Rachel to sleep really hard when she's running a fever. I just don't want her to wake up and find herself alone. I'll be back as soon as I can."

He sat in the space next to her. Her cheeks were pink from the fever. He took the cloth, placed it in a bowl filled with water on her nightstand, and wrung it out. Heat radiated from her forehead.

This was his fault. He should've compelled Rachel back inside yesterday, out of the rain. He shouldn't have left her that way. If only he'd stopped to talk to her last night. If that stupid book hadn't taken him by surprise, none of this would be happening.

He should've stayed with her, talked to her, to find out if she felt better after her fainting spell on Friday. He never even asked.

Something about the soft hum of her shallow breathing made him ache. He shouldn't be here, sitting this close, not wanting to leave. His biting remorse moved him from the bed to open the white wooden blinds shading her windows. A pushpin board hung on the wall with pictures of her with a few girls. But one in particular caught his attention. A young man, about their age, had his arms wrapped around her. He leaned closer, studying their expressions, studying her. She looked carefree, happy. Was that her boyfriend? Were they still together?

Lying next to a slim cell phone on the end table stood a framed photo of a man standing with Rachel. She looked several years younger and they wore the same orange and gray uniform. Paul lifted the book she'd been reading yesterday from her dresser and turned it over. That wasn't just an ordinary Amish book. It was one of those romance novels. Like the one he'd caught his cousin reading last spring. His mouth suddenly dry, he looked from Rachel to the book then back to Rachel again.

Then she shifted.

He dropped the book and it clattered onto the dresser. He reeled back and moved next to the bed, pulling the wet cloth from her head.

"Daddy?" The word came from her lips in a breathy rush.

Her weak, but frightened voice startled him. Heaviness settled over him as she drifted back into a restless sleep. He pulled the wet cloth from her forehead, rinsed it, and replaced it, careful not to wake her. Grabbing an extra blanket from the end of the bed, his fingers brushed against her covered feet. The cloth dampened her hair and stuck to her cheeks. After positioning the blanket on her, he gently pushed the wet strands of hair away from her face.

Rachel tossed and turned, pushing the blankets down. Maybe the additional throw was too much. When he reached over to remove the extra blanket, her eyes fluttered open. He stiffened, waited for her reaction, but she closed her eyes without acknowledging his presence. What if Mrs. Adam's was wrong? How sick was she?

He sat next to her and took a deep, pained breath, his guilt suffocating.

Paul took her warm hand, intending to place it under the covers, but she squeezed his fingers. Her skin felt smooth against his rough, calloused palm. He stroked her flesh, his awareness rising. Never had he held a girl's hand before.

For the next twenty minutes, he kept the tender flesh of her palm secure in his grasp. Her head shifted occasionally on her pillow, but she gave no sign of waking. He couldn't move as the thought of leaving Lancaster County, of leaving her behind, caused an agonizing twinge through his chest.

"I'm back."

He jumped up, and Rachel's hand slipped away from his. The unusual warmth he'd felt dissolved and now there was only a cold, stark emptiness. He backed away from the bed.

Mrs. Adams stroked Rachel's forehead. "Honey, I need you to wake up to take this." Her voice rang through louder, more determined than before.

Paul wanted to move closer, but stopped himself and leaned against the wall near the door. Would he be able to stay long enough to speak to her?

"Thank you so much for staying." She spoke in softer tones, her voice weary, though encouraging.

"I hope she'll be okay." He didn't want to leave. Not yet. But he had no reason to stay any longer. "I need to go into town. Do you need anything else?"

Mrs. Adams covered her mouth. "Oh, I forgot. Could you stop by the restaurant and let Mrs. Mavis know she won't be in today?"

His gaze shifted between Rachel and her mother. "The restaurant?" he asked, his voice wobbly.

"What's the name of that place?" She tilted her head toward the ceiling and let out a frustrated sigh. "The Plain and Fancy. She's supposed to work this afternoon."

She had a job ... at the restaurant? Paul grabbed his hat from the table. "I'll go right now."

"Thank you, Paul."

Why hadn't he thought of that before? The first day he laid eyes on her came back to him. She'd visited the restaurant to inquire about a job. That had to be where she spent all her time.

He hurried to town, eager to do as asked and come back. Maybe she would be awake when he returned.

Mrs. Mavis greeted him when he entered the restaurant. Her boisterous voice boomed from behind the counter. "Good morning, Paul. Will you be dining alone today?" The wrinkles under her eyes suggested many long hours of labor.

Under her kind gaze, his shoulders slumped. "No, I'm not here for lunch. Rachel Adams, she works here?"

Her eyes narrowed, but she offered her answer with a smile. "Yes, but she won't be in until this afternoon. Why do you ask?"

"I'm working for her mamm. Rachel's sick. Really sick."

Her plump cheeks fell. "Oh, the poor dear. I'm so sorry to hear that."

"Jah, me too."

"Please tell her we'll be praying for a speedy recovery. Thank you so much for letting me know."

Nelly's ears wiggled as Paul trotted down the highway at a steady pace. He bounced to the familiar rhythm, his thoughts consumed with the same Englisch girl who'd stolen all of his good sense. Paul pulled onto the familiar path and headed back inside. "Please, God. Let her be okay."

Mrs. Adams stayed upstairs with Rachel. He couldn't go to her room—it wasn't his place. He would have to wait for Mrs. Adams to come down. At least he had plenty to do downstairs, where he'd be close.

He glanced toward the stairs over and over, willing Mrs. Adams to appear. He picked up another floorboard, hammering it in place. He worked diligently and had finished part of the living room by the end of the day.

Mrs. Adams never came down so he left without knowing if there had been any change.

Paul brushed Nelly and gave her fresh hay before walking toward his uncle's house. The sun hid behind the tall pines, casting shadows across the dirt yard.

"*Was us ketz?*" Aunt Leah asked.

Paul laid his hat on the rack, buying time to hide his disappointment. He assembled a half-hearted smile for her. "Nothing's wrong, *mir lew uff hoffning.*"

"Nothing, we live on hope. That's your honest answer?"

A mixture of hay dust and heaviness had settled on his chest, and he cleared his throat. "Mrs. Adam's daughter is *mied.* Something smells wunderbaar."

"You go from sick child, to how gut the food smells. Jah, you're worried."

He paced in the kitchen. The sound of his shuffling shoes reminding him how much he wanted to march up those steps today and cradle Rachel close to his chest. "She's in God's hands. Can I help you?"

Aunt Leah slapped him heartily on the backside with her towel.

"Ach, Paul. You work hard all day and want to help in the kitchen. Have a sit down. Dinner's almost ready."

Tossing and turning all night, he dreamed of Rachel. She called his name over and over, but he couldn't reach her. Her tear-filled eyes accused him before she vanished into thin air. He sat up in a cold sweat. Moonlight beamed through his upstairs window casting a shimmering glow across the dark colors of his patchwork quilt. He collapsed into his pillow, crossing his arms behind his head, the dream still dancing across his mind.

The following morning, just after dawn, Paul arrived at the Adams'. Was Rachel feeling better? Would he get the opportunity to see her? These questions took the place of any normal emotions he had before yesterday.

Paul let himself in and peered down the hall. He checked Mrs. Adams' office. It was empty. He worked quietly, not wanting to disturb Rachel, but not so quiet that Mrs. Adams wouldn't hear his presence. During lunch, his tension wound tighter each time he crossed by the stairway. His unease was so rigid, by the time Rachel's mom appeared toward the end of his lunch hour, Paul nearly came out of his boots.

"Hi, Paul.

He straightened at the sound of her voice. "How is she?"

"She's better. Her fever came down some, but she's still sleeping a lot." A measure of relief flowed through her words. "I've been working from her room to keep an eye on her."

He mumbled under his breath, "Thank you, God." Then stronger. "Do you know what's wrong with her?"

"I called the doctor's office. There's a virus going around." She sighed. "She insists on not going, but if she's no better by tomorrow, I'm taking her."

"My aunt could check on her. We don't usually see outside doctors, except for emergencies, so she's our community nurse."

"That's very nice of you to offer. Rachel has the most outgoing personality of anyone you will ever meet, but when it comes to her needs, she doesn't want to burden anyone." Her brow crinkled. "And she's very stubborn about accepting help. But I will definitely keep your aunt in mind. I really enjoyed our visit."

His shoulders relaxed. "Mrs. Mavis sends her thoughts and prayers." He paused. "I was surprised to find out Rachel was working at the restaurant."

She stirred cream into her coffee. "Is it that obvious she's never had a job?"

"That's not what I meant."

"I'm only teasing. Her daddy never wanted her to have to work. They were always so busy with softball." She gave a part laugh, part cry. "She wanted to get a job, hoping to make some friends. It wasn't easy for her to come here. She's so unhappy." She poured Paul a cup and placed it in front of him before sitting. "It's been hard leaving her friends behind. Leaving everything behind."

She took the job to make friends, and he had cut her off completely. The memory of her words, her tone, her disappointment, twisted like a knife through his chest. It probably crushed her.

He took a sip of his coffee, but the strong, warm flavor gave him little comfort.

She folded her hands under her chin. "I've really left her to fend for herself."

He wanted to sit with Rachel, to be near her—to apologize.

She yawned. "I wanted to fix the loft in the barn for her. Give her somewhere to hang out, a place of her own. I don't know when I'll have time to get to it." She took another sip. "Would you be interested in helping me?"

"Jah. There's some extra wood. If you didn't want to save it, I could use that. What are her interests so I can give it a more personal touch." Something deep within cheered at the thought of learning more about her.

"What a wonderful idea!" She stood, grabbed a towel, and wiped off the table. "She enjoys reading and softball. Photography. She loves children. She's really smart. Has always made straight As. For as long as I can remember, she has tutored other students. And her heart ... she has the kindest heart." She turned and faced him fully, her eyes gleaming. "You just don't find the maturity she has in girls her age these days."

He'd seen that, just in the small amount of time he'd spent with her. And photography. That explained all the pictures. Paul stood, his outlook brighter than it had been in days.

"Oh, I almost forgot. I think Rachel was dreaming, because she never answered me, but she said your name. She must have thought you were still sitting with her."

Mrs. Adams walked away, leaving him speechless. His eyes widened, and he was unable to blink. Should he tell her Rachel called out her dad's name yesterday? That made more sense than her saying his name. She hadn't known he was there. Or had she?

Rachel only wanted to be his friend. He had treated her different from the moment he laid eyes on her. And all because she created feelings in him, feelings he'd never experienced—feelings he couldn't explain.

But maybe he could make it up to her. He wanted to create the perfect loft and was almost desperate to get started.

❦ 12 ❦

On Friday morning, Rachel hurried toward her car hoping to catch a glimpse of Paul working by the barn. She wanted to confront him, to make him understand she'd only read that book because her mom had suggested it. She hadn't even wanted to read it. Not at first. He didn't have to know that, or how much she enjoyed it, how being swept into that world made her think of him.

But none of that mattered. He wasn't there.

Returning to work was just what she needed. The restaurant gave her an escape. She'd go crazy in that house all day, thinking about Paul, about how he wanted little to do with her.

The familiar aroma of blueberry muffins filled her senses as she entered the Plain and Fancy, and she remembered with a pang of regret, she'd skipped breakfast again in a hurry to get to work.

Coffee would have to do this morning.

She had just finished tying her apron when an elderly man entered and took a seat in her section. His gray beard, matted with tangles, hung to his breastbone.

"*Guder mariye.*"

Rachel replied with confidence, "Good morning to you. What can I get for you today?"

"I'll have a ham and cheese breakfast sandwich, a sticky bun, and a cup of coffee."

She scribbled his order and slipped the pad in her apron. "I'll put your order in and be right back with your coffee."

The man's broad smile filled his full cheeks. "Danki."

"You're welcome."

A group of teenage Amish girls gathered around one of her tables. She gave the man's order to the cook, poured a cup of coffee for another customer, and returned to the floor.

She reached for her pad as she approached the Amish teenagers. "Hi, I'm Rachel. I'll be your server today."

"Wiegeht's, how are you? Is Kelli working today?" One of the girls asked.

Why would they be asking for Kelli? "She's on break right now, but she'll be back in few minutes." Rachel gave a polite smile.

One by one she took their order, trying not to imagine Paul courting one of them. They were all pretty, especially the blonde with eyes the color of blue ice. Wisps of wavy tresses spilled from her cap. She was probably the lucky one.

"I'll be right back with your drinks."

She exhaled as she returned to the kitchen. Did Paul think he was better than her because of his heritage? Her skin tingled as she recalled his piercing gaze, edged with a trace of warmth. She shook the thought and focused on the order.

Kelli returned just as she entered the kitchen.

"Some Amish teenagers are asking for you."

"Oh, it must be Belinda. She's a friend of mine."

"What do you mean ... friend? You have an Amish friend?"

"Sure. There are so many of them around here, you're bound to become friends with some of them."

Rachel placed the drinks on the tray and set it on the counter. A dull ache spread across her chest, Kelli's statement setting heavily on her heart. *Friend.*

Paul's words gouged more deeply.

"Do you hang out with her?" Rachel asked.

"Not a lot. I've gone to a few Sunday night singings before, but it's not really my thing. She invites me all the time though."

Rachel crossed her arms, her tasks forgotten. "What's a Sunday night singing?"

"It's like a party. They eat, play games, and hang out at each other's farms."

"Really? Isn't it like against a rule or something to be friends with us?" That's what she'd hoped. It would make her feel better. She was already in danger of caring too much what Paul Fischer thought. Especially after the way he carried her out of the sun, the way he looked at her when she'd opened her eyes, the way he sat with her through his lunch break.

"No, they're really nice. They just live different lifestyles than us."

"Oh." She paused, taking a deep breath, the ache cutting deeper. A strange desire to explore the lives of the Amish and find out what made them so different filled her. "Hey, if they invite you this week and you go, could I tag along? I've been stuck in the house all week." Kelli could never find out the real reason she asked. No one could.

Kelli moved toward the door. "Why wait for an invitation?"

"You're going to ask?" With her greatest effort, Rachel kept her voice even.

"Why not?"

Her smile transformed into a troubled frown. "And that would be fine?"

"I guess we'll find out."

"Okay. Here goes." Her chest beat erratically as she walked toward the girls' table, Kelli following behind.

They exchanged how-do-you-dos before Kelli asked the dreaded question. "Are you guys having a singing this Sunday?"

Rachel shoved her hands in her pockets and glanced at the other girls spaced around the table, her brain racing ahead. What if they said no?

"Jah, you coming?"

"Sure." Kelli nudged Rachel in the elbow as she glanced at the dark-haired girl sitting in the far corner. "This is my friend Rachel. She's new to town, and I wanted to bring her along. If that's okay?"

"Jah, Rachel. Please come." The others nodded, their smiles widening.

"I would love to. Thank you." Rachel escaped to the kitchen, to take a deep vital breath.

Would Paul change his mind once he saw her with his friends?

Later that evening, Rachel poured scented bubbles into the gushing flow of bath water. After lighting a candle, she climbed into the warm, silky haven. She'd been eager to make it home before three, but reached her house disappointed. Paul's buggy wasn't parked in the yard, and neither was Mom's car. Her iPod playlist hummed in the background, and the familiar constant ache weaved through the recesses of her heart. The image of Paul's protective concern when she'd fainted burned in her memory. Had she imagined the entire thing?

No, it was real.

She closed her eyes against the betrayal of longing, blocking from her mind the way he took her breath, the way his blue eyes turned her insides to mush. She inhaled the scent of lavender, pushing her fingers through the foaming moisture, thinking about the spell Paul had cast over her. It was unyielding, unbreakable.

An hour later, she sat on the front porch cool from staying in the bath long after the water chilled to the same temperature as the air. She soaked in the night music. Crickets chattering, horse and buggy's passing by, wind stirring the tree's leaves. How would Daddy like Paul? She pictured her dad standing across from her on the softball field. Hands on his legs, his eyes trained directly on her. He had a rare smile, the kind that gave you the feeling he believed in you. It conveyed confidence that love in its truest form lay beneath the surface. She missed him.

Oh, how she wished he were here to give her some man advice. Laughter filled her soul. Yeah, that wouldn't go very well. He'd made it clear that only a remarkable man would be good enough for his little girl.

The cool evening breeze forced her inside, and she found her mom sitting at the kitchen table working on bills.

Rachel poured a glass of lemonade. "How was your day?"

"Pretty good. How about yours?"

"It was okay, nothing too exciting." Rachel paused, the fluttery empty feeling in the pit of her stomach deepening. "Did Paul take the day off?"

Mom kept her eyes on her checkbook. "Yes, he asked for a few days off."

Rachel swallowed a mouthful of liquid, forcing herself not to react. "Really, for how long?"

"He didn't say, only that he would be gone a few days."

Gone? "Is he going out of town? When will he be back?"

"I don't know."

What if he decided to leave and never came back? What if she never saw him again?

❧ 13 ❧

arly the next morning, a loud crash woke Rachel. She blinked several times, trying to piece together what was happening. She eased herself into a sitting position and counted off the days.

Friday.

Paul? Rachel tossed back the covers, moved to the window, and gently adjusted the blind. His buggy wasn't there.

Rachel dressed and wandered downstairs.

Sitting in the middle of the floor, Mom was unpacking the last of their boxes, officially making this home. Rachel grabbed some breakfast before taking her own box to unload.

"I had a nice visit with your Aunt Barbara. Her little Katelyn is precious."

Rachel smiled easily. "How old is she now?"

"Four."

"She was only a baby when they last visited. Was Tanner there?"

"No, but Barbara insists your cousin can't wait to see you again. She's planning to bring him by one day, if she can ever get him settled with all his college preparations. Oh, honey, I'm sorry. I know school is a sore subject with you."

"It's okay," she said too quickly, but repeated her response, more slowly to balance her emotions. "It's okay, really."

"I don't know why it's taken so long to go through this stuff."

"I do. It's our whole life." She fiddled with a box filled with Dad's things, filled with memories. His ties, his baseball trophies, his smell.

Mom lifted the container from the floor. "Maybe we should put this one away for now." Her voice lowered and raw emotions swept across her face in slow motion, starting with disappointment, then anger, and ending with devastation. She stood and disappeared down the hall.

A sudden weakness washed over Rachel. Things had been better, more normal than at home. But now, the certainty edged its way to her core. Deep down, Mom still blamed her.

Another box overflowing with trophies caught her eye, and she leaned against the wall. The heaves fighting to escape ripped through her middle as silent tears tumbled down her cheeks, dropping in splashes on Paul's hardwood floor.

Mom returned and Rachel looked off into the distance to hide her tears, now drying and cold. Leaving behind a trail of salty stickiness, stinging with the realization that Daddy was never coming back.

"That's enough organizing for one day. Why don't we start a fresh pot of coffee, and you can tell me all about your job and new friend, Kelli."

Mom often seemed to ignore the pain by pushing it away and pretending things were normal. Yet it was obvious. The pain suffocated her. Daddy had been gone a year, but a day didn't go by there weren't tears in her mother's eyes. Rachel went along with the charade. She had no choice, or she would drown in her own grief, her own guilt.

"We have plans Sunday night." Her thoughts raced ahead to the anticipated time, and an unexpected shiver crawled up her spine.

"That's wonderful, honey. I'm so glad you like your job and that you've made a friend."

She bit her lip. "Me too."

Mid-Sunday afternoon, Kelli pulled into the drive, and Rachel ran out to meet her. She hoped the maxi dress she'd chosen would be appropriate for their party.

Jittery trembles filled every muscle as each second passed. *This is a bad idea.*

Moments later, Kelli parked her car in an Amish yard, right beside the barn. The large white house, twice the size of theirs, had no shutters. The front porch stretched from one end of the house to the other. A swing hung on one side, and three wooden rockers took up the space on the other.

"Come on and I'll introduce you to some of the other girls."

Twenty buggies parked along the path and onto the lawn. Rachel lingered by the car looking through the crowd at the Amish friends gathered together near the back door.

I shouldn't be here. What if my coming makes Paul furious?

Kelli linked their arms. Rachel staggered before grasping her hand. "Kel..." Before she finished telling her she'd changed her mind, several Amish girls met them at the car.

Belinda took Rachel's free hand. "Danki, for coming."

Others introduced themselves and Rachel recognized a few from the restaurant. The girls were so welcoming. They hugged both her and Kelli and took their hands and then guided them toward the crowd. Rachel blew out a breath as her stiff shoulders slackened.

I can't leave now, that would be rude.

Paul wasn't among the Amish men and disappointment assaulted her like a mallet. Maybe he was late. The sounds of arriving buggies kept her neck swiveling to inspect the new arrivals. Thirty minutes later, she gave up. He wasn't coming.

Kelli fit in easily. The Amish had friends with outsiders. They were pleasant and inclusive, which meant Paul simply didn't want to be hers. The sharp jab of regret slowly bled through her veins strengthening her determination. She *would* have that talk with Paul as soon as he showed up to finish their house. And she would get her answer once and for all.

A volleyball game started up on the farm's large yard and Kelli joined in. Rachel stood to the side next to the incredibly green and tall cornfield. She listened. No horns blaring, no speeding cars, just the sound of wind rustling through the stalks and laughter that seemed to stretch for miles. Cows grazed in the pasture and chickens wobbled through the yard, bobbing their heads with each step. Horses neighed, swatting flies with their tails, and a dog barked as he chased a few audacious birds. Dust whirled around the player's feet as they trailed the ball. Kelli's team was winning.

One of the girls sauntered across the yard toward Rachel. She carried the true image of an Amish woman. Her dark hair tucked under a bonnet, bobby pins sparkling against the late afternoon sun. The girl's light blue dress hung just above her ankles. "Rachel, I have baby kittens in the barn. You want to see, jah?"

"Yes. Thank you."

Inside the barn, the strong aroma of manure about knocked her back. She coughed, clearing her lungs.

"Ach, it takes getting used to, jah?" She gave her the kind of smile that someone would give their sister, their friend. Even though they were from different worlds, this girl seemed genuinely interested in getting to know her better.

"I've never been to a farm before."

"Come see the *bobblin*. Mamm will only let me keep one."

The small balls of fur inched closer to the orange and white mama cat sprawled out on a pile of hay. Their soft meows echoed through the wooden stalls.

"Aw, they're adorable."

The girl introduced Rachel to the rest of their animals before they left the barn.

As the sun set, everyone gathered inside another barn, and a young man lit a few lanterns. A smile crept across her face as she remembered from her novel they didn't use electricity.

The guys and girls stayed separated for the most part. Occasionally a couple would break away from the group, but they distanced themselves in a way. The parties back home were nothing like this.

Only one girl didn't seem to want to be there. And every dark glance in her direction told her she didn't want Rachel there either. What if she was Paul's girlfriend?

How would Paul feel about her being here, surrounded by his people, his friends? And why wasn't he here?

Kelli bounded toward them, her cheeks red from exertion. "Rachel, they're getting ready to sing. Belinda wants us to sit next to her."

A few girls stood one by one, each singing a solo. Some of the guys took a turn. Then the whole group sang together. Rachel hummed along to a few of the songs and closed her eyes reveling in the praise and worship.

It took her a second to realize someone was calling her name. A young man stood across the room, his gaze fixed on her. "Do you sing?"

She pointed a finger at her chest. "Me?"

"Jah." His smile was understanding. He had put her on the spot, and he knew it.

A wide smile stretched across her lips as she moved toward the front. "Yes, I love to sing. Is it okay if I share a song?" She didn't look at any one person, but searched the crowd of faces seated before her.

The others all nodded.

She took a deep breath while deciding on a song. And then the words to *Redeemer*, by Nicole C. Mullen came and she got lost in the moment with Jesus. When she opened her eyes, a few stood and greeted her with a hug.

Kelly nudged her after she took her seat. "Wow! I had no idea you could sing like that."

Heat burned Rachel's neck. "Thank you."

The crowd moved outside, one by one. She stayed next to Kelli, Belinda on her other side. "That was a beautiful song. A great one to end our singing."

Kelli hugged Belinda. "We're going to get going."

Rachel accepted a hug from Belinda. "Thank you for inviting me. I had a great time."

"You will come again, jah?"

She nodded, but then Paul came to mind. She may never come again.

"Did you have fun?" Kelli asked when she pulled onto the highway.

"Yes," she admitted. "I admire them for the way they choose to live. It doesn't seem to bother them at all."

"Yeah, I do too. Growing up plain makes it easier. It would be difficult to give up the things we're used to."

Her rising curiosity of one particular Amish man had her speaking before she had a chance to think it through. "My mom hired a young man to renovate our house. He's Amish."

"Really? Who? Was he at the singing?"

"No, I didn't see him." She looked through the window, hoping Kelli wouldn't hear her true feelings in her tone. "His name is Paul Fischer."

"Oh yeah, the construction guy. I know him."

She twisted her fingers with indecision for only a moment before blurting the question that demanded freedom. "What do you know about him?"

"I've only spoken to him a few times, but he's nice." Kelli flipped the visor up. "I would've thought he'd be married by now."

Rachel cleared the lump materializing in her throat. "Isn't he too young to be married? He's only eighteen." The thought of Paul married made her sick. Physically sick.

Kelli shrugged. "The Amish are usually married by the time they're eighteen."

Eighteen? "Oh, I didn't know that."

"He's probably engaged. Anna has tried forever to get him to court her."

Rachel's stomach lurched. "Anna? Have I met her?" The emptiness in her belly deepened.

"She was there tonight. The grumpy one." Kelli's words sank like a boulder into Rachel's soul.

It *was* her.

Rachel tried tuning in to the soft rock music streaming from the radio, still contemplating her decision about going to the singing. What if Paul found out? If her reading an Amish book upset him, she could only imagine how mad he'd be when he found out she went to one of their parties.

❧ 14 ❧

Rachel skimmed through her closet, searching for something to wear to the Central Market. She wanted something more modest, more Amish, but there was nothing. Everything was bright, bold, trendy. She settled on a pair of cropped denim pants and a pink top with a sleeveless jean jacket.

Paul didn't work on Saturdays and wouldn't come today. And then the truth hit her square in the chest—she missed him.

At least she wouldn't have to face him after their confrontation.

They couldn't avoid each other forever, not while he worked at the house. It had been over a week since they'd spoken. Maybe he'd forgotten about the book and things could go back to normal. As long as he hadn't found out about the singing.

The cool breeze left goose bumps on her arms while she raced to the car. Did Pennsylvania ever get as hot and humid as Florida? It had felt pretty close Friday. But not this morning.

Rachel drove into town, the radio playing her favorite Toby Mac song, just not as loud as usual. She slowed as a horse-drawn buggy pulled onto the highway ahead of her. Self-conscious, she lowered her music even more as she passed. *It isn't wrong to pass them.* "That's why they use the middle lane." She muttered under her breath while guilt afflicted her.

Minutes later, Rachel pulled into the crowded parking lot. She found an empty spot and glanced at the clock. *I'm early*.

Rachel opened the wooden door and searched for Kelli as the scent of grilled sausage and onions assaulted her senses. Counters lined each wall and she scanned the first few tables with an assortment of cookware, quilts, furniture, and clothing. Amish men and women greeted the browsing customers.

Rachel roamed by the first few tables filled with wooden birdhouses, windmills, and handmade dolls. One particular item held her curiosity. She lifted the oddly cute object. An outhouse with three words inscribed on the bottom of the door: *Shhh, open quietly*.

She glanced at the seller whose beard twitched. In the restaurant, she'd served several young Amish men with beards. Why didn't Paul have one? "Is it okay to open this?"

The young man's eyes twinkled. "Jah. But set it down first."

Rachel expected to find a small wooden toilet inside. These people were so talented. She pulled on the tiny, black handle and the wood exploded across the table. She jumped back releasing a small yelp. "I broke it." She picked up the scattered pieces and detected a mouse trap set inside the four walls, rather than the wooden toilet she'd expected to find.

The man laughed so hard he couldn't speak.

She giggled. "Very funny."

"Jah? You got it gut."

How many people had seen the joke played out on her? Flushing, Rachel scanned the room, her gaze catching the back of a young man who'd already rounded the corner. Paul? No. All the Amish men were dressed similar. She could've been mistaken.

But at the sound of her name coming from a rich, deep voice, she knew she wasn't.

&a.

Paul was standing at his table selling some wood carvings at the

Central Market when Rachel arrived. She stopped just a few tables down from him, but hadn't noticed him yet. Would she speak to him? Maybe he could talk to her. That would be the polite thing to do. No, he couldn't.

He hadn't talked to her in over a week. Not since the day he said those horrible things to her. This wasn't the time or the place to apologize.

Most of his family and friends were also there today, so it would be best to keep his distance, not risk curious eyes. His fascination with her was already too much. She was all he thought of lately. He would never be able to hide his emotions from his family. They knew him too well.

His cousin Troy approached his table. "Wiegehts?"

"Gut. Hey, do you want to earn some extra money? I have to leave for a bit."

"Go, I've got things covered, jah?"

Paul could always count on Troy.

Rachel didn't seem to be paying close attention to the tables. Instead touched item after item like she didn't know what to do with herself. He'd made the right decision to avoid her. What would he possibly say anyway? Then she turned and left the building.

Why was she leaving so soon? He had already given his table to Troy.

He opened the main door. She stood on the sidewalk facing the parking lot, but then moved to the side of the building, toward the wooded area. He hurried through the building and pushed past people on his way to the back. He reached the back door and hastened through the narrow alley that led to the other side of the building.

From the alley's depths, he spotted Rachel as she inched closer to the woods, and bending, she spoke softly to a small rabbit that scampered deeper into the trees. She wore those same flip-flops, and her feet were wet from the overgrown grass. Did she not own a pair of safe shoes? Memories of that Friday flooded back. How he'd lifted and carried her to the porch. Her soft skin, the feel of her in his arms as she fell into him, the adorable, confused look in her dark brown eyes.

Out of nowhere, an Englischer appeared and advanced toward her, a young man Paul didn't recognize.

From the wood's edge, Rachel turned to walk closer to the back of the building, but when the strange man called her name, her face seemed to glow in response.

Had she been waiting for him? Was he her boyfriend?

Paul stopped as heaviness settled in his body. It was like a vice closing around his heart, tightening with each second.

The two were speaking but the wind whistling through the alley overpowered their voices.

A desire to retreat to a quiet place to think drew him, but he couldn't move.

❧ 15 ❧

Rachel recognized Jason from the restaurant instantly. "Oh, hi." Rachel put on a smile trying to conceal her alarm.

His eyes searched her, and mental fuzziness gripped her when she realized her mistake. Too many yards separated her from the building, and she took a few jerky steps forward. There were no windows. No doors. Just a chain link fence that connected its rear corner to the wall of dark forest behind her, enclosing the space she occupied.

There was an alley, but no way was she going in there. Not with this guy trailing her.

She needed to move toward the front but would have to walk around Jason to get there. With another awkward step, Rachel inched closer to the back of the building. "Did you need something?"

"I thought you came out here to talk to me, since I called your name. I overheard you at the restaurant Thursday. I knew you were coming and hoped we could spend the day together." His gaze moved from her face to her torso to her legs in slow motion and then back again, an arrogant expression inching across his features.

She looked toward the front, longing for the escape it ensured. If only she could get past him. "I can't. I already have plans for today."

He didn't speak or budge, but kept his gaze locked on hers. She quickened her pace, but before she could get past him, he grabbed her arm with his thin, clammy fingers.

Her heartbeat thrashed in her ears. "What are you doing?"

And then the gap between them closed.

When she tried to pull away, he dug his fingers into her flesh as he pulled her closer to him, closer to the edge of the trees.

She twisted her body, but slipped and fell into him. "Let go of me." Her stomach heaved.

"Rachel?"

Paul?

Jason halted but tightened his grip as she twisted back to see Paul crossing the lawn from the back of the building. He jogged toward them, rapidly closing the distance, not slowing until he'd laid hands on her.

Paul secured an arm across the back of her shoulders and pulled her toward him. "Could I borrow her a minute?"

"Get lost, Amish boy. We're in the middle of something." Jason gave a tug, but she yanked back, broke free, and leaned into the safety of Paul's arm. "Fine. I'll catch up with you later, beautiful." With a sneer, he walked away.

Paul's hand slipped to her waist, and he kept his grip tight around her as he guided her in the opposite direction. Once they reached the rear of the building, he glanced over his shoulder before leading her to the middle of the alleyway and stopping. Rachel stared wide-eyed into the dead-end area. She would've been trapped. But then she noticed the door, the one Paul must've come through.

Rachel couldn't believe Paul was standing here—holding her. She had hoped to see him, to apologize, but this was not how things were supposed to go. Her hands were trembling, her head was aching, and at any minute that boiling rolling around in her stomach could—

Paul lifted her chin, persuading her to look at him. "Are you all right?"

Fear crinkled the edges of his wide eyes. It was the same fear soaring through her veins. She didn't want to let him know how frightened she felt. But what if he hadn't been there? What would she have done? Fighting back the nausea, she took several slow, deep breaths. She stared at him feeling dizzy, out of balance. A whirlwind of frightening images played in her mind. Jason dragging her through the forest, leaving her broken body for the vultures. She had watched too many movies.

Paul pulled her into a tender embrace that took her breath. "Rachel?"

The feeling was something she would never forget—the warmth of his body, his strong fingers stroking her head. He held onto her a few moments longer before she found her voice. "I'm okay."

When he pulled back, he kept his hands connected to her arms, his hard, callused hands a welcomed reminder of his strength. "Did you know him?"

She looked over her shoulder as another chill passed over her. "No, not really ... he's visiting his aunt."

"I wasn't sure. I didn't want to interrupt you at first."

Rachel bit her lip when she finally allowed her gaze to meet his. "He keeps asking me to go out with him."

His brows turned downward in displeasure. Gone was the compassion she'd just witnessed and in its place was vigilant determination. "What were you doing out here?"

"I'm meeting a friend. I was waiting for her." Tears burned her eyes, and she lowered her gaze.

"Do you want me to drive you home?"

She wanted to say yes. "No. We've been planning this all week. She's probably waiting for me inside."

The concern in his eyes was real. "I'll walk with you to the front."

"Where did you come from?"

He abruptly averted his gaze and cleared his throat. "I was standing near the back door and saw you."

She could've sworn he was struggling to maintain his composure. Why, she couldn't be sure. She pretended not to notice. "Oh ... I didn't know you were there. Thanks for waiting, for making sure ..." she stopped, unable to finish the horrific thought.

They walked to the front in silence. He paused when they reached the door and turned to face her, taking each of her arms. "Please promise you won't walk out here alone again." The gentle warning had the expected effect, but her fears must've been evident because he didn't let go.

"Don't worry." A nervous chuckle escaped her lips. "I won't."

He held the door for her before walking past her in the opposite direction. She followed his diminishing figure until Kelli touched her shoulder. "There you are. Where were you? I thought I saw your car."

"I'm sorry." Rachel wrapped her arms tight across her middle. The unseasonably cool air stirred through the building as she entered. Unexpected chills whipped through her body.

"Are you okay?"

"No." She glanced over her shoulder in the direction Paul had disappeared. A mixture of panic, disappointment, and longing consumed her. "It's a long story."

What if Jason was still in the building somewhere, waiting for her? She trembled. She wanted to go home, crawl in bed, and cry until she fell asleep but was too afraid to leave. Mom would be in Philadelphia for the rest of the afternoon.

They walked through the market, but she had trouble focusing. Instead, she searched for Paul and Jason the entire time, both with different approaches.

The scent of onions and grilled sausage no longer appealed to her. The only thing she found comfort in was that they were among the Amish and Paul was still here. Somewhere. She searched every face. Why did she tell him she was fine? She was anything but fine. She wanted to stay near him. It felt safe.

She held her waist with a white-knuckled grip, her gaze darting in every direction.

Amish women at a nearby table set out handmade dolls. Rachel could make out colors, but not details.

"Do you want to get some lunch?" Kelli linked her arm through Rachel's.

"Sure."

They sat across from each other at the market's restaurant, and Rachel explained what happened and how Paul showed up. "Maybe I'll go on a trip of my own the next time that Jason guy's in town."

"I've never known him to act that way. He's always been kind of quiet. We should report him."

"No. I don't want to do something irrational. I have an overactive imagination."

"I don't know. The way you make it sound, I'm not so sure of his intentions."

Rachel shook her head. "Really. It just scared me more than anything."

She glanced over her shoulder. Why couldn't she find Paul? Why hadn't she taken him up on his offer to drive her home? And what if she was wrong and Jason was still waiting for her?

❧ 16 ❧

Paul had wanted to reach out to Rachel when her eyes had filled with tears. It cut him deeply. Instead of shrinking away from him, her eyes locked with his and spilled over with ... trust. It had taken him by surprise. Especially after the way he'd treated her. And she barely knew him.

The Central Market filled quickly, and he moved through the crowd, his anger swelling. He stuffed a fried onion into his mouth, swallowed Coke from his glass, and leaned against the wall.

What would've happened if he hadn't showed up? How dare that audacious swine frighten her? Images of the Englisch guy forcing her into the woods filled his head and his glass shattered. Coke and shards of glass sprayed across the floor. Blood leaked from the cuts across his palm. A stinging sensation stretched from his wrist to his fingertips.

Thomas slapped his shoulder. "*Was in der welt*, Paul? You look *feraikled?*"

Paul forced a laugh. Disgusted was the exact word he would've used. "It was an accident, Thomas."

"You squeezed the glass to busting, jah?"

Paul ignored his friend's rhetorical question and focused on hiding the blood trickling down his hand. "I have to clean this up, before someone slips."

"I'll grab the sweeper. Take care of your cut."

Thomas left and Paul glanced at the table where Rachel sat with Kelli. Impatience stormed through him. How long could he follow Rachel without being spotted? He felt like a stalker. How was he any better than the other guy? Wasn't this what he'd been doing earlier, trailing her, watching her every move? Even though she'd needed him in the end, it didn't matter. It was wrong. What if she'd accepted his invitation to take her home? At least he would be able to keep her safe. What would his family say if they were found walking together?

He stumbled as his thoughts slammed to reality by Anna's high-pitched voice. "What're you doing? You working today, jah?"

"I'm looking for something."

"In the restaurant?" Anna's face twisted into a crooked grin. "Are you getting ready to have lunch?"

"Nein, I already did." The taste of onions still burned his tongue. He turned and walked in the opposite direction. He couldn't chance Anna recognizing Rachel.

"You're bleeding." She reached for his hand.

"It's nothing." He tucked his hand in his pocket, the rub against his rough pants stinging the cuts. "Well, I'm going to get back to work. See you around, Anna." He headed straight for the men's room. He ran cool water over the gashes, rinsing away any evidence of the earlier incident. Then he grabbed a handful of napkins and pressed them against the cut to stop the bleeding. He peeked around the corner, making sure Anna was nowhere in sight, before he proceeded to his table.

Thomas grabbed his arm and yanked his straw hat from his head, staring at Paul's hands. "You clean the cut?"

Paul groaned. "It was nothing."

"It wonders me."

"Jah, well, Thomas. *Schusslich*. I got in too big of a hurry."

Thomas shook his head. "Ach, you need to slow down."

"Jah, I will. Troy's working my table. I'll see ya later."

Paul stepped through the door and scanned the parking lot. Rachel and Kelli climbed into their cars and headed off, one behind the other. Paul climbed into his cab, careful to stay out of view.

His buggy was too slow, and he lost them. Too quickly. The fear in her eyes replayed itself over and over, and he couldn't shake the gnawing feeling the Englischer meant her harm. He held the reins tighter than normal, the leather strap aggravating the small gashes still oozing with blood.

Who was that strange man? How could he find out without anyone asking unwanted questions?

Driving by her house to make sure her car was there would make him feel better. He hoped. He reached her house and excuses reeled through his mind for reasons he needed to stop, but her mom wasn't there. Rachel would think nothing of it, but he couldn't. It would be wrong. So he guided Nelly two houses down and turned into his uncle's driveway.

❧ 17 ❧

Rachel's anticipation rose with each horse-drawn wagon that passed. A cool breeze made a whistling sound as it danced through the trees. Had Paul found out about her attending the singing on Sunday? He hadn't mentioned it on Saturday. Maybe he hadn't heard yet, and she could tell him first.

She sorted through her clean clothes, folding and placing them in the appropriate drawer, trying to keep her attention on something other than the sound of passing buggies. Time passed quickly, yet slowly. She thought about Saturday. Had imagined riding next to him in his buggy and hated herself all day for turning down his offer. His concern burned in her memory, and she'd memorized their entire conversation standing outside the market. It didn't make sense. She remembered every word, could still feel his arms around her. But she also remembered the words that had hurt her. Badly.

Rachel left for work disappointed when he never arrived and reached the restaurant five minutes before her shift. She left her bag in the break room and tied an apron around her waist. She searched the guests, the same way she did every day, making sure Jason wasn't among them. Her body lost its stiff posture when he never showed up at his usual time.

Then she turned, coming face to face with two Amish girls wearing dark gray dresses.

"Anna, let's sit over here."

It was her. The Anna? The one Kelli thought would be marrying Paul any day now. Anna wasn't the blue-eyed, blond-haired girl from last week, but she was pretty, and yes, Rachel recognized her from the Sunday night singing.

Soft freckles sprayed across Anna's cheeks and nose. Her auburn hair hid beneath the kapp, but wispy curls tumbled out in disarray. Anna's dark green eyes searched her with a contempt she didn't understand, the same dark look she'd given her at the singing. As the girl passed and chose a booth, Rachel glanced away and sighed. They didn't sit in her section.

Anna planted her elbows on the table. "Paul ... yes ... he ... I know ... asked me."

Anna's laugh echoed through the restaurant, grating on Rachel's nerves. What was she saying? Why couldn't her words level out at the same pitch?

Rachel tried to ignore the feelings, but her eyes kept stumbling in Anna's direction.

She tried concentrating on the woman sitting at the table in front her.

"I wanted iced water, not tea."

Rachel's eyes widened. "Oh, I'm so sorry. I'll be right back."

Thirty minutes later, the two Amish girls left. Rachel stepped outside for her break, the fresh air a welcomed change from the stuffy restaurant.

Paul had thought about asking Troy to join him for lunch at the Plain and Fancy, but decided not to. Rachel might be working. He hadn't been to the restaurant since she came to town that first day. He missed his favorite side dish, hash brown casserole.

He opened the blinds, bringing light into the dark room. Putting some space between him and Rachel could be all he needed.

There was only one problem. He didn't want distance between them.

He was sketching the plans for a new project when Thomas stopped by.

"Wiegeht's. Why are you working in here? I thought you hated office work."

"It has to be done." Paul nodded. "What're you up to?"

"Mamm sent me into town with a list." He removed a crumpled piece of paper from his pocket. "We missed you at the singing."

"I wasn't in the mood."

"There was a new girl. What was her name? Belinda called her Rachel."

"Rachel?" Coming out of his seat, he banged his knee against the desk. He stepped toward the filing cabinet, unnecessarily, and fussed with the drawer. "So? New girls come around all the time." *Not Rachel Adams, eefeldich.* "Was it the Yoder girl?"

"Not an Amish girl, an Englischer. The other girls liked her. Wavy dark hair and a natural tan, with big brown eyes. A beautiful girl with the voice of an angel."

His mouth flew open, his breath stolen. *Rachel was at the singing.*

"You act like you know her."

Paul steadied his gaze on the file in front of him. "I work for her mamm."

"Oh."

Rachel was there. Why would she go? She was singing? The tone of her voice came back to him clear as the cloudless sky. He brought a shaky hand to his forehead. He couldn't talk about this ... about her.

"Anna asked where you were. She hoped you'd take her home after the singing."

Paul's fingers felt numb as he thumbed through the folders. "Jah, well. I'll never make that mistake again."

"Was in der welt?" Thomas asked, a hint of anger pervading his tone.

Paul almost snapped, thinking of the way Anna gossiped, but softened his attitude. Thomas knew nothing of it, and he didn't plan to spread more rumors. "I just don't like her that way."

"It wonders me. Who *do* you like that way?" Thomas teased.

He slammed the cabinet before turning to face Thomas. "No one. I don't care for anyone.

Thomas crossed his arms. "Well, you aren't getting any younger. You'll be the only one left not married."

"I can't get married until I meet the right girl," he said without thinking, and Thomas caught the slip.

"That doesn't make any sense. You've already met them all. There are no more girls to be choosing from. Unless a new girl moves into the community."

A new girl *had* moved into the community. "Ach, Thomas." He cleared his throat. "I'm just not ready yet. Will you leave it be?"

"Okay, don't be so touchy. I'm just saying, Anna would take some handiwork, but she's already smitten with you."

"Well, thanks for the advice, but I can handle my own love life." That was the furthest thing from the truth. That Adams girl had everything in his head and heart warped. No one had ever held his interest until now. Why did she have to be an Englischer?

A few hours later, he leaned back in his chair, staring through the office window, his mind preoccupied with one thing.

Her.

Then out of nowhere she sat on a wooden bench in front of the restaurant.

Tugged like a puppet on strings, he moved closer to the window.

Rachel stared into the sky, her skin glowing against the sun's rays like buttercups scattered on an open field. He took a deep breath. Beautiful. Jah. Thomas had described her exactly. *Mox nix!* Her beauty is irrelevant. He shifted his feet, leaning forward, closer.

It wasn't only her beauty he couldn't resist, but there was something else, something he needed, something he craved. He wanted to know everything about her. All of her hopes, her dreams, her fears. What made her happy, sad? Today there was something pressing on her. Was it because of what happened at the market? Was she still shaken? He could see mysterious pain etched across her face.

Even still, as people passed, she smiled at everyone. Not just a habitual average smile, but her compassionate Rachel smile.

Everything about her drew him in, like a force compelling him.

❧ 18 ❧

Rachel stood at the sink washing the breakfast dishes when a buggy pulled into the yard. Her gaze zeroed in on the man driving the rig.

He's here.

Her legs wobbled, and she gripped the counter to steady herself as Paul and another young man climbed from the wagon and unloaded the siding. She leaned against the counter. They'd be outside all day. She definitely shouldn't go out there.

Rachel moved to the living room with a book. A non-Amish book. She glanced out the window often, peeking as Paul hung the siding.

He stood on a ladder leaning against the front window. He climbed a few rungs, and his shirt loosened from his waistband. His black jacket lay sprawled across the swing. With each climb her heartbeat quickened. He stopped after only a few rungs, placing himself in her perfect view. She turned away when his gaze fell on her. With a tight grip on her novel, she took careful strides up the stairs.

Rachel sat on the bed with her phone. She hadn't told Samantha about her crazy feelings for Paul yet, but it was time. She could trust Samantha to never tell a soul. No matter how far away they were from each other ... she could be sure of that.

Their texts went on for several minutes before Rachel found the nerve to spill her heart. She told her about fainting in the garden. How Paul didn't want to be friends after catching her with an Amish novel, but then rescued her from Jason. How something about being with him stirred feelings she'd never experienced.

Samantha couldn't wait to visit and see this mysterious perfect Amish man for herself. If only Rachel could take his picture. A collage of pictures. She could fill a scrapbook with images of him. But that wasn't allowed. Her memories would have to suffice.

She moved to the window and looked across the yard. Samantha sent her final text. The one that made it hard to feel the ground beneath her feet.

You're in love. Finally.

Paul had infused Rachel's senses for the past few weeks like no guy ever had. But in love? The thought frightened her, especially when he didn't even want to be friends.

Paul no longer worked on the front of the house. She had peeked through each window in search of him. He stood by a makeshift table set against the barn. She stepped back.

Rachel wanted to talk to him, to be near him. She needed a good reason to go outside. It would be uncomfortable weeding her garden with two men toiling around outside, so that wouldn't work.

The porch needed sweeping. She pushed the broom from side to side, in long unhurried strides. But even with the slowest of motions, it didn't take long. Only two minutes. Paul hadn't even noticed she'd been outside.

What else could she do? Nothing that wouldn't be completely obvious.

Maybe there was something in her car she needed right now. Paul would be in her clear view from where it was parked. He was sure to see her and maybe he would approach her. Maybe he wanted to talk to her as much as she wanted to talk to him.

After ambling across the yard, she climbed inside her car, leaving the door propped open. She took her time finding something. She just hadn't decided what yet.

She peeked over the steering wheel and caught Paul watching. She bent quickly, her pulse throbbing. After a few seconds of hiding behind her hair, she leaned forward. The heat was stifling, and she pushed the door open a little more. Maybe he thought she was getting ready to leave. She was wasting her time. He wouldn't come over here.

A CD.

She grabbed her favorite Natalie Grant disc.

Paul's blood pumped faster when Rachel climbed into her car. Kevin had also stopped working and gazed in her direction. The admiration on Kevin's face made Paul regret bringing him today.

Kevin cleared his throat. "Do you mind if I introduce myself?"

No, I don't want you to talk to her. How would that sound? Paul had no choice and simply nodded.

A broad smile filled Kevin's face. "We're going to the same school this fall."

"Really?" Paul's voice sounded unstable even to his own ears.

"A mutual friend of ours told me she'll be graduating with us. I never had the opportunity to talk to her at the restaurant."

Dread slammed across his chest, and with each glance in her direction, reality settled over him.

Kevin was an Englischer.

Rachel stepped from the car and came face to face with a young man. But it wasn't Paul. The young man's blond hair fell across his forehead and was swept to one side.

She tried to hide her disappointment. Paul seemed intent on the materials laid out in front of him, and she concentrated on his subtle movements.

"Hi. I'm Kevin Williams," he said, with a slight quiver in his voice. "We'll be going to the same school this fall."

"I'm Rachel. It's nice to meet you." She held up the CD. "I was in the mood for some Natalie Grant."

Kevin glanced at the clear square case. "How do you like Lancaster County?"

"I do. It's different."

Kevin fumbled with his phone. "Are you on Instagram and Twitter?"

"Yeah."

"I'll find you and follow you." He smiled as if he was wrestling to keep his teeth from breaking through the barrier of his lips. He failed. "Rachel Adams, right?"

She leaned in closer to look at the profile picture.

"That's me." She glanced toward the barn. Paul was staring at her. They held each other's gaze momentarily, and she had to remind herself to breathe.

"So, Rachel, would you like to go with me?" Kevin waited for her answer, but she hadn't heard his question.

She tried to make eye contact with Kevin, but she missed by a millisecond. Her thoughts were on the man working by the house. "I'm sorry, go with you?"

"There's a concert next Saturday night. Would you like to go with me? I could show you around and maybe we could get something to eat." His tone shifted from friendly to flirty.

"Oh, next Saturday. I'm sorry I already have plans, but thank you. It's so sweet of you to invite me. It's going to be nice knowing a few people before school starts."

"It's a small school, but I'm sure you'll like it." Kevin rubbed the back of his neck. "Maybe some other time."

Her gaze kept floating between Paul and Kevin. "You're working with Paul today?"

His eyes brightened as he leaned closer. "I usually work wherever he needs me. Today, I got lucky."

Her stomach plummeted. "Well, *I* better get inside so *you* can get back to work. I wouldn't want to get you in trouble. I'll see you later."

Rachel had imagined all sorts of scenarios when she'd stepped outside. But she walked away with nothing that she'd hoped to gain from her expedition. Except another invitation.

It just wasn't from the right man.

Paul tried to listen, paying close attention to Rachel's facial expressions. She smiled a lot. It bothered him. He hadn't cared that she caught him staring. How could he possibly stand the thought of Kevin dating her?

What was her reason for saying no? Did she turn him down because she didn't know him well enough? What if she *had* agreed to go with him? Even though she hadn't, it was only a matter of time before she agreed to date someone. Whether it happened here in this plain Dutch country or next year when she went off to college, the day would come when she would.

The image sent a pain through him so deep, it took his breath.

He'd been handling this situation all wrong. He had to stay. If he were to leave now, an even larger gash would take its place. A gash so deep, it might never mend.

As Rachel walked toward the house, she stared at him. Her gaze didn't falter as he stared back. Paul only wanted to enjoy the pleasure flowing through him. Her eyes were full of questions, questions for which he had no answers. Her hair fell off her shoulder, the long straight strands covering part of her face.

The rest of the day, he waited anxiously for her to come back out. He thought of twenty excuses to go inside. But he didn't give in. He dipped his chin, the satisfaction of her *no* to Kevin still humming through the air between them.

He then endured hours of torture listening to Kevin's plan to ask her out again, to make her fall in love with him.

Ignoring the envious thoughts rearing their ugly heads, he considered the possibility of spending more time with her. His pulse spiked every time he was anywhere near her.

He'd just have to find a way to deal with that.

❦ 19 ❦

On Monday morning. Rachel changed into her running clothes and stepped outside to the warmth of sunshine. The birds laughed at her and the flowers smiled in sympathy. As Rachel ran, she thought about her conversation with Samantha ... her conversations with Kelli. No matter how she tried to forget Paul, his image continued to dance in her mind—him talking to her, protecting her, holding her.

She stopped mid-run and bent at the waist, her chest heaving. "I'm in love with him."

Warmth crept up her neck, and she stretched four fingers across her lips realizing she'd spoken those words out loud. She checked her surroundings before resuming her jog.

After her run, Rachel showered and slipped on a pair of jeans and a long-sleeved white fitted top, dwelling on the monotonous life that belonged to her now. She never wore jeans in Florida midsummer.

She settled with a slice of toast for breakfast. The butter melted against her tongue, the strawberry jam sweet.

Paul's hammer pounded against the siding as she ate. She finished her orange juice, the tangy liquid cool against her throat.

At least he was here.

What did it matter though? Now, even when she thought of him, an overflow of emotions strangled her.

Singing softly, she washed the few dishes left from last night. The song intensified as she emptied the sink. The drumming of her heart quickened when Paul crossed the yard, close to the kitchen window, the only one ajar.

Hoping to find a nice spot to do some reading, Rachel grabbed her book and blanket and stepped onto the porch. With each step, she studied the path leading into the woods. The trees were full of flowers hanging over the trail, inviting her. It would be a perfect day to explore the area and would steer her away from Paul. Especially when all she wanted was to be near him.

She missed Florida. The ocean, the palms trees blowing in the breeze, the sand beneath her toes as she walked on the beach so many early mornings and late afternoons. She even missed the guys who *wanted* to be friends with her. A trip to Florida would give her a fresh dose of reality, unlike this fantasy world where nothing seemed right.

Paul worked his way to the back side of the house and wouldn't notice her. She peeked in his direction anyway, unable to resist. He never looked up.

The cool air brought with it a feeling of hopefulness mixed with the doubt that plagued her. She stepped to the edge of the woods when the dull sound of footsteps reached her ears.

"Rachel." The whisper of her name in that deep, velvet voice soaked through her skin, and she slowed her pace as if controlled by an invisible wire.

She hesitated before turning to face him. When she did, his pools of deep blue threatened to swallow her whole. But she snapped out of it quickly. "Hi."

"Are you sure you want to go in there?" His protective nature satisfied a needy place within her.

Rachel closed her eyes for a full second, unable to bear that unmistakable connection that drew her to him. "There's a trail. I wanted to see where it would take me."

"Oh." His eyes drifted from hers and reached through the trees behind them then came back to rest on her. Head tipping, he studied her, unveiling something deep and raw within his eyes.

She licked drying lips. "Why are you looking at me like that?"

He blinked and the mask fell back into place. "Because we're different." The abrupt words didn't match the way he'd studied her.

"Different?" She stared at him, moisture building behind her eyes. She hated this. Her brittle laughter followed. "It's too bad that bothers you. Your other friends don't seem to care."

Confusion bore a groove between his eyes. "Why would you say that?"

Why *had* she said that? She didn't want him to find out about the singing. "No reason. I'll see you later." She turned and hurried into the woods, biting back stinging tears.

❦

Paul stood only a moment by the edge of the woods unable to resist joining her.

"You shouldn't put yourself in unnecessary danger."

She paused and turned to face him. "I'm not putting myself in danger. I'm just going for a walk."

"Just like you run on the road every morning. A street filled with traffic, I might add." He raised an eyebrow and nodded toward the road. "I'm not sure you're the best judge of your own wellbeing."

She stomped toward him, her hands clenched in tight knots on her hips. "I am perfectly capable ... well, it doesn't matter. You shouldn't say things like that."

"Why not?"

"It's rude." Her hands loosened by her side, and her gaze lowered. "You make it sound like I try to endanger myself."

"That isn't what I meant. I just wish you'd be more careful." His eyebrows lifted, but he couldn't keep the stern look for more than a few seconds. Not while looking into those eyes. "Would you mind if I joined you?"

Passion still burned in her eyes, but had weakened. He captured the tormented lesion buried within. He had hurt her feelings.

She lifted her chin in a challenge. "No. I wouldn't want anything horrific to happen to me."

He had expected an argument and faltered when her reply reached his ears. But somehow he restrained the grin begging for release. "Gut. Me either."

Finally that smile of hers burst through in full force, followed by a sound that reached deep within him. Her amused laughter.

Everything had always been plain and simple, until now. There had never been any question. His life was set in stone, the life God had chosen for him to be born into. Even if he left his uncle's home, it wouldn't change anything. He was Amish and would be joining the church eventually. He waited for no particular reason. He just hadn't made the commitment. He never had the desire to find out anything about the Englisch world like some of his friends had.

He thought differently now, for the first time. He tried to imagine courting someone else, anyone else. He couldn't. He drowned in his thoughts as they strolled side by side down the trail.

"Have you been back here before?"

"No." Gone was the hesitancy in her voice. It was now laced with wonder.

"What did you think of the young people's gathering?"

Rachel stumbled to a halt and turned startled eyes on him. "You know about that?"

Something in her tone made him move closer, and he had to physically restrain himself from reaching out to her. "A reliable source told me there was a beautiful Englisch girl there. I knew it had to be you."

He studied the gentle curve of her cheekbone and the way moisture collected on her lower lip when she caught it between her teeth.

She stilled, and he cherished that extra moment. With careful movements he shifted forward, closer. "I don't mean to embarrass you."

The play of emotions etching across her face changed from shock to dread to warmth all within one long breath. "You aren't angry?"

Her response surprised him and it took a moment to find his voice. "Why would that make me angry?"

"Because I went after you told me you didn't want to talk to me anymore."

He laughed. But his gut wrenched at the truth. "I didn't say that."

Her tremulous lip was the only indication of her regret. "You don't have to pretend with me just because you work for my mom."

"Rachel, you're absolutely *eefeldich*!"

She slung her head around, turning her back toward him.

"Wait." Paul took her arm. The urge to take her into his arms pierced through him, to hold her like he had at the market. Having her wrapped in his arms was as comfortable as it was riveting. This time he had to resist. "I didn't mean that the way it sounded. I wanted to ask you something."

She faced him, her eyes storming, as she propped a hand on her hip like she was offended. "What did that word mean?"

His smile widened. "Eefeldich? It means silly or ridiculous."

"Oh." A hint of a smile curved at her lips as her gaze fell then she grasped his fingers. "What happened to your hand?"

"Oh, it's nothing. Just a little accident."

Her lips turned downward into a full pout, and he wanted in that moment to take away her confusion, to be completely honest with her. "Are you planning to go to another singing?"

She stared at him blankly. "No."

"Why *did* you go?" Paul had hoped he was her reason. One moment, one glance into her eyes and he would know the answer. It was absurd to want this, but he couldn't stop himself.

She hesitated, then her head tilted to one side. "I don't know."

"If you decide to go again, I would like to take you myself."

Shock crossed her face. He had to stop himself from laughing. He was floating on a cloud, one he wanted to ride a while. The consequences, he would suffer later.

"What?" She shook her head. "Why?"

"I haven't been in a while, and I thought I could bring you on Sunday, to introduce you to all my friends. I know how fascinated you are with us." What if she said no? He teased her, instead of being honest, and pointed at the novel in her hand. "Is that as exciting as your Amish romance novel? I've heard how scandalous books about my people can be."

A slow smile broke across her blushing face with such striking beauty that for a moment, he could only stare. "I thought you didn't want to be my friend, Paul."

A thrill surged through him at his name falling off her lips. "I said we shouldn't be, not that I didn't want to be."

Rachel's laugh was bleak. That same unmistakable laugh he'd memorized. He'd made her angry. "Well, I feel much better now." Then her eyes softened with confused interest.

"We're from two different worlds. To be friends ..." He lost his way in the depth of her eyes, then shrugged. "But it's impossible not to. Will you go with me on Sunday?"

She stiffened in surprise. At least he hoped it was surprise, since she still hadn't answered him. And then her answer formed on her lips, and he could almost taste its honeycomb sweetness.

"Yes."

Yes, she'd said yes. It was electrifying and terrifying. Now what?

They came to a stop near a creek, and Rachel's face glowed with radiance. He had hurt her feelings many times since their first meeting. He preferred this expression over all others.

"This is so beautiful. It's like a small paradise in the middle of the woods."

The easy position of her shoulders, the way she threw her hair back with her fingers, he was confident that, finally, for the first time in his presence she seemed relaxed.

"Look at that perfect patch of grass across the water."

He tore his gaze from hers. "It's nice."

She stepped forward, testing the first board of the bridge.

"Let me."

Moving to the side, she allowed him to cross the planks ahead of her.

He needed to be careful. She had a way of making him forget all of his Amish commitments, his loyalty. "They seem to be in good shape."

"They do." She ran her hand along the rail. "Where were you?"

"When?"

Rachel looked happy, comfortable. When their eyes met, Paul felt the same magnetism, the same attraction as their last encounter. "Last week?"

The connection between them made him take a step closer. "I was working on something else."

"Another job?" The hesitancy in her facial expression gripped him.

"Jah. Something like that."

Her gaze fell, and he had to stop himself from lifting her chin. "I wasn't sure if you were coming back."

He remembered how he had thought about leaving, and how his chest hurt at the thought of never seeing her again. Paul uttered a delighted chuckle. "I would never leave a job unfinished."

The light sound of her laughter stretched through the moment, deepening his desire to take her in his arms. "I didn't think you would."

Paul had a hard time clinging to his fine line of restraint and had to go before he did something he'd regret. He moved aside to allow her to step off the bridge, then he crossed to the other side. "I better go. You have some reading to do." Her gaze fell to the book in her hand. Paul didn't want to leave her alone. He didn't want to leave her at all, but he had no choice. His feelings were on the edge of becoming transparent. "I'll see you later."

"Okay." Disappointment crossed her face. Was she disappointed he was leaving? The possibility made him smile.

With a glance over his shoulder, he met her gaze one last time. "I'm glad you're feeling better, Rachel."

Her baffled expression amused him, but as he reached the edge of the yard, the reality of the situation set in.

It only took five minutes to drive to his house, but he needed every second to sort through his feelings.

What had he done?

This was completely wrong. He had arranged his dilemma into categories. The first one was obvious. He was Amish and she was not. Nothing he could do would change that fact. And that caused the second problem.

A relationship with her was forbidden.

Of course there was always the exception. He could leave the only family he had to join her world. He could do this with the chance of losing her eventually anyway. Some didn't believe marriage as a lifelong commitment. Just like Caleb's wife. What if Rachel didn't? What would he have then? Very rarely, an Englisch person joined the Amish community.

No! He would never allow her to join.

What would this cost him, cost her? How could he pull her into this situation with a good conscience?

It could destroy them both.

Rachel woke earlier than usual on Thursday. Paul arrived just as she returned from her morning run, and she pretended not to notice him standing by the barn. She needed to weed her garden but hated for him to see her like this. Her face burning from exertion, her skin soaked in sweat. But she needed to get it done before the temperature rose.

She stood by the rows for only a moment then turned. Paul was standing right behind her and she bumped into him. She had a hard time ignoring the thoughts screaming in her mind when their eyes met, so she focused on the smooth line of his jaw.

He held to her waist, his firm hands pulling her closer. A tingling sensation trickled through her torso.

"What's wrong?" he asked, the warmth of his fingers still tight around her middle.

"Nothing. Why?" She inhaled, remembering to breathe.

"You gasped?"

It took a moment to gather her thoughts. "I did?" She paused and then laughed as she remembered. "I was reading a message from a friend."

"Oh? A friend from Florida?

"Yes, Sam ... Samantha. My best friend."

"Is everything okay?"

"She just said something that really took me by surprise." Rachel would never admit that their entire conversation had been about him.

"You should try not to make noises like that, unless you're in danger." He took a step back, his hands slipping from her. "You scared me." He smiled that unforgiving smile, his eyebrows pointing inward. "I haven't forgotten the last time we stood here in the garden."

Heat filled her face. She liked the idea of him checking on her. Rachel wasn't ready to lose this moment with him, not yet.

When he turned, she followed him. "Wait."

Could she do this?

She wanted it so desperately the words flowed from her mouth without consent. "Would you like to have dinner with us tonight?" *What? Rachel? What are you doing? Fix this.* "You've been working so hard for my mom."

He grinned. "I would like that. What time should I come?"

"How about six?" Rachel twisted her hands together.

"Okay, I'll see you later, jah?"

Unable to give an audible answer, she walked to the house in a daze. Thrilling and agonizing sensations flowed through her at the same time.

Rachel found Mom in the kitchen, sitting at the table, sipping a cup of coffee. How would she ever pull this off. "I invited Paul to dinner." There. It was out. Now, how would Mom react?

"What a great idea!"

"Really?" What had she done? A fluttery empty feeling filled her stomach. He started speaking to her again and now he was coming for dinner. One minute she nearly exploded inside with the possibility of spending more time with him. The next minute she hated herself for hoping for more.

"He's been a big help to me. It was nice of you to invite him."

"Okay, well, I'm going to grab some apples ... from the tree ... outside."

Rachel filled the basket, her every motion guarded, uncertain.

She glanced at Paul before walking inside and caught him watching. She tightened her grip on the basket.

After she searched Pinterest for a new recipe, she made a list for the market and kissed Mom on the cheek. She left for work excited and nervous at the same time. She had trouble distinguishing between the two lately.

Paul's buggy sat in the same spot when she pulled into the yard after work. He was hanging a piece of siding. To avoid the risk of her tongue running off in the wrong direction, she waved and headed inside.

She had to settle down. It was already four o'clock, and there was so much to do. She slipped into the house and started on dinner. This night could be perfect, if she could just stop shaking. He's Amish, she told herself over and over as she watched his buggy pull out of the drive an hour later. It was impossible to think he would ever be interested in her.

Rachel pulled the boiled potatoes from the stovetop when Mom entered the kitchen. She blended them with butter and milk. "Do these need salt?" She handed a spoon filled with the creamy white potatoes toward her mom.

After a taste, she licked the spoon clean. "No, they're perfect." She glanced under the pot lids. "Sautéed squash with peppers. Yummy. What smells so good in the oven?"

She scrunched her nose. "An easy chicken recipe. I'm worried."

"Why?"

"I should've stuck with my usual recipes. It's been a while since I've cooked for ... someone else."

"Nonsense. You have nothing to worry about. You've been cooking since you were eight. It's natural to feel nervous when cooking for others. I'm sure it will all be delicious."

If only she had her mom's confidence. This wasn't any person though.

This was Paul.

Friends back home who tried to date her held no comparison to him. Rachel's dad had teased her all the time for being so picky, but never believed anyone would ever be good enough. How would he feel about her interest in an Amish man? If only he were here now. Would she confide in him? It had been a year, but it seemed like only yesterday.

Rachel pushed the aching thoughts aside and glanced at the clock. Five forty-five. Paul would be here in only fifteen more minutes.

Moments later, Paul's buggy came to a stop in their driveway.

A gasp leapt to her throat. "Oh no, he's early. He's going to come in, and I'm not finished."

"Sweetheart, it's only Paul."

"Mom, this is different. Can you keep him company?" Her mom wouldn't understand, and she couldn't explain right now. How would she ever be able to explain this to anyone? "Please, Mom?"

"Well, okay, if that's what you want me to do."

The steady knock startled her, though she'd been expecting it. When she didn't hear voices in the hallway, Rachel peeked over her shoulder and quickly turned away. Her breathing was suddenly uneven. Paul stood in the doorway of the kitchen.

"Hullo, it smells gut." His voice, that deep compelling tone, filled the space of the kitchen.

"I hope it is." She dried her hands on a towel and faced him. "I'm trying a new recipe."

"I'm sure it'll be delicious." Paul wore no hat, his hair still damp. He handed her a big bouquet of white daisies. "These are for you."

She took the hand-picked beauties. "Oh, how thoughtful!" With a swift inhale, she drew in the sweet scent, a tremulous smile breaking through. *He brought me a gift.* "Thank you so much."

Her mom stood behind him, smiling and holding her hands up and mouthing the word *sorry*.

"They're beautiful. Here, let me put them in some water." Mom took the flowers from Rachel's unsteady hands. "Paul, I don't know why I haven't thought about inviting you before now."

Paul turned toward her mom. "Danki, for having me. I've been looking forward to it all afternoon."

He took the platter of chicken from Rachel's hands and set it on the table. Rachel turned off the stovetop and double-checked the counters to make sure she hadn't overlooked anything. Then she joined them at the table.

Paul pulled Rachel's seat out and took the chair across from hers. He had taken his jacket off and she couldn't help but notice how his tan arms made a bold contrast against his white shirt.

"Paul would you mind asking the blessing?" her mom said, once they were all seated.

"O Lord God, heavenly Father, bless us and these thy gifts, which we shall accept from thy tender goodness. Give us food and drink also for our souls unto life eternal, and make us partakers of thy heavenly table through Jesus Christ. Amen. Our Father."

It was the most beautiful prayer she'd ever heard.

After passing around the dishes, they ate in silence for a few moments.

Paul only took a few bites before he set his fork down and met her mother's gaze. "This is delicious."

"Rachel did it all. I can't take any credit," Mom told him, smiling.

Rachel's cheeks burned in response.

"I kept hearing about it, but now I'm finding out for myself, jah? You're an excellent cook, Rachel."

She'd become used to the Amish slang, but his compliment with that accent, intended for her, made her heart flutter.

Amish women had to be good cooks. They were all homemakers, at least from what she'd read. She could never compete with that. Images of herself as his Amish wife filled her mind. She cleared the crazy notion.

I can't think that way.

She took a small bite of chicken, after cutting it into the smallest portion possible. Sweat warmed her scalp as her thoughts raced forward to after dinner possibilities. To them alone. Together.

Picking up her glass, she took a sip of water then set it back on the table, but this time closer to his.

Something about tonight made her feel like a young girl in love for the first time. And she was enjoying every minute of it.

Paul was staring at her when she glanced up, and she held his gaze. It was something she would never have done ordinarily, especially with him. But in this moment she felt invincible, until her fork slipped from her fingers and clattered across her plate. Rachel's cheeks burned as she reclaimed it.

"You're coming along with the siding."

Thank you, Mom.

"Jah, I'll finish in the morning. Then I'll start the screened-in porch, and I plan to have everything else completed by the end of the week."

After taking her last bite, Rachel excused herself to wash the dishes. Did that mean he wouldn't be here working every day? She ran sudsy hot water in the sink, thankful for the chance to escape for a few moments.

Not expecting the thrill that coursed through her veins when Paul moved in the place next to her, she awkwardly grabbed the hand towel.

Rachel shook her head. "You don't have to do that."

"I want to help." His gaze locked on hers, the faint lines around his mouth slackened. Then his lips curved up in a slight smile.

"It looks like you two have this. I'm going to take a much needed break." Mom kissed her cheek. "Thank you for dinner, sweetheart. It was so good."

"Absolutely delicious, jah?"

"Thank you."

Heat rose up her neck as she scrubbed each dish with more care than usual. As she handed them to Paul, his hand grazed against hers time and time again leaving behind a trail of longing. Her imagination was without restraint. They were standing so close, his clean earthy scent made her head swim.

"It's nice ... you helping. My dad used to wash dishes with me." Her dish rag slowed over the plate. "I don't know why I shared that." She usually avoided talking about her dad.

"Because you miss him."

"Yeah." She tipped her head up to look at him and prayed he wouldn't voice the questions swirling in his eyes.

His smile was soft, understanding. "Then I'm glad I offered."

The thrill escalated higher.

After the dishes were dried and put away, she crossed her arms and faced him fully. His eyes, when they met hers, were like the sea's tide drawing her under.

She took a subtle step to the side, breaking the spell he held over her. "Would you like to sit on the porch?"

He propped an elbow on the counter. "That sounds nice."

The dish towel fell unwillingly from her fingers. He reached for it and placed it into her hands.

"Thank you." Her gaze scanned his face, examining every faint freckle, every dimple. She imagined running her hand across his freshly shaven chin. *What's wrong with me?*

Once outside, he moved past her and took a seat on the swing and patted the seat, inviting her to join him. She sat as softly as she could, trying not to touch him though everything in her screamed to.

They rocked in silence for a while. A soft neigh and occasional shift of hooves stirred in the distance. He pushed the swing back and forth with his foot. Being this close to him was intoxicating. She pushed a stray hair away from her face and buried her hand beneath her leg.

"How do you like living in Lancaster County?"

She licked her dry lips. "I do." *Now that you're talking to me again.*

"Have you been to Hershey Park yet?"

The man she looked at now was so different than the man she encountered that first day. More friendly. More open. More handsome every time she looked at him.

When their gazes collided, she found it hard to breathe. But she pressed through the tiny bit of air left lingering in her lungs. "No, not yet. Have you ever been?"

He looked at her with a peculiar expression. "No, but I'm sure it's fun."

He was Amish. Of course he hadn't been to an amusement park. That was a stupid question.

"I have traveled to Hershey on several occasions and seen some of the rides from a distance."

She laughed softly and looked up at the stars. "I visited an amusement park every year growing up."

"Really? Which one?"

Rachel ordered herself to concentrate on his questions, and not on the man sitting close enough to graze her arm every time he gave the swing a gentle push. "Disney World in Florida."

"Jah. I've heard of that. It's big. And has many places to visit."

"We lived about seven hours away. We spent a lot of weeks in Orlando. Walking the long streets, taking in all the sights." Her daddy standing next to her waiting in line, his gentle tug on her sleeve pulling her forward. It was as if it were yesterday. "There was never enough time to do it all."

"It sounds like you miss it."

She missed him. Every day. Every hour. She glanced at Paul. "Yes, I miss those days a lot. We take too many things for granted. Even the smallest of things may one day be the very thing we miss the most."

Paul took her hand and gave it a gentle squeeze. Warmth penetrated through her fingers, shooting sparks up her arm. His touch captured her full attention. "Those are wise words to live by."

He released her hand and they sat in a comfortable silence for a few moments before he spoke again. "It's getting late. I should go."

Rachel stood, rocking the swing with her motion. "I'll be right back." She returned a few seconds later with the wrapped dessert and handed it to him.

"Danki for inviting me. It was delicious. You're a wonderful cook." He leaned into Rachel pressing his arm against hers. "I know my aunt will appreciate the pie. And I'm glad I'll get another piece." He took a few steps and turned. "Make sure to tell your mom *gut nacht* for me."

"I will."

He hesitated at the bottom of the steps. "I had a really nice time."

Standing by the door, she waited until his buggy disappeared. She stretched out her fingers, the feel of his hand in hers still lingering. A piece of her broken heart poured out tonight, a very tiny piece, but it was exposed, and she hadn't even realized it until it was over.

She had given Paul a window into the deepest, darkest part of her heart. And for the very first time, though it still hurt, thinking about her daddy didn't feel like it was strangling her.

❦ 21 ❦

As Rachel served breakfast to her customers, every memory of last night replayed itself. The time flew by as the first crowd came and went and then at twelve, started all over with the lunch crowd. Eggs and bacon became plates of pasta. Toast became sandwiches. And cups of coffee became Cokes and milkshakes.

Rachel was refilling a drink in the kitchen when Kelli snuck up behind her and propped a hand on her hip. "Why are you in such a good mood?"

"No reason."

Kelli laughed and turned her attention to the salads on the counter. "Fine, don't tell me. I'll find out soon enough."

If only Rachel could confide in her. She couldn't though—at least not yet. Maybe never.

Rachel glanced through the circular glass panel at the top of the door before she pushed it open. She stopped in her tracks when Paul and an Amish girl sat down at one of her tables.

Her head spun as nausea and dizziness swept through her at the same time.

She set the drink tray down and grabbed the counter to steady herself. After taking several deep breaths, she took the tray and found the strength to push the door open that led to the dining room. She delivered her drinks a few tables down. Lips pressed tight in an effort to hide the trembling, she focused ahead.

God, please be with me.

The girl sitting across from him wasn't at the singing. Of course she was beautiful, with dark brown hair, ivory skin, and probably perfect in all her Amish ways. Something Rachel could never compete with.

Rachel approached the table, her gait slow and cumbersome. She tucked her hands in her apron. "Paul?"

"Hullo, Rachel. How are you?"

"I'm ... fine." Her voice wavered. "Thank you." She pushed her lips into a tight smile and clung to her order pad with such intensity the paper crinkled.

"I knew you were working, so I asked for your table. I wanted you to meet Mary." He kept his eyes on the girl.

Rachel had gone from a complete high to a complete low in a matter of seconds, and her body hadn't caught up with her emotions yet.

"Hi, Mary."

Knowing there was no way out of this, Rachel stood in place drowning in desperation. She should have sent Kelli to take their order. Why had she thought she could handle this?

"It's her birthday. I promised to bring her to lunch." Paul leaned forward, propping his elbows on the table. "This is her favorite restaurant."

"How sweet of you, Paul. Happy Birthday, Mary."

"Danki." Mary's genuine smile made her feel worse. Then the girl glanced at Paul with admiration.

I can't do this.

She could get Kelli to take over anyway, and she'd tell Ms. Mavis she was physically ill. No. Paul would ask questions. What if he figured it out?

Rachel thrust out her chin and scribbled their order onto the black pad, the rest of their conversation a garble of Pennsylvania Dutch.

Escaping to the kitchen, Rachel stood against the counter, trying to calm her raging thoughts.

Kelli put her arm around Rachel. "What's wrong?"

Rachel tried to blink away her tears but one escaped. Facing the counter, she cleared her throat. "Nothing. I'm just tired. We've been so busy today." Rachel hated lying, but she couldn't tell Kelli the truth.

"Do you need a break?"

"I'll be fine. Maybe I'll just fix something to drink." Rachel wiped her face with her sleeve.

"Okay, if you're sure. Let me know if you change your mind. I can handle your tables."

"Thanks, I really appreciate it."

Rachel stayed busy with her other tables and only visited Paul and his girlfriend to take their orders and deliver them. She couldn't. They talked and laughed like they'd been together forever, killing her more with every glance in their direction.

She was polite, nothing more.

Finally, they finished their meal. Rachel pushed her feet toward them, one grueling step at a time. Raising one of the hands clenched at her sides, she delivered their bill.

"It was nice to meet you, Mary." Her voice didn't match her feelings, injured and begrudging, and she allowed a reluctant grin. "I hope you have a wonderful birthday."

"Danki. It's so nice to finally meet you too. Mamm wanted to say danki for the delicious apple pie you sent home with Paul last night."

"The pie?" The relief in her voice was obvious, but she didn't care. "You're ... you're Paul's cousin?"

Paul chuckled and heat rushed up her neck.

"Jah." Paul placed the money into her palm keeping his hand in hers just a bit longer than necessary, then winked. "See ya later, Rachel."

"Bye." The word came out so soft, she wasn't sure he heard.

She had to have one last glance.

No, she shouldn't. She couldn't.

She gave in.

He had stopped at the front entrance and stood there motionless, watching her.

That smile, the one that penetrated through her soul, took her breath.

Then he disappeared behind the door.

Rachel reached the register and unfolded the money. A piece of paper was wrapped inside. She tried to swallow, but instead took a deep breath and allowed the moment to fill every inch of her. *He wrote me a note. No. It must be some mistake. Maybe he gave me his shopping list by accident.* She opened it and scanned it quickly, then started again at the beginning and read slowly wanting to savor each word.

Lunch was good, but your cooking is better. Looking forward to Sunday. Your friend, Paul.

Rachel read it once as the flutter in her belly grew. She placed the money in the register and read the note again before sliding it into her apron pocket and returning to the kitchen.

In a daze, she made it until two. Pulling the ponytail holder from her hair, she climbed in her car and drove home, the convertible top down. Her hair blew in the wind. Was she dreaming? Rachel felt for the note in her pocket. It was still there.

Kelli insisted on coming over after witnessing Rachel's near breakdown. Rachel wanted so badly to talk to her about Paul, because she knew more about the Amish.

If only she could tell her everything.

Paul's buggy wasn't parked in the yard when Rachel returned home. For the time being, Rachel could still pretend that this was real. If he were here, her reality would be forced to come down from the cloud that had settled under her.

Rachel ran upstairs to shower and change into a sweatshirt with a pair of shorts. Kelli's red jeep pulled into the yard a few minutes later.

Rachel met her at the door. "Come on, I want to show you something."

They climbed the loft ladder in the barn. Kelli followed, her smile glued in place. "Wow, this is so cool." Kelli's blond ponytail slung back and forth with the motion.

Rachel's mouth hung agape as she recognized the changes herself. She hadn't been up there since that rainy day Paul caught her reading the Amish romance.

Kelli broke into her thoughts. "Did you do this yourself?"

"No, ... my mom must have." But she couldn't have. A wooden plaque, carved with her name, hung directly above the bench. A small table with a lantern and two chairs were set in the other corner. Throw pillows and a new rug she didn't recognize were the only indication of her mom's touch.

"This is like your own hangout, huh?"

"Yeah, it was my mom's idea." Rachel removed the plaque from the wall. "She must have bought this in town at the flea market." Why hadn't she mentioned this? "Come on, let's go in. I wanted to straighten your hair."

Kelli pulled her fingers through a few strands. "Straighten my hair?"

"Yeah. I have a hot iron."

She had planned to go to cosmetology school. But things were different now. Rachel didn't know what she wanted. Not anymore. Her life had been planned out perfectly, until that day. Then everything changed. And nothing had been the same since.

Once in the house, Rachel led her to the kitchen. "Are you hungry?"

"I'm always hungry."

They grabbed some chocolate chip cookies and rushed upstairs to her room.

"Wow, that's an insane wall of pictures. Are you into photography?"

"My dad gave me a camera for my fourteenth birthday." She exhaled a lungful of air as she plugged in the straightener and then walked toward the display scattered across the wall. "It's a collection from up until last year. I don't really play with it much anymore."

"You should. These are really good."

"Thanks." Rachel studied a few of the pictures, the memories rushing back like a thousand piercings mixed with a steady torrent of gratitude. What if she didn't have the hundreds of pictures to stare at every night as she drifted off to sleep?

She zeroed in on a picture of her daddy, standing tall on a ladder, working on an addition to the garage. He was always building, designing. And he was good. Mom always said he was the hardest working man she'd ever known. Then her gaze shifted to Jordan. Her best friend. He'd kept his distance since the funeral. It bothered her that he chose to stay away, because she hadn't understood. It hurt for a long time, but it wasn't his place to be there for her.

"Is your mom a designer or something? Everything's so beautiful. I absolutely love your room. I love your whole house."

Rachel cleared the memories for the moment. She'd come back to them later. She always did. Every day. "Yeah, she used to. I guess it will always be in her blood."

Kelli's eyes widened. "She's really good."

"Comes so natural for her." Rachel shrugged. "Maybe some of it will rub off on me."

"Before school starts, I'm making a trip to Philadelphia to go school shopping. You want to go?"

"Sounds fun."

"Great. Maybe we can grab dinner on the way back." Kelli sat on the vanity stool, her cheeks full with a silly grin. "So tell me ... what's going on?"

"What do you mean?" Rachel couldn't stop her own smile.

"The Amish guy at the restaurant today." Kelli's grin nearly glowed with amusement. "Oh, you mean Paul. He's the one I told you about. He's doing renovations for us. My mom."

"And?"

"And what? That's it." Rachel tried to keep her voice even, but the words fell out with noticeable delight. Could she trust Kelli with this? What if she laughed, or worse, told all her friends? She would never be able to show her face in school or anywhere in Paradise ever again.

Kelli rolled her eyes. "You expect me to believe that? I saw you. The way you gawked at him."

Rachel combed through Kelli's tangles. "What? I was *not* gawking." Especially not at first when she'd thought the unthinkable. Mary was his girlfriend, or worse, something more.

"Ha! Oh, *yes*, you were. You can tell me. I won't say anything. I promise."

Did Paul see that in her expression? "Of course I like him. He's really nice." Rachel measured Kelli's reaction, waiting to see if she needed to retract on her admission.

"He's nice." Kelli puckered her lips out and made a spitting sound. "Yeah right. Does he know?"

Rachel burst into laughter as she pulled strands of Kelli's hair through the iron. "I hope not." She slammed her lips shut. How could she have let that slip?

"You really *do* like him. He *is* gorgeous."

"Yeah, but it doesn't matter. It would never work." She pulled a few more strands through, her fingers now trembling.

"What do you mean? He couldn't keep his eyes off you."

"What?" Rachel bit her lip to contain her excitement. She had imagined that exact scenario, but never thought it would actually happen.

"Every time I looked his way, he was watching you. At first it creeped me out because of that Jason guy, but I knew there was something different about this one."

"Really?" She leaned against her dresser, her thoughts drifting to those last few moments. "He was?"

"Yes, he really was. Amish or not, I almost gave him a piece of my mind."

"No, you didn't." Rachel pulled the last few strands through the iron. "What do you know about their rules and stuff?"

"They don't approve of romantic relationships between, you know, couples like you and him, but you two might be an exception. What if he gave up his Amish upbringing to be with you?" Kelli's voice softened and she placed a hand over her heart, her face tilting toward the ceiling. "That would be so romantic."

Rachel thought of his note again and soared on an emotional wave as all sensible thoughts flew from her mind. Her hopes rose with each moment that passed. "He invited me this Sunday ... to the singing."

Kelli's mouth and eyes widened stretching her brows high into her forehead. "What? Really?"

"I know." She couldn't quite bring herself to believe it was anything more than him just being nice. "But I'm sure it's no big deal."

"Not a big deal? He asked you for a date."

"No." Rachel whispered gutturally as glee tickled her throat. "It's nothing like that." It was better not to get her hopes up.

"Whatever." Kelli rolled her eyes, her bigger-than-life smile stretching across her face all at the same time. "You better tell me every single detail Monday."

"Yes, ma'am." Rachel released the iron and brushed through Kelli's hair. "There. How do you like it?"

"It's beautiful." Kelli sifted the golden locks through her fingers. "It's so soft. Can you come to my house every morning before school?"

Rachel laughed.

At least she'd made one friend this summer. Maybe even two.

❦ 22 ❦

Twirling in place with the small wrinkled note held tight against her chest, Rachel repeated the phrase. *He's looking forward to Sunday*. A tingling rush skittered across her chest.

She read Paul's note at least ten more times before hiding it in her jewelry box on the dresser.

She assessed each piece of clothing in her closet and decided on a navy long-sleeved V-neck. She slipped on her favorite pencil skirt that hung just below her calves. It would be perfect for an Amish singing on a cool night. Well, almost.

Rachel curled her hair and finished off her makeup with a layer of pink lip gloss. She glanced at the time and a quivering emptiness filled her stomach.

Rachel didn't want to read anything into his intentions, but couldn't help herself. She couldn't remember the last time she'd felt this happy, this carefree.

The buggy's familiar rhythm traveled through her open window. She rechecked her hair, brushing through the long layers one more time, careful not to straighten her bouncing waves. She took several deep breaths before running downstairs and meeting Paul at the door.

"Hullo. I saw these and thought of you." He handed her a bunch of wildflowers. The yellows, blues, and orange bounded through the green just like her heart—leaping all over the place.

She took them, concentrating on the assortment in an effort to hide her warming cheeks. "Thank you."

He followed her inside.

"Oh, how lovely." Her mom reached for the arrangement. "I'll put these in water for you."

"Mrs. Adams, I promise not to have her out too late."

He crossed and uncrossed his arms. Was he nervous?

Mom lifted the bundled flowers to her nose. "You two have a nice time."

Paul led her toward the buggy, and Rachel waved at Mary sitting in the backseat. Paul took Rachel's hand to help her inside. When she tried to step up, she couldn't spread her feet apart enough to reach the step.

His smile faded.

"Maybe I should change. I won't be able to climb ... Oh!" The exclamation escaped as Paul scooped her up beneath her knees and lifted her into his arms.

The deliberate presence of his hands reached through the material of her skirt, her blouse, as he held her against his chest. She wrapped both arms around his neck, her pulse racing. His strength shocked her when he released one hand to grab the wagon and took one unwavering step up, their faces almost touching. His slight grunt of effort was soft in her ear.

Her hair fell across her face when he released her, and he swept the loose strands out of the way, his fingers grazing her cheek. She gripped the edge of the seat, lightheadedness colliding with the soft buzz floating around her head. It took a moment to catch her breath, so indwelled was she on the intimate moment.

Paul grasped the reins, his eyes scanning her face as if admiring every feature. "You haven't changed your mind about going?"

"No, I've been looking forward to it all day," Rachel said, breathless.

"Me too." Not until he gave her a gentle smile did he steer his horse toward the road.

Mary leaned forward against the front seat. "So have I."

Rachel turned to look at Mary. She had almost forgotten Mary was there ... had almost forgotten all her troubles.

The company of this Amish man had a way of making everything brighter.

Paul lost all of his good sense when he lifted Rachel into his arms. It had been necessary the day the snake appeared in the garden, but this was totally different. His heart pounded against his chest when her fingers had curled into the hair at the base of his neck. He could still feel them there, and it was sending his mind to places it shouldn't go. As Paul released her, he breathed in, hoping to capture her scent. A fusion of soft, sweet, and exotic soaked through his senses. Maybe he could keep it forever, if he inhaled hard enough.

When they arrived at the farm, Mary climbed from the buggy, but that skirt made things difficult for Rachel again. And he was more than happy to help. She slid into his arms, but even while wanting to pull her closer, he was careful not to linger. The thrill of knowing Rachel was here felt dangerous. In her presence, he felt more alive than ever before, and he couldn't imagine ever going back.

Mary grabbed Rachel's hand and pulled her along like they had been friends for months. There was no need to worry about Rachel; Mary's friends were delighted to see her. Most had already met her at the last singing and all took turns giving her hugs.

Anna marched toward Paul, her disappointment evident. Paul strode toward the barn, careful to keep his voice even. "Hi, Anna."

"Paul."

Anna webbed her fingers between his and almost leapt closer. Unease wrapped around him as her grip tightened on his fingers. Paul yanked his hand from her firm hold, and his gaze wandered in Rachel's direction before he faced Anna fully.

"What're you doing?"

Her lips curved in satisfaction. "I just wanted to say hullo."

Paul's nostrils flared as Anna sashayed away. He met Rachel's gaze for the briefest of moments before she quickly turned away.

Had Rachel witnessed the exchange with Anna? Had that been for Rachel's benefit? Had Anna sensed the truth?

He wanted to march over there and set things straight with Rachel. *There is no Anna and me*, he wanted to say. *There will never be anyone for me but you.* But he couldn't. He had to be the plain Amish man everyone expected him to be.

How quickly he'd been reminded that this would be no walk in the park.

Paul blew out a heavy breath, then smiled as he passed Mary and Rachel. The pain he'd thought he detected in Rachel's eyes was now gone. Maybe she hadn't seen Anna's scheme after all.

Paul talked with his friends, trying not to be drawn to the fact that Rachel stood right across the lawn from him. What he experienced was a once-in-a-lifetime thing. The other guys only spoke of her briefly. They cared nothing about the Englisch girl.

She was the only thing filling his mind.

❧ 23 ❧

Rachel attempted to breathe normally. Why had she agreed to come here? Why did Paul even invite her? Did he intend to rub the girl in her face?

The picture of them holding hands, standing so close to each other, clenched a knot in her middle. She wanted to go home.

Rachel forced herself to concentrate on the conversation the girls were having.

Mary took her arm. "They're starting a game. Let's get on the same team."

"I'm no good at volleyball. But I enjoy watching." Rachel pointed toward the bench set against the barn. "You go ahead. I'll be fine."

Mary joined the others, and Rachel leaned against the barn. She tried to soak in the competition taking place before her, but to no avail. Her mind was focused on the man standing on the other side of the farm with a group of guys and the blonde-headed Amish girl trying to keep his attention.

When the game ended, Mary spoke to Paul briefly before joining her.

"They're getting ready to start singing. But Paul's ready to go."

Ready to go? Rachel had convinced herself to ignore Paul and the hovering Amish girl. And was even looking forward to the singing. Maybe it was for the best. It would be harder seeing him sitting next to the girl.

One of the young men from her last visit approached. "Hullo, Rachel. I was hoping you would be willing to share with us again tonight."

"Oh, I'm sorry." She glanced at Mary. "We're ... we aren't going to be able to stay."

"Share again?" Mary tugged on her arm. "You sing?"

"Jah. She's wunderbaar-gut."

"Ah." Mary laughed. "I must hear this wunderbaar-gut voice of yours sometime."

Anna moved toward them. "You're leaving already?"

"Jah." Mary turned and grabbed Rachel's arm. "Anna, you haven't met Rachel."

"Nice to meet you." The young woman gave Rachel a ready smile before turning her full attention back to Mary. "See you later. I need to catch Paul and tell him gut *nacht*."

Heaviness settled on Rachel's body. She wouldn't look. No matter how much she wanted to. She couldn't.

Rachel and Mary reached the buggy first, and Rachel lifted her skirt high enough to climb in before Paul caught up to them. He would not have to lift her inside again. Especially now. She was ready to be alone, to sulk in her disappointment.

As soon as he climbed in, he faced her. "I'm going to drop Mary off on the way if you don't mind."

What was he up to? An absurd urge to challenge him zipped through her, but against her own will she mumbled, "Okay."

When they arrived at Paul's house, her eyes widened. He lived only two houses down from her. How didn't she know?

Mary hugged her from behind. "Bye, Rachel. Let's get together soon."

Rachel reached deep within and pulled out her most sincere smile. "I would love to." Paul was turning the wagon around on the path before Rachel spoke again. Something true. Something safe. "Your cousin's really nice."

"Jah, she's like a sister." He slowed the rig as they approached the highway.

When she noticed Paul watching her with admiration, every feminine instinct she possessed escalated and a portion of doubt dissipated.

"Would you mind riding with me for a while? I want to show you something."

Her curiosity had her nodding, and she welcomed the cool breeze. Maybe the heat that rose to her face would go unnoticed.

"Where in Florida did you live?"

"Pensacola." A comfortable tugging pulled at her heart strings.

"That's many miles from here."

"Yeah, it was my mom's idea to move here." Why had he invited her if he had a girlfriend? Why wasn't he driving Anna home? Wasn't that how the Amish courted?

"So, you're not happy about being here?"

The moisture in Rachel's mouth dissolved. "No. Well, yes, I mean I like it. It's just different."

"But you miss your friends?"

The mention of her friends brought a sudden rush of sadness. "Yes, I miss them a lot."

Rachel wished she'd worn her jacket. The cool air created goose bumps along her arms or maybe it was the idea of sitting next to Paul in his horse-drawn buggy. Holding her arms tight against her chest, she tried warding off the chill. He removed his jacket and handed it to her. He wore only a white T-shirt under his coat. Her thoughts scattered as he lay the jacket across her lap, his hand brushing against hers as he pulled back.

"It's cool. Take it."

The warmth of him seeped into her thighs, but the urge to take it and wrap it around her wrestled against her good manners. "But you don't have any sleeves."

"I'm used to it." His muscles flared as he worked the reins leading his horse. "I'm sure you're used to warmer weather in Florida."

Rachel pulled the jacket on, and the sleeves settled somewhere near the tips of her fingers. His warmth still lingered, his scent comforting. She forced herself not to pull the black wool to her nose.

"School will be starting back soon. What grade are you in?"

"I'm a senior. How about you? Did you graduate last year?"

His eyes crinkled, the soft lines falling perfectly onto his flawless cheek. "No, I finished school a while back. We only go through the eighth grade."

Regaining some control over her bundle of nerves sitting this close to him, she turned slightly to face him more fully. "That's not fair. I would've graduated several years ago."

"You're fortunate to be able to finish school. Don't you like it?"

She shifted, tucking her legs closer to the seat. "I do, but I'm nervous about starting this new school as a senior."

His sapphire eyes sparkled. "I wouldn't worry too much about that. You'll make friends easily and probably forget all about your Amish friend."

Rachel's pulse picked up speed. "I would never forget about you." *Did I just say that out loud?*

"What makes you so sure?" he asked.

Her stomach did a flip flop. She couldn't imagine her life now without him in it.

"You're so beautiful when you're embarrassed. I should do that more often." He held her gaze longer than usual, laughing lightly. "What're you planning to study in college?"

"I've always wanted to do cosmetology. Hairstyling, cutting, and color."

He reached across and let her hair drift between his fingers, causing her pulse to leap all over the place. "I can definitely see that. You have beautiful hair. I wonder if you could do something with my mop."

What would it feel like to run her fingers through those dark brown locks, curling beneath his hat? *Paradise.* It would feel a lot like paradise. The thought nearly sent her over the edge.

Literally.

The wheel hit a rut and bounced her on the bench. Paul's arm was around her before she registered the need to grab onto something. He tugged her closer. "Don't you go falling out of my buggy."

An electric charge surged through her body. His arm fell away and she straightened, her shoulder still tingling from the stroke of his fingertips.

He pointed out different farms and drove by her new school. But she wasn't really paying any mind, her thoughts zigzagging in all sorts of directions.

Then the batting cages came into view and dug up fresh wounds. "There's the softball fields." She spoke the words out loud, not meaning to.

"You play softball? Are you planning to play here?"

"I haven't decided. Maybe." She thought about how hard that would be. How every time she'd stepped onto the field since the accident she thought of her daddy.

"I bet you're really good." A trace of admiration brightened his tone.

"What makes you say that?"

"There's this determination about you." He smiled as if he was carefully searching for the correct word. "It's intriguing."

A flurry of fierce emotions swept through her middle. Exhilarating. Mystifying. Refreshing. Feelings she could definitely get used to. "I've played since I was five and loved every minute. I still practice. Every single day."

"I'll be looking forward to seeing you play." He leaned over and tipped his face to the side, closer to her, heightening all those emotions. "This is the Conestoga River Covered Bridge."

The sun set against the sparkling water as Paul pulled the buggy to a stop on the other side. But with one glance at her skirt and without another word set the horses on their way again. He led them along winding roads as the moon lighted their way. He pointed out farms and bed and breakfast hotels.

The time flew and nine o'clock snuck up on them. As bad as she dreaded the evening to end, he pulled into her long driveway. She wanted this night to last forever.

"Thank you for the tour."

Paul pulled the buggy to a stop and hurried around to help her down. "I wanted to be the one to show you Paradise." His words lingered as his gaze fastened to hers. "Maybe you'll let me show you the rest of Lancaster County." Holding Rachel's waist in his hands, he gently lowered her to the ground. He stood at least eight inches taller.

She took a deep breath. "I would love that."

At the front door, she turned, not sure what to say. He stared at her with such intensity, her mind whirled in confusion.

Rachel stopped breathing when he lifted his hand and hesitated, before softly tracing her cheekbone down to her chin with the tips of his fingers. He turned without a word, leaving her standing there mesmerized.

He climbed into his buggy and turned once more. "See you tomorrow."

"Oh, your coat!" She called out as he took the reins.

"I'll get it tomorrow. Looks better on you anyway."

Rachel forced herself to open the door but took one last glance as he drove away. His dark hair curled at the ends and touched the tip of his white shirt. She thought about running her fingers through it again.

Once safe inside her bedroom, she fell facedown onto the bed, hugging her pillow, and replayed the entire night. She didn't wake until three in the morning, still fully dressed, still wearing Paul's coat.

Rachel slipped from her clothes, sleepily replacing them with her pajamas. Nestled in his jacket, she savored her memories of last night a few minutes longer.

This place was beginning to feel like paradise.

＃ 24 ＃

Monday morning, Rachel busied herself straightening her bedroom as thoughts of last night stirred through her consciousness. Had it really happened? Paul's jacket lay sprawled across the bed, but the feel of its wool against her skin remained. His fingers against her cheek still burned, and his expression would be etched in her memory forever.

Paul pulled his horse and buggy into their yard, and Rachel stayed near the window as he unloaded tools from his buggy. A few times he glanced toward the house.

Did he hope to see her, too?

Thirty minutes later, she walked toward the garden.

Paul stepped from the barn and headed straight for her.

"Good morning."

"*Gut-morgen* to you." A smile tugged at the corners of his mouth and an excited tickle seeped into her belly. "What do you have planned for the day?"

"I was gonna pull a few weeds ... before work tonight." Their gaze met for a long tender moment. "I thought about fixing a picnic lunch to have down by the creek. You can join me if you want to?"

"A picnic lunch?" A hesitancy caught her as his eyes held hers in a peculiar way. "I would love to. See you at noon." He left her with a teasing wink.

"Bye." Her pulse tripled sensing his eyes following her as she continued toward the garden.

Rachel slipped on her gloves and checked the perimeter before taking a step into the first row. Using extra caution, she pulled the green leafy vines back with a stick in case something was hiding underneath. She shuddered at the thought of finding a snake.

When Rachel returned to the house, she started lunch.

Thirty minutes later, her mom walked into the kitchen. "Something smells good. Fried chicken and potato salad, yummy."

"Paul's going to join me down by the creek for a picnic. You could join us, if you'd like."

"I knew you two would become friends." Something changed in Mom's face, and a quirky smile lifted her lips. "Weren't you out in the garden earlier? Your makeup and hair looks exceptionally nice for working outside."

Rachel wiped her forehead with the back of her hand. "I have to work later. There wasn't much to do. Just a few weeds."

Mom placed an encouraging hand on her shoulder. "I'll let you two have your picnic, but please fix me a plate."

Rachel spooned the potato salad into a container. "Did you tell Paul I was sick?"

"Actually he sat with you while I went into town to buy some Tylenol."

She paused mid-scoop, the words landing on her heart like a feather in the wind. "He sat with me? In my room?"

"He was worried about you." Mom swiped a spoonful of the creamy potatoes before Rachel could lower the lid. "When I returned from the store, he was sitting on the bed ... holding your hand."

Rachel leaned on the counter, her gaze glued to her mom's. What? Paul? Holding her hand?

Mom licked the spoon clean, rinsed it, and dropped it into the dishwasher. "Delicious. By the way, how did you like the loft?"

Rachel tried to absorb the information. He'd sat with her and held her hand, the day after he told her he didn't want to be friends. She forced herself to focus. "I love it, Mom. You made it perfect."

"Honey, I wish I could take the credit, but Paul did it."

"Well, of course he helped. You can't use a hammer." She laughed out loud, regaining her composure. "But you gave him the ideas."

"No, actually they were all his. I only told him I planned to do something with the loft for you, and he took over. He even made the plaque with your name."

Rachel stiffened and her heart gave a leap. "He made that?"

"He did a great job. And it was very thoughtful of him to take some time away from all my other projects, so make sure to thank him."

Don't worry. "I will." And will be looking forward to it.

Rachel finished preparing lunch, hovering on a cloud, one spinning with unspoiled emotions. She took out her favorite plush blanket, stuffed silverware and napkins inside the basket, and made two quarts of fresh lemonade. Slipping the beverage into the refrigerator, she soaked in the warm breeze, relishing in her newfound delight. Rachel wanted to see the loft again, that plaque. It would be from a different perspective this time. It was still early so she slipped through the back door.

The expectancy of what she would find, of what it could mean, enthralled her.

Why had he done this?

Rachel removed the rustic wooden sign from the wall and traced the letters. He had carved beautiful designs of flowers and hearts on each side of her name. Squiggly lines made their way through the whole piece of wood. It had a beautiful shape with curvy edges. Rachel hung it back on the single nail as something inside her quivered.

A lantern sat on the table. It had to be his. The words her mom told her earlier soared through her mind. He'd held her hand. Why did she always sleep through the good stuff?

Rachel returned to the house, grabbed the picnic basket, and hurried out the door to find Paul. He rounded the corner of the house at the same time.

"I've got lunch whenever you're ready to take your break."

"I hoped you'd say that. I couldn't wait any longer. It's all I've been able to smell for the last hour." He reached for the basket. "Here, let me."

"Thank you."

Paul took a deep breath. "It smells delicious."

She could feel his eyes on her, but she studied the scattered white blooms spilling from the trees.

They were silent as they strolled down the path. After they crossed the wooden bridge, Paul helped her lay out the blanket in a patch of lush grass.

He took off his hat, his hair tousled from the removal. The perfect squareness of his jaw, the smoothness of his skin, the absolute confidence of his mannerism fixated her.

"Can we pause a moment in silence for the blessing?"

"Yes, of course." Rachel bowed her head. Though guilt plagued her at her obvious appreciation at an inappropriate time, her words flowed. *Thank you for this meal. Thank you for your love. Thank you that you've led me to new friends. I'm so sorry ...*

"Amen."

Rachel opened her eyes. "Amen." Her cheeks burned. "Is that an Amish tradition?

"Jah."

"We pause in silence at school occasionally. I like praying that way. When someone else is speaking, I sometimes repeat what they say. But praying in silence is personal, you can really talk to Him." She unfolded the basket. "I talk too much."

"Nein, not at all. I enjoy listening to you."

The smile she'd been fighting blossomed. "My mom told me you fixed the loft."

He nodded and cleared his throat.

"It's beautiful."

"I'm glad you like it."

She moistened her lips. "You left your lantern up there?"

"Nein, that belongs to you now. I thought it would be nice to have in case you wanted to sit out there after dark."

His response warmed places within her she hadn't known were cold. "You didn't have to do that."

"Ach, I didn't do it for you only."

"What do you mean?"

His smile reached through her. "If I ride by your house after dark and the lantern's shining, I might stop to visit."

Her cheeks burned at his admission. "No, you wouldn't."

"You wouldn't want me to?" Paul seemed to dare her to respond.

"Well, of course I would. You can visit anytime you want." Was this a game?

He cocked an eyebrow. "I have your permission then."

"That's for certain sure." She couldn't hide the laughter demanding to be set free.

"Not bad for a new Lancaster County Englischer."

"You're nothing like I would've imagined an Amish person to be." All at once she realized how that must have sounded.

A deep grunt vibrated in his throat, then shifted into a hearty chuckle. "You mean like those perfect Amish men in your books."

She dipped her chin, her neck and cheeks flaming. "I didn't mean ... I only thought ..." Her words were tangled in her head and spilling rapidly all over the place. Then he took her hand and that flame plummeted into her chest and expanded through her middle.

"I'm teasing you. And I'll take that as a compliment. I think ... I hope." His eyes skimmed over her face, then his lips twitched as his gaze settled on her mouth.

She could only nod. Her heart gave a little leap every single time he looked at her that way. But just because he'd agreed to have lunch with her in the middle of the woods, didn't mean anything had changed between them.

After finishing a chicken leg, he wiped his mouth. "This is gut."

"Thank you." The last thing she needed was to read anything into his intentions. He'd barely agreed to be friends.

"You did this all yourself?"

Rachel paused with her spoon halfway to her mouth. "You seem surprised." She planned to enjoy every minute she had with him, and being herself was becoming easier and easier.

"Mastering fried chicken isn't easy. But this is some of the best I've eaten." He winked.

She re-dipped her fork into the potato salad and trapped a potato between the tines. "My mom always insisted I help her in the kitchen. She wanted me to fall in love with cooking."

"It paid off. That's for certain sure."

One thing she knew for certain sure. She had fallen for the man sitting across from her.

After they finished eating, Paul leaned back onto his side and faced her. "I wonder about your father."

His question threw her for a moment, and she tightened her lips and inhaled hard. There was only one way to say it. Bluntly.

Her mind drifted back to that horrible day. "We, my dad and I, were in an accident as we were leaving softball practice on a Saturday afternoon. He died."

"What happened?" he insisted, his gaze drawing the truth from her.

She stood and crossed to the bridge watching the water break against the sides. "It was my fault."

Paul moved into the space behind her. She could feel his presence. It was comforting having him so close, and the words she'd kept to herself, the words she'd never spoken came easily. "I was complaining about being late to a birthday party. He was the coach, so practice ending later than usual was his idea." Rachel leaned into the railing, the memories coming back as if they'd happened yesterday. "I was so self-ish. He was only trying to make me better, our team the best. He was so good."

Her smile came effortlessly, picturing Daddy standing across the field at third base. His face stern, watching her, teaching her, loving her. "I never told him how much it meant ... him coaching me all those years. I took him for granted. I thought he would always be there coaching my team ... cheering for me." Hot tears stung the back of her lids. "I pulled out into the intersection, even after he told me to wait. The light was green, so I didn't listen. A man driving a truck ran through his red light and crashed into us. If I had listened and waited, he would still be here today. My mom would have her husband. I took him from her." Her heart pounded. She had told him everything. Watching Paul's face, she searched for signs of judgment or disap-proval. But there was only sympathy, compassion. Then he reached around her and placed his hand over hers. Tears escaped at the comfort he offered.

"You can't blame yourself. It was an accident."

She closed her eyes, images emerging that had haunted her dreams. His blood-streaked face, his chest moving, then stopping. "It was my fault. I should've been the one to die, not him."

Paul's arm stiffened, and he fixed his gaze on her. "God doesn't make mistakes."

Grief settled over her like a fresh tidal wave. A broken sob burst from her throat before she could stop it. And then, Paul folded her against his chest and she wept, soaking his shirt with her tears.

Heavy silence lingered between them while her sobs faded away. "I'm so sorry. I didn't mean to fall all to pieces on you." Her voice suddenly wobbly, she pressed her hand against his chest. "I ruined your shirt."

He gripped her arms, his touch gentle, yet strong. "No, Rachel." She lowered her lashes unable to make eye contact with him. "I'm the one who's sorry. I'm sorry you had to go through that. Please don't blame yourself. It isn't up to you to decide when God calls his children home. And praise God for your memories, for the life and love that you shared. If your dad is anything like your mom, he wants a full, happy life for you. Not hurting and hating yourself for something you never had any control over." He looked at her, really looked, like he wanted to make sure she would agree.

Rachel's gaze fell to his hands, and she stared until her vision blurred. She digested all he said, and finally a measure of calm returned. "My mom connected everything in Pensacola with a memory of him. We agreed it would be best to move." Suddenly tremulous, she wrapped her arms tighter around her middle. "We both needed a new start." The piercing sorrow of reliving the memory finally eased into a dull ache. "I'm sorry about the emotional breakdown."

"Don't be ... I enjoy talking to you. You seem to feel things deeply. It's a unique, beautiful thing. You're beautiful."

"Thank you." The trembles heightened a hundred fold. "What about your parents? My mom said you lived with your aunt and uncle."

"I was young when my parents died. Only four. I don't remember much about them."

Her heart squeezed and she took his hand. "I'm so sorry." Rachel tried to imagine what it would be like to live a whole life without her parents. At least she had her memories.

She focused on the streams of light breaking through the tall pines. They were standing so close to each other. Rachel turned and made a bold attempt to look him in the eye, but missed by a few inches. Her gaze halted on his lips. *This isn't helping.* "Come on. Let's finish our picnic." Her hand still connected to his, she pulled him toward the blanket.

She soaked in the moment as long as she could, then released his fingers as they sat down. She missed his touch instantly. "How did you learn to build things? You're so good at it."

"I've always worked with wood. It's something I've enjoyed for as long as I can remember."

"I know you renovate houses, obviously. But I overheard that guy Kevin calling you boss."

"I'm a building contractor. Several Englischers work for me, but I only have a few guys. I'm just getting started."

"How much do you want to grow?"

"That's the complicated part."

"It shouldn't be. Your work is beautiful. You're very gifted, Paul. You can go as far as you want." Rachel watched the play of emotions stretching across his face. Passion, hesitation, longing.

"Tell my uncle that." His gaze settled somewhere deep in the woods. "He's completely against this."

"That's hard to believe." Paul was different, he had a determination she'd never witnessed in other guys his age. It wasn't just his Amish upbringing, there was more to it than that. She reached for his hand, longing to feel his touch again, longing to show him how she felt for him. She squeezed it gently before letting it fall away. "Your work speaks for itself. There's no doubt, you can do anything you set your mind to."

His gaze bore into hers. So intense, she feared she would dig her fingers through the short layers of hair surrounding his neck and kiss him hard on the mouth if she didn't do something. Fast. "So Kevin works for you?" She leaned onto her side, breaking the connection. "You've never brought him before and haven't brought him back since, not that I've seen anyway."

"I needed him that one day. Most of your mom's renovations only need one hand. I have the others, like Kevin, working on other projects."

"Oh. I was wondering why he never came back but that makes sense. Kevin introduced himself that day he worked here." She thought about his invitation. So caught up in her desire to be close to Paul, she'd almost missed his question. She must've seemed so rude. "He said we'd be going to school together."

Paul pulled himself onto his knees. "Jah, he mentioned that." His chin dipped to his chest. "Well, it's getting late. I better get back to work." He packed their things into the basket. His gaze no longer held the same glimmer as before. They were blank, devoid of any hope. Then he looked around with a hint of confusion.

She took the basket from him when they reached the yard.

"Thank you for lunch, and the wunderbaar gut company. Your cooking could give my aunt's a run for its money."

"You're welcome." Her response faltered on her lips.

He took her hand this time and squeezed it gently before letting it go. "Have a gut night at work." He turned and headed in the opposite direction.

What just happened? She should be thrilled. He'd called her beautiful. But something was wrong. Rachel went inside, put her things away, trying not to let the sudden change in his behavior bother her.

Paul crept to his uncle's barn eager to be alone. He slammed the hammer into a piece of wood. It slipped and hit his finger. *Dummkup!*

He'd once again made an idiot of himself. He'd had a wonderful time with Rachel and was delighted she'd asked him to join her for lunch. But why would she want to spend time with him? An Amish man. When she could have an Englischer like Kevin?

The disappointment was cold and bracing, more painful than his throbbing finger. He couldn't blame her. What would she possibly see in him—a plain Amish man who could offer nothing worldly, everything she'd ever known.

Mary traipsed into the barn. "What're you doing?"

He winced at the pain inching up his arm. "Working on something."

She leaned against the wooden shelf. "Something for Rachel?"

"Ach, Mary."

"I thought you liked her." There was a certain determination in her voice.

"I work for her mamm. She's a nice girl. Of course, I like her." He loved her. He wanted to protect her. To spend his life making her smile.

Mary rolled her eyes. "You know what I mean. Like I like *Thomas*." She dragged her fiancé's name out. It rankled his nerves.

He started to grab another piece of wood, but stopped mid-reach. "I'm that obvious?"

"Jah." Mary sat on the stool, her eyes glimmering. She looked like a little girl listening to a story, impatient to find out the ending. "It's okay if you like her."

"No, it's not," he snapped.

"You haven't joined the church."

Mary shouldn't be pushing him. She should be discouraging him. Crossing his arms, he challenged her. "I'm going to. Besides, it goes against everything we've been taught." His tone was sharper than he intended. Her gaze fell, and he regretted his tone. "We had a picnic lunch today."

The brightness in her eyes returned. "Really? Whose idea was it?"

"Hers, but it was no big deal." Paul didn't want to be a bad influence on Mary, or lead her to stray from their Amish heritage. Something his uncle would blame on him, something his uncle would never forgive. But he needn't worry. She was engaged to his best friend, Thomas. Could Mary feel the same way for Thomas that he did for Rachel?

It would be better for Rachel to be interested in someone like Kevin, but that didn't make him feel any better. He could barely stomach the image of her with anyone else.

Mary settled on the bench beside him. "What did you talk about?"

"We did more eating than talking." He wasn't at liberty to tell Mary much. He respected Rachel. Respected her mom. And to talk about their private conversation wasn't the Amish way.

"Did she have a good time at the singing?"

"I don't know. I guess so. You spent more time with her than I did."

"Anna and her cousin visiting from out of town came in the store today. You won't believe what Anna said."

"Speaking gossip again?" Paul wasn't interested. He picked up his hammer and slid two pieces of wood together. "You know I don't care to hear her stories."

"It was about you."

His lips twitched. "Me? What would she have to say about me?"

Mary's lip turned up into a sour pout. "She's planning to kiss you right on the mouth next time she gets you alone."

"What?" The hammer slipped from his grip, clattering against the table. "She told you that?"

"No, she told her cousin, Meg. They didn't see me. I was standing near the back."

"Eefeldich. Is she serious?"

"I knew she liked you, but it surprised even me." She frowned. "She's also been hanging around with that Englisch crowd that likes to party."

"Ach!"

"I think she's hoping you'll try to stop her."

Paul had told her about how Anna manipulated him Sunday night. Mary didn't seem to think Rachel saw them, but she wasn't sure.

"I'll have to make sure I'm never alone with her."

Mary chewed her lower lip, and the wrinkles between her eyes deepened.

"What is it?"

"Nothing." Mary looked as if she wanted to say more, but changed her mind. "I'm sorry things are so difficult for you right now. Have you thought about telling Rachel how you feel?"

Over and over again.

❧ 26 ☙

Rachel stepped outside the restaurant for her morning break. Two birds flew to the ground to peck at a scrap of bread. Blades of grass sparkled in the sunlight from a light rain God had provided earlier. Sudden movement from across the street caught her eye, and she took an instinctive step forward when Paul stepped off the curb.

He hadn't noticed her yet. Should she speak to him? She started to cross the street but stopped when a young Amish woman came around the corner and approached. The girl laughed as she leaned against him. It was the same girl from the singing. The same girl who'd been talking about Paul to her friend. The same girl who hurried to tell him good night.

Anna.

Rachel spun around, the swell of disappointment crushing. Only two more hours until she could go home. Without waiting another second, she moved toward the restaurant door, taking one last glance in his direction. They were no longer there. Good. It hurt too much seeing him with someone else.

After arriving home from work, Rachel took a shower and started downstairs for a snack. She had been unable to eat anything at lunch after seeing *them* together. She was no longer in the mood for company, but had no choice. Her aunt and cousins were on their way.

Rachel had only taken a few steps down the stairs when she noticed Paul standing in the kitchen doorway. Her footsteps halted, and she swiveled on the ball of her foot to retreat upstairs.

"Rachel." His velvet smooth voice reached her from the floor below.

She paused for a long moment, before taking a deep breath and slowly turning back. Then she made the mistake of meeting his gaze. The depth of his blue eyes confused her. Rachel tried not to trip over her feet as she finally made her way down the steps. She reached the last one, and he moved in front of her. "Are you okay?" he asked, breaking the silence.

She stared through the window at the sedan pulling into the drive. "My aunt and cousins are here to visit."

He chuckled. "Are you not happy about seeing them?"

"No, I am." She twisted her fingers together. She would never admit what was really wrong.

"I didn't realize you had family close by."

"They live in Hershey."

"Oh." Paul gripped the edge of the stair railing and rubbed the wood as if he didn't know what else to do with his hand. "That's wunderbaar-gut. But I would expect you to be happier." His dancing eyes urged her to give in.

"I am happy."

He took a step closer. "Nein, something's troubling you."

Pull yourself together. "No, really, I'm fine."

He cleared his throat and looked away. "If you say so."

She imagined falling into his arms. She stopped short and clenched her hands behind her back. What was she doing? What was he doing? He'd been with that girl only two hours ago. Now, he was standing here mesmerizing her with his stare.

She gave herself a mental slap on the wrist. He wasn't doing anything wrong. She was reading what she wanted into this. And she definitely wanted this.

He stood there a moment longer, looking at her with an intensity that stirred a longing within her and threatened to weaken her knees. "Your family's coming in. And I've got to get started on that porch. I'll see you later." He lifted a tummy-fluttering smile and was moving away before she could voice a response.

Mom entered seconds later with Aunt Barbara, Tanner, and Katelyn just as Paul disappeared down the hall.

Aunt Barbara pulled her into a hug. "Look at you. You're absolutely gorgeous."

Rachel hugged her back. "Aw, thank you so much. It's so good to see you." She bent, facing her youngest cousin. A beautiful little girl with big brown eyes and straight dark hair. "Hi, Katelyn." The child stepped behind her mom, keeping her focus on the floor. "Of course you don't remember me. I'm Rachel." Katelyn's cheeks puffed into a crooked smile as Rachel stood and reached to hug Tanner. "Hey, you. It's been a long time."

"Too long. You've changed so much."

Rachel stared up at him. He was taller than she remembered. "Look at you. You're like in college now."

"You'll be there next year. Have you thought about where you're going?"

"No, not really." She had planned to go to Pensacola State her whole life. But the thought of leaving Lancaster County now caused her physical pain.

The sound of Paul's hammer reached her ears and the air in the house thickened. "Katelyn, would you and Tanner like to go for a walk. I have a really cool secret place." She shoved the persistent vision of Paul standing with his girlfriend to the back of her mind and focused on her cousins.

Shy eyes glanced up at her, a hint of excitement filling them. "Okay."

Rachel offered her hand and Katelyn accepted it, her smile timid.

Once Katelyn warmed to her, she treated Rachel like she'd known her, her whole life. She wanted Rachel's full attention, and Rachel was happy to give it. Katelyn was a good distraction.

They played hide-and-seek when they reached the creek. Katelyn and Rachel hid together behind a big bush surrounded by tall pines.

After Tanner counted to twenty, he ambled toward them. Katelyn's squirming feet against fallen branches would give their secret place away.

"Where could they be?" A lighthearted grin broadened his Pennsylvania accent.

A soft giggle eased from Katelyn's lips, and she covered her mouth with her hand.

Rachel gave her a knowing look, and Katelyn slipped to her bottom, her hand still firmly in place. That is, until Tanner jumped in front of them reaping a wild scream from them both.

They moved to sit on the thick patch of grass, and Katelyn told her all about preschool. Her excitement over going to pre-kindergarten was precious.

Maybe it was seeing Tanner again after all these years or maybe she hadn't noticed before, but Tanner reminded her of Daddy. They had the same features, the same lanky frame. Maybe it was just the idea that he was a part of her family. Part of a family she could still hold onto. Part of a family she didn't want to let go.

Back in the yard, she avoided looking in Paul's direction and instead watched Katelyn skip across the yard. Inside, Mom and Aunt Barbara had cookies and milk set out. Rachel grabbed a couple of water bottles and a few cookies before heading back outside to the front porch.

"How do you like Lancaster? Are you making friends?"

Rachel handed him a bottle and looked across the yard. "Yeah. I've made one really good friend at the restaurant. We'll be going to school together."

"That's great. I'm sure you'll fit right in." Tanner stretched out his long legs. "I'll have to introduce you to Eric Matthews. He's one of my best friends and will be graduating with you. I'll try to bring him by the restaurant before school starts. Maybe you'll have some classes together."

"Yeah, that would be great." This certainly wasn't how she expected her last year of high school to turn out. "It's going to be so awkward starting a new school as a senior."

"I'm sure. If you need anything, let me know. I'll be right there."

"Thanks, Tanner. It's really good to see you again and so nice having family here."

When they left an hour later, Rachel stayed on the front porch swing. The afternoon breeze blew her hair, but it didn't ease the dilemma that had come back in full authority. When Paul came toward the front porch, she stiffened and pressed a hand against her stomach.

Paul had waited patiently for her family to leave before approaching her. Rachel had seen Anna with him today. He was certain. "Hullo."

She hesitated before meeting his gaze. Her expression was cautious, not trusting.

"Hey." Her gaze fell back on the bottle top she twisted.

"How was your visit?"

An innocent smile crossed her lips. "Good."

Paul sat on the swing next to her hoping she wouldn't mind. She slid over still playing with the drink bottle. Being this close to her triggered strange yearnings.

He crossed his arms to keep from taking her hand and pushed the swing with his foot. The sudden movement caused her to shift into him. She straightened, placed the bottle on the porch, and tucked her hands beneath her legs.

A desire to reach out and hold her manipulated his self-control. He rotated his jaw trying to regain power of his reactions. "What has your thoughts tied up?"

Rachel was watching him, her lips parted slightly, like she wanted to speak. But her mouth closed. Her eyes were warm, full of questions. And all he could think of was kissing her.

Could she be experiencing the same longing?

"I was thinking about Katelyn. And how I miss her already."

He had expected some form of confession about seeing him with Anna today. Paul smiled at the relief relaxing the lines on her face. "What about the other cousin? He looks about our age. Will he be going to school with you?"

"No, he graduated last year. He has a friend who will be though. He's planning to introduce me."

"Oh." He cleared his throat.

She would have many male friends. Why had this never occurred to him before now? The thought sent another wave of emotion through him. One he didn't like. Paul had a hard time imagining the rest of the world when he was near her.

"Oh? What's that supposed to mean?"

"You'll probably have so many friends before the year is over, you won't be able to keep up with them all." His words were only a disguise attempting to diminish the dark brooding cloud that swept over him.

"Even in Florida, I only had two close friends."

The same battle seemed to rage in her expression. She was curious and wanting and confused and nervous all at once. Just as he was.

Her face tilted and locks of dark brown waves fell into her face, a few sticking to her lashes as she raised her gaze to meet his.

Without permission, his hand lifted, touched her forehead just above her eyebrow, and pulled the few strands away. It was challenging to pull back, to stop himself from moving closer than he already was. Paul imagined wrapping his arms around her waist, pulling her close, and breathing in the scent of her.

For many long seconds, neither of them spoke a word.

He stood, shaking his head. *What are you thinking?*

Paul forced himself to walk away. He stood at the bottom of the steps before he turned around. She looked at her feet, her cheeks a deep shade of pink.

"I need to get back to work." His voice was low, his throat suddenly hoarse.

"Okay." She wavered as she stood.

Paul left before he could change his mind and go back to her. He would have to learn some control.

No mistakes. He could make no mistakes.

❧ 27 ☙

Rachel's imagination had worked overtime since her talk with Paul yesterday. As she descended the stairs, something occurred to her—Paul had already come inside.

Pulling her fingers through her hair, she treaded down the stairs. He stood at the bottom, just like yesterday, and smiled in a way he hadn't before. It was as if he'd been waiting hours to see her.

"Hullo."

She pictured herself tumbling down the stairs and landing in his bulging arms, like on the cover of some cheesy romance novel. A soft chuckle escaped her lips. She shook the vision free not wanting to trip and say something stupid. She'd fallen enough in his presence.

"What's so funny?" Those eyes gripped her with their compelling gaze.

Her tongue refused the truth. "Nothing."

"I don't believe you." He gave her a crooked grin.

"I promise. It's nothing." She leaned against the banister content to stare at him.

He frowned. "Okay, but it's such a shame."

"What is?"

"That it was nothing."

"What do you mean?" He was teasing her. And she liked it. She could stand here forever with him like this. His eyes were warm, filled with a strong energetic power that drew her in. An occasional urge would swell within her, and she'd have to look away.

"I hoped I could make you smile like that again."

Heat flooded her face. How did he do that? She could be perfectly fine, but one glance from him sent her into another dimension. He was definitely flirting. It just didn't make sense if he and Anna were together, unless Kelli was right? Could Kelli be right? This very minute it didn't matter. Nothing did. Only her and him. In this moment.

"Are you off today?"

She moved past him, deliberately brushing against him in the tight space and tipped her face up to look at him. "Yes." She laughed, fighting the attraction drawing her closer. "Kelli and I are going school shopping in Philadelphia."

"Oh? That's a long drive." Rachel couldn't help but smile at his stern expression. "Will you be calling your mom when you arrive?"

Her heart skittered against her chest at his protective tone. "Yes."

"And when you leave?"

"I tell her where I am at all times."

"That's good. I would be worried sick if you were traveling that far, and I had no way to know you were okay."

She could get used to this. Especially when she was the object of his consideration.

Paul leaned against the banister and crossed his arms. "It's a good thing you have that little phone."

Kelli pulled down the path, altering their attention.

"Have a nice time, and a safe trip." He delivered his words slowly. And every muscle tightened as he pressed his way past her, leaving only inches between them. "And make sure you come back."

She followed every inch of his diminishing form. No one had ever made her feel the way Paul Fischer did.

Rachel's thoughts were crowded with images of Paul with too much time to think on the long ride to Philadelphia. The way his fingers trailed down her cheek, the look in his eyes, that crazy sexy smile of his that could almost buckle her knees.

"How are things with the handyman?"

Rachel scanned the open road, heat burning her neck. "There's not much to tell. We're friends. At least when I'm trying not to avoid him."

Kelli rolled her eyes and head all while keeping her gaze on the road. "Why on earth would you do that?"

"I don't want to make a fool out of myself. And I don't want to push myself on him. He might be engaged to that girl, what's-her-name."

"Anna?"

Rachel knew the girl's name. She had it memorized. But hearing it out loud caused a knot to tighten in her middle. "I saw them together yesterday."

"Really? What were they doing?"

"I don't know. She approached him." And fell all over him. "I didn't stick around to watch." She hadn't wanted to see his reaction to Anna —to see him take her into his arms. The thought made her sick.

"I'll ask Belinda."

"No," Rachel said, too quickly. Of course she wanted to know. She just wasn't ready to find out. Not yet. "You don't have to do that. I can ask his cousin, Mary." But it wouldn't be any time soon. Maybe never.

Rachel dialed her mom's number as soon as they parked an hour later. "Hey mom, we're here ... he did ... Okay, I'll call you when we're leaving. ... Love you, too. ... Bye."

"What did your mom say? Who is *he*?"

She inhaled hard. Then blew the breath out in slow motion. "Paul has asked her twice if I called."

"You're kidding me?" Kelli squealed. "He really likes you."

"It makes more sense for him to like Anna."

"I don't think so. Anna's just pushy."

Agonizing chills escalated through her body with each thought or mention of Paul. And Anna. "Do you know a guy named Kevin that works with him? He said we would be going to school together?"

"Kevin Williams?"

"That's him. I think Paul was trying to set me up with him?" It was impossible to not talk about him or think of him. Paul now occupied permanent residence in her mind, her heart.

"Why in the world would he do that?"

Rachel grabbed her purse from the back seat, desperate for a diversion. When Rachel finally faced forward, she caught Kelli's raised eyebrow still in place. "I don't know. Because Kevin asked me out. It was just weird."

Kelli's mouth dropped open. "Kevin asked you out? What did you say?"

"I told him I had other plans."

"What? Kevin Williams asked you out and you told him no?" She cackled. "I probably wouldn't tell anyone else about this. At least until you get to know everyone."

"Why not?"

"Because he's the hottest thing at Conestoga Creek High, and all the girls will instantly despise you."

Rachel definitely wasn't planning to tell anyone. "But what's even weirder. Paul hasn't brought him back to my house since that day."

"Paul wouldn't try to set you up with someone. Not when he's in love with you."

A panicked flutter skipped through her heart. "He's Amish, Kelli. He even told me we shouldn't be friends."

"But he's talking to you now. He took you to the singing and then on a buggy ride, so apparently he gave up on that."

"He's just trying to be nice. He was with Anna yesterday. They're together. I'm sure." But memories of him flirting, their conversations, the alluring magnetism of his eyes roared above all other sensible thoughts. *Make sure you come back.* She nearly soared at the five little words playing havoc in her mind, her heart, her soul.

Kelli pulled into a parking spot. "Does Paul know that Kevin asked you out?"

"I didn't tell him, and he hasn't said anything about it." Rachel climbed from the car. "Let's have lunch first. Then we can walk off all those calories."

They found a corner table in the courtyard and ate their chow mien lunches.

"I need some warmer things for fall. Things I didn't need in Florida." The thought of home hadn't hurt so much. The pain was easing. "What kind of styles do you wear to school around here?"

Kelli waved, shaking her head all at the same time. "I love your style. You have the coolest clothes. They scream confidence."

"Really? Thanks." The compliment made Rachel feel good, and she glanced at her outfit. Jean capris with a blue and green dress that hung a couple of inches above her knees. "So I shouldn't buy a few Amish dresses."

"Only if you're planning to marry the handyman."

Yes! In my dreams.

After lunch, they wandered through the mall.

"Come on, this is my favorite store," Kelli said, moving forward.

Off one of the first racks, Rachel grabbed a light blue sweater and held it against her chest and studied her reflection in the mirror. Would Paul like this? Of course he wouldn't. He liked plain clothes and plain girls.

Two hours later, armed with a few bags from different shops, they headed to the parking lot.

Kelli pulled onto the main highway heading back to Paradise. "You should come to church with me sometime?"

She twisted in her seat to face Kelli. "Really? I would love to."

"We have a large youth group and an awesome drama program. We have so much fun."

"We did some drama. I miss that." Rachel pulled her hair back.

Kelli scanned her with a sweeping glance. "We perform at different venues. You should join our team. Your voice is amazing."

"Really? Thanks." Rachel stretched and crossed her legs. A familiar joy leapt through her middle. It was almost like having Samantha here. Almost like being home.

They arrived home an hour later. Rachel showered, put on her pajamas, and with her book in hand, settled on the bench inside the barn. That was the best way to learn about the Amish without asking too many questions. And the easiest way. Rachel was glad Paul had put the lantern out, it was already dark.

Her bookmark guided her to her saved page and within the first paragraph she was transported into another world. One that wasn't so complicated—one she dreamed of joining.

The barn door woke Rachel with a start. She caught herself before falling off the bench. *Mom.* How long had she been sleeping?

The ladder creaked, following the shuffling sound of footsteps climbing to the loft and coming to a stop near the top.

"Paul?" She needed a moment to recover from her state of shock.

He took the last step, bringing them only feet from each other. Whatever she was about to say stumbled to a halt. His sleeves were rolled to his forearms, his collar loosened at the base of his neck, his gaze raking over her and settling on her lips. She struggled to find the right words. "What are you doing here?"

"I rode by and saw the lantern burning."

"Oh." Her voice sounded childish even to her own ears.

He covered the bottom area of his face with his hand. Rachel crossed her legs, her pajama pants riding up with the motion. She had already washed her face and pulled her hair back in a pony tail. It reminded her of the first time she'd met him.

"How was your trip?" His voice rumbled with pleasure.

"It was fun." Was he really standing there? Or was she dreaming?

He leaned against the wall and crossed his arms. "Were you planning to sleep out here tonight?" The teasing tone of his voice hurt only a little.

How could she have come out here dressed like this? Never in a million years had she expected to see him tonight.

"I'm sorry, would you rather that I didn't come?"

"No," she said with a sharp staggering breath. "I'm just surprised to see you."

"I rode by to make sure you were home." His voice sounded alluring, whether he meant for it to or not.

"You wanted to make sure I made it home?" Rachel pressed her lips together to keep them from quivering.

"Jah. And when I saw the lantern burning, I couldn't resist stopping." His faint smile enthralled her as his stare returned to her pants.

"If I had known you were coming, I would've kept my clothes on." Searing heat burned her neck and rapidly expanded to her cheeks.

He must think I'm an idiot.

She loosened her hair from the pony tail holder allowing it to fall free, to cover her face.

Paul took the seat next to her, leaving only inches between them. He leaned forward, his neck stiff, but then he faced her. "You have plans tomorrow night?"

"No, I ... I don't have any plans." Her body trembled. Did he want to spend time with her, again? "Why do you ask?"

"Kevin said he invited you to a concert at the theater, but you couldn't go. You had other plans." His voice was low and bleak. "I just wondered what plans you had."

Had he really just said that? "I was going to clean my room. I thought I would rearrange it."

"That doesn't sound as fun as a concert." He cocked an eyebrow. His smile was mocking as he stared into her eyes.

"You *want* me to go with him?"

He leaned back, his gaze never leaving hers. "Jah, if you want to."

She swore she saw a battle fuming in his eyes—the same battle wrestling within her. But none of it made sense. "I would've accepted if I wanted to go, but I didn't, so I turned him down."

"Oh." Paul regarded her with a wistful smile.

"Oh?" Rachel gulped air into her lungs. "There you go with that *oh* thing again." She pretended none of this bothered her, but her pulse was racing, her lungs constricting, her skin tingling. "Are you trying to set me up with him?"

He stood and leaned against the wall. "Not exactly." He hesitated. "I just thought ... never mind, I don't know what I thought."

Her throat closed and she couldn't speak.

"Could I see you tomorrow after you rearrange your room?"

Rachel straightened, determined not to give in to his charm. "I have to work."

He studied her face. "But I thought you just said ...," he whispered hoarsely. "What time will you be home then?"

His question reverberated through her thoughts and she bit her lower lip. "I get off at three."

"Gut, I'll see you tomorrow then." An easy smile played across his mouth as he took her hand. He moved toward the ladder never taking his eyes from hers, and she inhaled a lungful of air. Their arms stretched in the distance between them until their fingers fell away with his last step.

❦ 28 ❦

Rachel awoke on Saturday morning weary from a sleepless night. As she waited tables, her conversation with Paul, the way he had taken her hand, replayed over and over in her mind.

At the end of her shift, she started to walk through the restaurant to leave, but stopped mid-step at the unmistakable sound of Paul's name, through Anna's distinctive, shrill voice.

It beckoned her closer to the wall, separating her and Anna's table. She had to know what the girl was saying.

"The other night Paul took me home ...." The last few words fell away as disappointment stopped Rachel from moving. She covered her mouth, the weight of Anna's words crushing against her chest.

What did Anna mean, the other night? What night? In between all those times he spent flirting with her he had been courting Anna?

Maybe there was some mistake. He couldn't be courting Anna. Yes, he could.

The other girl's voice sharpened. "He kissed you?"

Paul kissed Anna? The words battered the tender wound encasing her heart.

"It's only a matter of time before he proposes. I can tell he's hinting around to it."

Biting back an unruly sob, Rachel hurried across the restaurant floor and sprinted to her car. Once safe inside, she grasped the steering wheel and pressed herself against the seat and drove home, instead of what she wanted to do—prop her head against the wheel and give in to the tormenting sobs welling in her chest.

Rachel had conjured a complete scenario in her delirious mind of exactly what she wanted. Him wanting her as badly as she wanted him. But she had been wrong. About everything.

Every flirtatious look, every unrelenting need to be near him, every daydream of him kissing her, holding her, loving her. There was no one else to blame. She'd done this to herself.

Paul pulled into the driveway moments after her, and she wiped the tears from her cheeks. Paul would not see her like this.

Conflicting emotions tore through her middle. She'd seen him with Anna. Three times. She should've known better. He was one of those Amish guys only seeking a thrill.

Paul met her at her car door. Every instinct screamed at her to run into the house. To never look back. But she couldn't.

Heart thumping in her chest, she glanced up at him. "Hey."

"Hullo." He opened her car door, and she stood. Appreciation shown in his eyes as he coveted her face, from her eyes to her nose to her lips. Rachel brushed past him. She couldn't help it. No matter how much it would hurt, she craved that connection she always felt when she touched him.

"Can we walk to the creek?"

"To the creek?" Her voice quivered with anger. "Okay."

Just don't look at him.

They walked quietly through the woods. This time, she kept a safe distance between them and concentrated on the trees around her. The sun's rays fought against the deep shadows of the green brush hanging above them. The flutter of birds and other creatures moved deeper into the cover of the trees at the sound of their footsteps. But none of that bridged the gap between her anger and sting of disappointment.

Once they reached the bridge, Paul leaned against a tree. When his gaze met hers, his brow crinkled. "How was work?"

Horrible. Especially the last few minutes. "Good." It seemed like days ago she'd been to the restaurant. Time warped in his presence. She took a step back, her mind reeling, her heart breaking.

He moved closer. "Is something wrong, Rachel?"

"No." He'd made no promises to her. She could pretend he'd never made her feel this way. But he made it impossible looking at her that way? "Why would anything be wrong?"

He advanced toward her. "You've been crying."

"I'm tired." Hot fresh tears streamed down her cheeks, and she averted her face. He didn't move. And now they stood only inches from each other. Rachel took an involuntary step back, needing more distance. She shifted her focus. Anything other than him, his magnetism tugging at every natural desire she possessed.

"You don't look tired, you look upset."

She recoiled from him, stretching even more distance between them. "I know we're friends now, but you shouldn't ... we shouldn't ...," she said between sniffs, struggling to suppress her tears. "How would this make your girlfriend feel?"

"My girlfriend?" His voice hitched a whole octave.

"I saw her today. She came into the restaurant as I was leaving."

"That's *narrisch*. What are you talking about? I'm not courting anyone."

"Maybe not officially, but taking girls home in your buggy leads to courting. And a kiss where I come from, proves your affection."

"Hold on ..."

"I thought you being an Amish man, strong in the faith, would make you more honorable. Maybe I was wrong about you. Especially if you're willing to deny it." She swiveled on her feet and swiped at another errant tear. Crying over him, in front of him, was the last thing she wanted.

"How can I deny something I know nothing about?"

She spun to face him, a loud grunt escaping her throat, surprising even her. "How could you? Playing games with that poor girl's affections? Anna's probably sitting at home waiting for you right now."

His eyes widened. "Anna?" It was nothing more than a whisper, then the shock on his face miraculously transformed. And her breath caught in her throat.

He slammed his hands against his thighs. His deep, boisterous laughter startled her. "I'm not courting Anna."

Rachel jabbed her fist into the curve of her waist. "I overheard her telling a friend that you took her home the other night and kissed her."

"I had to take her entire family home after a church service, because of a busted wagon wheel. But that was over a month ago."

"But ... "

"But ... nothing." He brought his hand to her cheek and gently brushed away the wet tears. "I'm not courting her, or anyone, and I most definitely haven't kissed her." Something in the sound of his voice, in his gentle touch, made her legs weaken. "What about you?" There had been no time to marvel in his response. "Are you interested in Kevin?"

Rachel closed her eyes, inhaling slowly through her nose. She opened them and focused on his day-old stubble, turmoil sweeping over her. "What? I thought I made that clear last night."

"You only said you didn't want to go to the concert."

His question, its meaning were like a blow, slamming the truth to her core. Rachel's hands flew to her hips. "I really don't appreciate you trying to fix me up with him."

Paul reared back as if she'd slapped him. "I assure you, that's not what I'm doing."

Her hands fell to her sides. "Then why do you keeping talking about him?"

"You'll be going to the same school." A heavy sigh emphasized his words. His gaze drifted away from hers, deep lines creasing between his eyes. He turned slowly, slipping his hands in his pockets. "He works for me and talks about you constantly until *ich kann nimmi schnaufe*." He pronounced each syllable, the pitch of his voice deeper, as though each word was significant.

Rachel's heart fluttered. "What? What does that mean?"

"He talks about you ... until I can no longer breathe."

A smile danced across her mouth, spreading faster than she could stop it. "You want me to go out with him because he talks about me ..."

"Ach, nein. I don't want you to go out with Kevin." Paul advanced toward her and placed both hands on the tree, behind her, bringing his face only inches from hers. "I don't want you to go out with anyone unless ... that someone is me." His voice lowered to a whisper, but she had no trouble hearing him.

Warmth, delight, and a longing she'd never known flooded her.

He lifted her chin compelling her to look at him. "I have strong feelings for you. Feelings I've never known. I tried to stay away, to get you out of my mind, but I can't." His hands rested on her waist. "I don't want to stay away."

Rachel blinked against the sudden erratic rhythm of her heart. She swayed on her feet and covered her chest, trying to quiet her pounding heart. "You don't have to."

His gaze shifted to her mouth. Lips parted, he closed the distance between them and pressed his mouth against hers. It was an intoxicating mixture of passion and tenderness. His hand stretched across her lower back, scaling upward to the base of her neck. He webbed his fingers through her hair, intertwining the strands between his fingers, holding her tighter. Raising on her tiptoes, she wrapped both hands around his neck. His kiss deepened with urgency, and she trembled in response. Too quickly he loosened his hold on her.

She lowered her lashes, unable to meet his gaze. She stared at the shadow of his day old stubble instead, unable to speak.

He pulled her into an embrace, breathing against her hair. "I've never felt this way, ever."

Paul tucked her head beneath his chin. She concentrated on steadying her breathing, her trembling lips. He had kissed her. Actually kissed her. And it was amazing and staggering all at the same time.

"You have no idea how long I've wanted to do that." He slowly worked his fingers through her hair tilting his head downward until their cheeks were touching.

Their erratic breathing blended in the space between them. She was dazed by the warmth of his arms around her.

With the tip of his nose he traced his way back to her lips giving her another soft kiss, and then another. When he pulled away, she fought to regain her composure.

"I want you to be mine, Rachel Adams."

There was nothing she wanted more than to stay like this with him forever. Edging a few inches backward, he added distance between them. But he grasped her hand, bringing it to his chest. The touch injected a new dose of fire through her veins.

"Is this okay? I don't want to make you uncomfortable."

She executed a small nod, unable to speak. He answered her with a smile, then cradled her hand and gently brushed his lips against each of her finger tips. She reminded herself to breathe.

The way he looked at her made her feel like the most beautiful woman in the world. A look that spoke directly to her heart. A look that said, he would never tire of looking into her eyes, even after a lifetime.

She couldn't place her finger on the exact moment her feelings for Paul changed, but as he slipped his fingers between hers and led her down the path, she became certain of one thing—she never wanted to lose him. Not ever.

Paul was alone now, and the voices in his head were like daggers. What was Anna thinking? How could she spread lies about him? He could still see Rachel now. The way her damp lashes blinked, believing the worst of him. The way she'd examined his reaction when he'd told her the truth. The way it had strengthened his reaction toward her. He had wanted to taste her lips, to hold her, to take away her doubt.

And then when that moment finally came, it had been earth shattering. It felt as if his world were suddenly tilting into the very place it was always meant to be.

His emotions were too energized, too exposed. Being the Amish man everyone expected was the furthest thing from his mind, but it was the one thing he couldn't ignore. He had to be careful returning to his uncle's house. His family could suspect nothing. But it would be hard to hide. The love gushing through his soul was greater than any consequence he would have to face.

The sweet taste, the delicate sensation of her lips shadowed Paul's guilt. When she'd kissed him back it had almost been more than he could handle. The yearning to be closer had nearly suffocated him.

Almost as suffocating as having to tell Rachel that they could tell no one.

❦ 29 ❦

When Rachel arrived at the restaurant, her emotions still smoldered on the edge of pure, untainted bliss. Then she noticed a plate of cinnamon rolls set on the counter with five balloons floating in mid-air. "What's this?"

Kelli grabbed her hand and pulled her forward. "It's for you. This is your last day ... for awhile. Mom wanted to do something special."

Kelli's mom closed the distance between them and hugged her. "We're going to miss you so much."

"I'll be back to visit."

Mrs. Mavis held her at arm's length. "I most certainly hope so."

When Kelli's mom left the restaurant floor, Kelli spun to face her.

"You are absolutely glowing. Did something happen?" The door bell jingled, and Kelli sighed. "You'll have to tell me later."

Rachel laughed, but the expression on Kelli's face stopped her short. Something was wrong. Then she noticed her cousin and another guy had come in.

"Hey, it's about time you came." She waved her hands through the air. "It's my last day."

She glanced back at Kelli, but she had already disappeared.

"Today? Really?" Tanner pulled her into a hug, and then Rachel led them to a table in her section.

"Yeah, since school's starting back."

"Gotcha. Aunt Beverly's idea, huh?"

"Something like that."

Rachel glanced at his friend, and Tanner took the hint. "This is my buddy, Eric Matthews."

Eric scooted into the booth. "I hear we'll be going to school together."

"Yeah."

"You'll like it. It's a small school but everyone's friends with everyone."

Maybe it wouldn't be so bad. She hoped being the new girl wouldn't make a difference.

Eric rested his elbows on the table. "How are you liking Amish country so far?"

"It's fascinating."

"It took me a while to get used to it, but eventually it grew on me."

"You're not from here?"

"Not originally. I'm from a big city back east." He offered no more details, so she didn't press him. "I'm sure we'll see each other plenty once school starts."

Rachel smiled, thankful to have one more face she'd recognize the first day. He would be easy to spot. Tall, dark, and good looking. She took their order before returning to the kitchen. Kelli was fixing a cup of coffee.

"How do you know Tanner Mitchell?" Kelli's expression pleaded for an explanation.

"Tanner's my cousin, well, my second cousin. Our moms are first cousins. You know him?"

"Not nearly as much as I would like to. I have always had the biggest crush on that boy."

"What?" Rachel couldn't hide the laughter in her voice. "Tanner?"

"Yes." Kelli squealed.

"Do you know his friend Eric, too?"

"Yes, he's graduating with us." Kelli leaned back on the counter.

"Eric's a super nice guy and Tanner's your cousin. I cannot believe this."

Rachel laughed. "It's been a few years since I've seen him, until he came over the other day."

"Tell me what happened with Paul."

The doorbell jingled again.

"We'll have to talk later." Rachel pushed the door open with her hip, her hands holding the tray crowded with glasses of orange juice, coffee cups, and a pitcher of coffee. She cast one last glance at Kelli. "Paul's taking me to dinner. Tonight."

Rachel returned to the dining room to find she had two more tables, so she couldn't talk to Tanner much either.

The afternoon plodded on at an irritably slow pace. When she finally arrived home, she moved to the front porch swing and was reading a chapter from her Bible study book when Paul pulled into the yard. Rachel fiddled with the book's edge, casually observing Paul's steady movements. He unloaded a long stack of timber, his muscles bulging under the strain. Then he carried them toward the back yard. What if he thought he'd made a mistake? He hadn't looked in her direction, and she glanced at the front door. Could she slip back inside without him noticing?

Before she had the chance to move, Paul walked toward the front porch and took the steps two at a time. He leaned against the column, keeping a safe distance, never taking his eyes from hers. She tried to smile, but her head swam with doubt. Why wasn't he moving closer?

"You haven't changed your mind about going to dinner?"

"No, I've been looking forward to it all day." Her voice sounded formal and foolish. Would they always fall into awkward moments?

"I have a few more things to finish, and I'll head home to shower and be back to pick you up. I can be here at six." He took a step closer and without thinking, she leaned forward. "Is that gut?"

"It's perfect."

"All right." As he walked away, his familiar chuckle reached her, heating places she hadn't known existed.

. . .

Thunder rumbled overhead and dark clouds hovered over them as Rachel climbed into Paul's buggy. Not until she was settled in the cab did Paul release her and walk around to his side.

Once he reached the main road, Paul took her hand and squeezed it gently. "My cousin Mary knows about us."

Rachel swiftly glanced at Paul, the butterflies in her stomach taking flight. "She does?"

"Jah. I told her about you."

She grabbed hold of his sleeve. "What did she say?"

"She knew the day we came into the restaurant together."

A thrill of hope ruptured through her. "How could she have known then?" She laughed. "I thought she was your girlfriend."

"I should've introduced you."

"What about your aunt?"

"I haven't told her yet. It's complicated." His voice was grave, like he was struggling to speak. "It's not because I don't want them to know. I do. They just don't agree with Amish and Englischers dating. I have to find a way ..."

His last few words faded, and suddenly the excitement vanished, and in its place doubt materialized. How could they have a relationship when he couldn't tell his whole family? Rachel focused on the cornstalks, feeling lost. He was even taking her to another town, one where he wouldn't be recognized.

"Please don't let this bother you. I just don't know how to handle it yet."

She gripped the buggy seat. What did that mean? His family would never approve of her. Maybe he didn't believe they would last long. When he glanced at her, the haggard look on his face apprehended her. It was going to be difficult for him. It *was* difficult for him. But he was here with her, no one else, not an Amish girl. He was here with her.

They reached the restaurant, and he helped her down. Then he slipped his fingers between hers, and his touch soaked through her skin, creating an avalanche of uncertainty. The vulnerability in his eyes was innocent, sincere. How could she be so selfish? Within those few seconds, the gentle caress of his callused fingers brushing against her palm caused her negative thoughts to vanish.

They chose a corner booth, and Paul took the seat next to her. "I hope you don't mind." The moment seemed surreal. She was on a date with Paul Fischer. "The only thing about sitting next to you is I won't be able to stare into your beautiful brown eyes all night." He took her hand and squeezed it. "But I had to make a choice between the two."

A sense of yearning trailed across her skin, tickling the back of her neck, and sinking into her belly. "You think I have beautiful eyes?"

"Jah. The most beautiful I've ever seen."

"Paul Fischer?"

The deep voice startled Rachel, and she stiffened and sat straight back against the wood booth. Anxiety swirled in her stomach, creating a merciless churning. She yanked her hand away from Paul's and clamped them together in her lap, but it was too late. There was no denying it, they were together. On a date. Her face burned as she stared at the menu.

"What're you doing all the way out here in Millersville? Aren't you still working in Paradise?" The deep male voice boomed across the restaurant, and Rachel was sure at least three tables in each direction heard every word.

Paul cleared his throat. "Jah, I'm still in Paradise. We're just out to dinner."

"With a beautiful young lady?"

Rachel met the man's gaze and pushed her lips upward into a full curve though it felt more unnatural than anything she'd ever done. He was wearing a T-shirt, jeans, and a ball cap. Definitely not Amish.

Paul's voice broke their eye contact, and she stole a peek at him, his expression calmer than she'd expected. "This is Rachel Adams. Rachel, Caleb Lapp."

Maybe Paul wasn't worried about being seen with her in public away from his community. Maybe he only had to worry about his Amish friends. But Lapp sounded very Amish.

"It's nice to meet you, Rachel. I'll let you two have your date. Just wanted to say hullo. See you around, Paul."

Paul wasted no time stealing her hand from her lap. "Do you care if I have this back?" The churning in her stomach stopped. If he wasn't going to let it bother him, neither was she.

. . .

When he pulled into her driveway after dinner, he rushed around to help her down. Her feet were steady on the ground, but still he held to her waist, compelling her to look at him.

Then they strolled to the other side of the buggy escaping the overhead light spilling all around them. Her pulse quickened, creating a tingling flutter in the pit of her belly. "Stop looking at me that way."

The corners of his lips curved into a charming smile. "Why?"

Her body reacted even as the words were forming on her lips. "Because if you don't, I'm going to kiss you."

He leaned forward allowing their bodies to meld as he pressed his lips against hers, his hand groping through her hair and settling on her neck. But the kiss didn't last nearly long enough.

"I'm sorry, Rachel."

Sorry. Where had that come from? So consumed with the thought of kissing him, it took a moment to realize why he apologized.

They had a problem.

A real problem. One she didn't want to face it right now, but had no choice. "What do you want to do?"

"This. I want all of this," Paul whispered huskily. "You, me, us together. Things will work out. Somehow. Trust me."

His hand rested against her cheek, and her confidence heightened. Before she could stop herself, the question she'd been wanting to ask him burst forth. "How does a person become Amish? Can someone just decide and take an oath?"

"Nein, it doesn't work that way." The sternness in his voice surprised her. It left no room for argument, and the hard set of his jaw expected her full cooperation. "A person is born into this lifestyle. You don't choose it."

What if they were to marry? She couldn't assume he felt that deeply for her. And asking him would be presumptuous. No. She wouldn't go there.

His answer left her feeling horrible. She wanted to be with him, and they would have to work that out. She certainly didn't want to be the reason for him getting into trouble.

❧ 30 ❧

Saturday morning, Rachel started a load of laundry, cleaned the kitchen and bathrooms, and had just finished dusting the living room when a knock on the front door startled her.

They never had visitors.

Her mom was in New York this morning, so Rachel was home alone. Kelli was working today. And Paul wasn't planning to come until hours later.

Her legs weakened. They were barely strong enough to hold her upright. With shaky fingers, she moved the curtain away from the front window but couldn't see anyone. What if it was Jason?

Loud pounding came again in three solid jolts and a sensation spread across her neck, like spiders crawling all over her skin.

I'm being ridiculous. It's probably Paul.

Rachel cracked the door open just a little and froze. There was a split second when her breathing ceased.

Jordan Baker, one of her best friends from Florida, stood on her front porch.

"Hey beautiful." He grinned, pushed the door open, and pulled her into his arms. They stood in an embrace for several moments before Rachel pulled back, her pulse still pounding in her throat.

"What're you doing here?"

He stuffed a hand into the pocket of his jeans. "I had to come. To make sure you're okay." His eyes were cautious, more serious than she'd ever seen them, and her gaze flitted across his familiar features. He set his chiseled jaw the way he always did just before he tipped his head to the side, and something faltered in his expression.

"You're really here. I can't believe this." She scanned the area behind him. "Are you alone?"

"It's just me." He took her hand.

Rachel knew why Jordan looked at her that way. "What are you doing here? Where's your mom?"

"She's home, but sends her love. And I'm here because I'm transferring to Penn State."

She took a step backward, causing their hands to separate. "No, you're not."

"Yes. I am." He squinted against the afternoon sunlight. "I'm going to their College of Medicine in Hershey, Pennsylvania."

"What?" She squealed. "You're moving here? To Pennsylvania? Hershey's only forty minutes away." She waited for him to tell her it wasn't true, that it was a joke, but his eyes weren't lying. And she knew him better than anybody. He would never tease her about something like that.

"I'm on my way there now, but I had to see you first."

"I can't believe you're really here. What happened to Duke?"

"Nothing. It's a great school. But so is Penn State, and I needed a change."

It didn't make any sense, but Jordan was standing right here in front of her. She couldn't get a grasp on it.

"Are you going to invite me in?"

"I'm so sorry." Rachel reached for the handle and leaned into the heavy door, pushing it with her hip. "You must be so tired driving all the way here from Florida." Rachel sat on the couch, and he took the chair across from her. "How did you know how to find us?"

"I told your mom I was coming and made her promise not to tell. I wanted to surprise you."

"Well, it worked. You 'bout scared the living daylights out of me."

Most of the tension drained away, and was replaced with shock. "Why haven't you called?" It was silly to ask. He had no real reason to call her. He was in college now, enjoying a different life.

"I'm sorry, Rachel. I should've been there for you. I just didn't know what to say. I kept putting it off and before long, too much time had passed." His confession took her by surprise. He thought he owed her something. He leaned forward, studying her face. "How're you doing?"

"I'm okay. Things are different here. It's as if I'm living in a new world."

"How's your mom?"

"She stays busy working. That helps. But Daddy not being here still hurts." She tried not to let the repressed feelings surface.

He dropped his gaze.

"Hey, guess what? I had a job over the summer." Rachel blurted, trying to change the heavy atmosphere they were spiraling into.

He lifted his head. "You working? That would be something to see."

"What's that supposed to mean?"

"I'm only kidding. What were you doing, selling knickknacks or something?"

"No, I was a waitress." She tilted her head and spread her fingers across her chest.

"I'm sure you're the cutest waitress around here. You're as beautiful as ever."

"I've been cleaning all morning." Her already shaky voice faltered. "I'm a mess."

"You're always beautiful. You always have been." He winked.

"What about your girlfriend? Florida's a long way from Pennsylvania. North Carolina was far enough."

He leaned back and frowned, the dimples in his cheeks deepening. "Really, Rachel? Are we still talking about this? I don't have a girlfriend."

"Well, you may not think of what's-her-name that way, but she sure thinks differently."

"Well, there's nothing I can do about that."

Rachel laughed out loud, still shocked that Jordan sat across the room from her. "I've missed you so much."

Jordan held her gaze with such intensity she had to look away. Rachel started to tell him about Paul, when the familiar sound of his buggy pulled into the drive. She jumped off the couch and grabbed Jordan's arm. "Come on. I want you to meet someone."

She ran out the door, excited, but Paul's expression wasn't what she'd expected. It was somber, distant.

Leaving Jordan on the porch, she reached Paul's buggy just as he climbed down. "Hey, you." She took Paul's hand and kept pace beside him up the steps. Jordan's gaze was zeroed in on their interlocked fingers. "This is Paul. Jordan's a really good friend of mine from Florida."

They shook hands. And both looked confused.

She lifted onto the balls of her feet and clasped her hands. "And guess what? Jordan's transferring to Penn State."

"It's nice to meet you." Paul finally gave Jordan a friendly smile. Then he directed his attention back to her. "I just wanted to stop by to say hullo. I was going home to get washed up. I'll be back in about an hour if that's all right."

"I'll be ready." Emotions swelled in her at having both of them there. She understood the real reason Paul stopped. He wanted to check on her, having found a strange car in her driveway.

Paul waved at them both again before pulling out.

"Who was that?"

"Paul. I just introduced you, silly." She took the seat on the swing next to him.

"Why would you introduce me to him though? Who is he?"

"Mom hired him to do renovations."

"You were holding his hand." Jordan's expression was contorted. He stared at her, his eyes sparking. He'd never looked at her that way.

There was no hint of teasing in his voice and, suddenly defensive, she squared her shoulders. "We're sort of together."

"You're dating him?" It all happened at the same time. He asked the question, and the root of his troubled look resonated like a light bulb exploding in her face.

He was angry.

"I guess you could call it that."

With no warning, he stopped the swing with a sharp motion and faced her. "He's Amish, Rachel. And driving a horse-drawn buggy."

Now she was angry, and the feeling was foreign. She'd never been angry at him. "I know that. I'm not blind."

"Why would you be dating an Amish guy? Aren't they different?"

His reaction surprised her. She had made a mistake telling him. "No, they just don't use electricity, and their religious beliefs are … kind of the same, but still different." She wasn't even sure about their beliefs.

"His family's okay with you and him dating?"

Why was he asking so many questions? How could he have known that would be a problem? "Well, no. His cousin knows." That uncertainty crept in again, and her stomach rolled.

After several seconds, Jordan's eyes softened, and he resumed pushing the swing with his foot. "So my favorite girl, who's never fallen for anyone, falls for an Amish guy."

Hot tears pricked the back of her lids.

"Don't cry." He pulled her against his chest. "I'm not trying to make you feel bad. If this is what you want, I'm happy for you."

Her stomach settled, and her mind quieted. This was her friend. He wouldn't do anything to hurt her. Not intentionally. Then, not wanting him to question her further about her relationship with Paul, she changed the course of their discussion. "I've missed you so much."

"I transferred because I couldn't stand being so far from you."

Rachel rolled her eyes at his exaggerated response. "I don't know about that, but I'm glad you're here. When will I see you again?"

"How about tomorrow?"

After enduring the weight of a conversation gone wrong, his answer gave her a huge swell of relief. "That's perfect." Having Jordan here would divert her inevitable anxiety. Paul would be busy with church services all day, surrounded by other Amish girls.

Girls he was allowed to date.

❧ 31 ❧

Rachel smiled at Paul's dim expression as she held to the porch railing.

"So how close were you and this Jordan guy?"

"We grew up together. He was always like a big brother. Our moms were best friends." She realized how it must have appeared—why he would have these questions. "He went away to college last year. We moved out here before his classes ended, so I haven't seen him much since the funeral."

Paul dug his boot into the dirt. "He thinks a lot of you."

"He's a really good friend." The words sounded shallow as she thought how Jordan hadn't come around since the funeral. He had always been there, but maybe he dealt with her dad's death in his own way and couldn't handle it.

Paul's gaze pored over her face, and a light flutter danced across her chest. "Come with me. I want to show you something." He took her hand and helped her in his buggy.

After a ten-minute ride down the road, Paul parked in a field. They pushed through the first brush of trees and reached a path a few yards into the woods. It reminded her of the trail on their property—not visible from the road.

Tall pines covered the trail so well she would never be able to find it herself. They came to the end, and it opened to a breathtaking sight.

They circled a big tree, and there behind it flowed a small waterfall. Frothy, cascading water plunged into a pool of water. Rachel stood on tiptoe to get a better view. On one side, a pool gathered and a doe stood lapping water, then bounded away as Rachel's feet settled on the ground.

"It's beautiful."

A swift, cool breeze blew hair into her face, and Paul pushed the long strands back. "Yes, it is."

She leaned against Paul, soaking in the moment. They had to find a way to make his family understand. Rachel looped her arm through his and rested her head against his chest. The water crashing on the rocks below created a symphony of music. Two big rocks covered with moss stood on the bank of the creek.

"These seats will do." Paul motioned for her to sit. "After you."

Removing their shoes, they faced the stream, their feet dangling in the water.

"Did you and Jordan ever have feelings for each other?"

She spun on her bottom to face him. The blue of his eyes, darker, troubled. "We were only friends." Telling him about the childhood crush would only complicate things. "Why?"

"It's all right if you did." Paul laced his fingers between hers. "I just wanted to make sure I wasn't going to have some competition. You're so beautiful. I can only imagine how many disappointed boys you left back in Florida."

"That isn't true. But I like hearing you say it." Rachel stroked his shirt sleeve with her other hand, creasing the fabric all the way up his arm. "Are you not happy my friend, Jordan, is here?"

"That's not it. I'm just a little anxious this friend's a male."

"You wanted to be my friend." Her cheeks burned. "Okay, well maybe not at first."

A groan leaked from his throat. "And that's probably what's got me asking so many questions. I couldn't imagine my life without you in it."

She didn't say anything, but drank in his words so she could replay them when they were apart.

Paul stood and slipped his shoes on. "I have something to show you."

She followed him. He stooped and placed his hand against the old oak. Rachel inched closer and traced their initials carved on top of each other, complete with a heart encircling the two.

"You did that?"

Paul's eyes roamed her face as if he ached for her, then all of a sudden, his mouth covered hers stealing every doubt, exposing every longing. With both hands gripping her waist, he tugged her closer and deepened the kiss. She wanted to stay in his arms forever. To forget about keeping their relationship secret, to forget all her fears, to forget everything.

Rachel was already swinging on the front porch when Jordan arrived Sunday afternoon. "Did you get settled in?"

"Yes." He pressed his hands against his legs, his gaze somewhere on the porch floor. "Where's Buggy Boy today?"

She didn't want to talk about Paul. Jordan didn't approve of their relationship, and it would be better to steer clear of that discussion. She also didn't want to think about why they weren't together right now, why she couldn't be at his church services with him. How she couldn't stop wondering if Anna was there prancing around him, begging for his attention.

"They have long church services. It'll be later before he can come over." She tried to sound upbeat. But what she wanted and what she was getting were two very different things. Familiar anxiety twisted through her stomach.

"How serious are you two, anyway?"

"I don't know, pretty serious, I guess." *I love him.*

"How does that work with him being Amish? I mean, won't he have to leave his family or something?"

She raised her eyes to the deep blue skies, squinting against the bright sun. "Not if I join the Amish church."

His firm hand on her shoulder brought her head back down. "What? You can't do that."

"Why couldn't I? It would be a whole lot easier." Rachel bit back the rest of the words she wanted to say. *It was the only way to be together.*

"That's his idea?" Anger filled his voice. "Is he pushing you into doing that?"

The conversation was disheartening. "No, he hasn't said anything like that. Can't we talk about something else? I don't want to fight." She leaned into him with a gentle push.

"Okay."

The next few hours, tension hovered over their visit, corrupting his whole mood. She wished she hadn't said anything at all.

❧

Paul's conversation with Rachel yesterday had replayed in his mind throughout the night, depriving him of sleep and did little to encourage him. Jordan was the male in the picture. The one hovering over her. Much too close.

Rachel's features beamed with childlike enthusiasm that Jordan had come. Everything about their relationship was complicated, but a romantic relationship with Jordan would be easier. For her.

It was impossible to think that through any deeper. Imagining her with anyone other than himself bruised his heart.

They could run away, marry, and move to another community where no one knew them. But her mom. Mrs. Adams had already lost too much. With Jordan, Rachel wouldn't have to choose. Nothing about her lifestyle would change.

Banishing the rampant jealousy attempting to shroud him, he returned his focus to the minister.

After the service, things only got worse. As always, Anna made a point to serve his table. All the other guys mooned over her. Why couldn't she latch onto one of them and leave him alone? He'd tried to make it perfectly clear that he wasn't interested.

"I wish Anna would look at me like that," Jonathan said.

I wish she would too.

It didn't matter how much Paul ignored her, she still clung to him.

His aunt and uncle suspected he was courting her. It was wrong to mislead them, but it avoided suspicions about Rachel.

"I'm looking forward to the singing tonight." Anna rubbed his shoulder, and he eased away, forcing her hand to fall.

He'd had enough of this and wanted nothing more than to see Rachel, so he excused himself. Paul turned to look once more at his family and friends as he drove onto the highway. Dread, the weight of heavy lumber, settled on his shoulders. Anna had been the only one who noticed him leaving.

※ 32 ※

Rachel's mind drifted back to the preacher's sermon. He talked about being unequally yoked even in dating relationships. It was as if the lesson centered on her relationship with Paul. He couldn't even tell his family about her, about them. How long could their relationship last? In her heart of hearts, she longed for Paul to be the one God had designed for her. But how could he be, if they were unequally yoked? She grabbed her Bible from the porch swing, but set it back down.

This will only make me feel worse.

Paul came after lunch, much sooner than she'd expected. "How was your service today? Where did you meet?" She hated her reason for asking, but couldn't stop herself.

"Gut. The Zook's held it at their place."

"Really?" Insecurities raced through her head, sparking an impulse to know the truth. "Anyone I know?"

"Sort of. Unfortunately."

Those insecurities heightened a notch. "Who?" Her fingers curled, and her nails scratched her flesh. She cleared her throat against the disturbing feeling trying to steal her breath.

He looked straight ahead. "Anna's their daughter, but they also have a son Joseph who's a few years younger."

She twisted in her seat and squeezed her eyes shut desperate to veil the raw emotion inching to the surface.

So that was it? Paul had been at Anna's house all day, while she'd worried about them being together. Even if he didn't have any interest in Anna, how could Rachel compare to her? Paul had tried to avoid telling her and looked uncomfortable when he finally did.

"There's no reason for you to worry." Taking her hand, he squeezed it gently and brought her fingers to his lips, brushing tender kisses across her knuckles. "I'm the one who should be worried. When you start school tomorrow, all those Englischer fellows will be trying to steal my *aldi*."

The warmth in those sapphire eyes had her melting. She crinkled her brow. "Aldi?"

"My girlfriend." He kissed her forehead, then her nose, before his mouth claimed hers, intense, yet tender, with a sense of desperation. He lifted her chin, compelling her to look at him. The tenderness in his eyes shocked her. "I love you, Rachel Adams. I always will." Taking her hand again, he weaved his fingers between hers.

Her confidence blossomed at his affirmation and an easy smile spread across her face. "I love you, too." Rachel's head spun at the three words still reverberating through her mind. *He loves me. He said it. He loves me.* She straightened, her fears diminishing with a statement that she'd remember forever ... a statement that changed everything.

Her father's voice echoed through her mind. Don't ever let anyone still your joy, sweetheart.

Her jealousy of Anna had almost ruined her day. She would not let an Amish girl she didn't even know steal her joy. It would've destroyed everything. And as Paul was leaving she made a promise to herself. She would never allow her jealousy to have a foothold like that again.

Rachel threw herself in bed, wishing tomorrow were the first day of summer instead of the first day of school. But no matter how she longed to add summer days to the calendar, her summer was officially over as soon as the sun rose over the horizon.

Not finding Kelli's car in the full lot, she parked between two cars where a group of kids stood talking. They all stopped and stared as she climbed from the car.

"Hi," one of them said, but Rachel wasn't sure which one. With hesitance, she looked their way and smiled before walking toward the building.

The hardest part would be trying to find her classes. Everyone crowded the halls, catching up from the summer. Many of them gawked as she passed.

Rachel found Kelli filling her locker. "I feel like an alien."

"We don't get new students very often. Especially ones dressed as cool as you." She laughed. Heat burned Rachel's cheeks. "Quit worrying and guess what, your locker is right there, three down from mine."

That was definitely the highlight since she'd arrived. Then they compared schedules.

"What? We have no classes together." Kelli ran her finger over each line item. "No wonder. You have all AP classes."

Rachel forced a laugh covering the disappointment swelling through her middle.

"At least we have the same lunch." Kelli pointed to the room across from where they were standing. "There's your first class. See you at lunch." Kelli called over her shoulder before hurrying in the opposite direction.

Rachel entered a room full of students. There was nowhere to look without meeting curious glances.

Kevin sat near the back. Remembering her conversation with Paul, she didn't particularly want to be seated near him, but she couldn't help but feel relief at seeing a familiar face.

"Hi, Rachel," Kevin said as she took the open seat.

"Hey, we got a class together." She pulled her schedule out and studied it.

"What class do you have next?"

"Um ..." Rachel searched the details. "Trigonometry with Ms. Jacobs."

"Oh, I have her third period," he said, not hiding his disappointment. "I'll show you how to get there."

"That would be awesome. Thanks."

Kevin didn't try to speak to her again until after class, but fell in step with her as they exited. They strolled along quietly. She was surprised by his silence. He'd been so talkative when they'd first met.

"Here it is. Maybe, we'll see each other at lunch." His response sounded hopeful as he grabbed the handle and opened the door. He seemed totally different ... not as confident. As he walked away, a few girls caught up to him.

It had been easier sitting by Kevin, even if she barely knew him. In this class, she knew no one. She found a seat near the front and had settled in, content to stare at a book until the lesson started. But then her teacher called her to the front of the class and insisted she introduce herself.

"I'm Rachel. Rachel Adams. And I'm from Pensacola, Florida."

One of the students raised a hand. "Why would anyone leave Florida to come here?" The girl's eyes rolled, emphasizing she would've never made that choice. But only months ago, Rachel wouldn't have either.

A few students laughed and heat radiated up her neck as she returned to her seat.

But that same girl had been in Rachel's English class. The girl caught up to her when the bell rang and walked with her to the cafeteria. She chatted about living in Paradise, about teachers, about all the cute guys that went to the other high schools. And Rachel nodded at the appropriate times, feeling thankful that this girl had made an effort to talk to her.

In the lunchroom, Eric, Tanner's friend, was sitting at Kelli's table two seats down from her. Kevin sat on the opposite side of the room.

Kelli leaned forward, propping her elbows on the table, her chin settling in her hands. "How're your classes so far?"

"Good."

A few others approached the table and took some of the remaining seats. Kelli introduced Rachel, and then conversations veered in different directions all around her. She was content to listen. Senior year was the biggest topic, other than highlights of summer vacations. She was thinking about her summer with Paul. What was he doing right now? Was he missing her as much as she was missing him?

Rachel glanced at Eric, and he met her gaze with a smile. She wasn't sure if he remembered her or not. Then he moved from his seat and grabbed the one directly across from her. "Hey, Rachel."

"Hey."

"What do you think of our little school?"

"It's nice."

After lunch, Eric walked with Rachel to her next class, and thankfully, he contributed most of the conversation. "I heard you play softball."

"Yeah. I did."

"Tanner was telling me how good you were. Are you planning to play here?"

She hadn't thought that far ahead, but then she remembered Paul telling her he would come to a game. "Maybe. I haven't really thought about it."

"The way Tanner talks, the girls could sure use you."

She slowed her pace and faced him fully. "What *are* you, the scout for Paradise High?"

He laughed hard. It was contagious and before she knew what was happening, she had joined him. "No." He shrugged. "I'm on the baseball team. Nothing wrong with wanting our school to succeed in all sports."

"That's very noble of you." Rachel smiled. "I promise to think about it."

"Good."

She wanted to ask about Tanner. Did he have a girlfriend? Did he ever talk about Kelli? But she couldn't. She didn't know Eric well enough to ask such personal questions. Even if they were about her cousin.

The rest of the day passed by at a steady pace, and she started recognizing a few of the faces. Some of them even spoke and asked how she liked Lancaster County. And her answer was always the same. *I love it.*

Because of a certain Amish man, she had found her own private paradise.

❦ 33 ❦

When Paul stopped by on his way home from work, he took Rachel's hand, led her toward his buggy, and pulled her against him. A flurry of tiny butterflies skittered through her stomach.

"How was your first day?"

"Better than I thought it would be. Everyone was friendly."

"Gut."

She embraced the warmth of his fingers intertwined with hers. "The hardest part was missing you."

"We'll see each other plenty. You'll start thinking I'm a *pescht*."

"I would never get tired of spending time with you."

"How did you know what that meant?" His eyes warmed, and the vivid blue darkened as he leaned even closer.

She smiled, her face heating under his affectionate gaze. "Didn't you hear? I'm a smart girl. I've been studying your Pennsylvania Dutch."

"Ah, I'll have to be more careful with my words." His voice deepened. "I might say something I'll regret forever."

The playful banter between them was exactly what she'd needed after missing him all day.

"I have some good news."

She laughed when his grin split as wide as the cornfield. "What is it?"

"I've been awarded a job in Hershey. An important job I've been praying about for months." He grabbed her shoulders and pulled her into his arms.

Rachel stiffened. He must've felt it because he squeezed her tighter. "In Hershey? Oh, wow."

He pulled back and looked down into her face. "You remember meeting my friend, Caleb Lapp?"

She nodded, remembering how she'd been so worried about the man seeing them together.

"We've handled small commercial projects for one of my customers over the last year. He's been impressed with everything we've done and has offered us a maintenance contract. Plus, the opportunity to bid on future outside projects they have coming up. Which means guaranteed work for our company for a year as long as we continue to produce high quality work."

Rachel blinked back the moisture collecting in her eyes. This was no time for crying. This was a time for celebration. But she couldn't help wondering how much of his time would be taken? He would be working in Hershey. It would be impossible to see him every day. She gulped hard, the truth scorching as it traveled down her throat.

"I've dreamed of having my own construction business ever since I could remember." He grasped her hands. "But I never thought it would grow this fast, this soon. And this is just the beginning."

She couldn't help but smile. He was so happy. She'd never seen him so passionate. "What does that mean?"

"It means, I'll be able to support myself, my future family. You, me, us." He cupped her face with both hands. His tender kiss sent her insides roiling, but he pulled away before she had a chance to respond. "It will demand more of my time, but in the end it will be worth it." His face was so close, she could feel his breath grazing her cheek with every word. "I owe so much to you."

"Me?"

"You make me want to reach higher, to follow my dreams, to never give up. You make me better, Rachel."

She didn't want to dampen his excitement, but she had to know. "You'll drive your buggy back and forth to Hershey every day?"

"For now. I need to keep things as smooth as possible with Uncle Abram. At least until I can afford to get my own place."

Her head spun with fear. Driving that far would be dangerous. She'd seen for herself how careless drivers could be—how so many gave little consideration to the horse-drawn buggies.

"Don't misunderstand." He advanced toward her, and she had to tilt her head back to see his eyes. "I appreciate everything my uncle has done for me. But he doesn't approve of my career choice and reminds me every chance he gets. The tension between us will continue until I'm out on my own."

And it would only make things worse when his uncle found out about her.

The next day was better and worse. Better because Rachel remembered how to find her classes. Better because she no longer felt like an outcast. Better because today the teachers actually taught new material. But worse, because she couldn't stop thinking about Paul and how she couldn't look forward to seeing him later. A few hours every weekend wouldn't come close to satisfying her yearning to be near him. But maybe spending time with his cousin, Mary, would ease some of the sting.

Eager to get Mary alone, Rachel invited her for a visit.

"Come in. I made us a snack." Rachel grabbed some glasses from the cabinet contemplating a way to bring up the question—how to become Amish. There had to be a way ... and she had to find out.

"Chocolate chip cookies. They smell gut." She smiled, turning her gaze back to Rachel. "Danki."

Heat flooded Rachel's cheeks as the awkward questions hovered in her mind. She lowered herself into the chair across from Mary. "Paul told me he confided in you about us?"

"Actually, he told me about you the first day he worked here."

Rachel paused in her feat to grab her glass. "The first day?"

"The first day." Mary loosened the straps on her bonnet.

Rachel pushed her cookies away, no longer hungry, but suddenly fascinated to hear everything. "What did he say?"

"Paul thought it would be better if he didn't work for your mom because of you."

The image settled on Rachel, like a cool ocean breeze on a hot summer day. His gaze had avoided hers at first. She knew even then there was something about him she wanted. But when had her crush transformed into something deeper, richer? "You're okay with this?"

Mary beamed. "It's obvious how much he cares for you. He wouldn't be doing this if he didn't."

"He said he couldn't tell your parents yet."

"We're taught to refrain from romantic relationships with anyone outside our Amish faith. Most people don't have a true understanding of what that means. It's more complicated than the simple life we choose to live."

Rachel didn't want to tell Mary that she'd gained all her information from an Amish romance novel. "Paul isn't very open about his Amish faith, but told me we believe the same. That the Bible is the living word of God."

"Jah. And there's nothing more, except our main focus is living our whole life for God, with all our heart, body, and mind. That doesn't just apply to us, but to all Christians. My father, whether Paul believes it or not, loves him like he's one of his own. But Daed is firm in his belief that Amish should marry members of our community." Mary stared off into space for a long moment then placed a hand on Rachel's. "Paul doesn't want you to get hurt."

He's worried about me. The unanticipated notion shook her, but a staggering relief surged through her. "Tell me about you?"

"I'm to be married in November."

"You're engaged?" Rachel leaned forward.

"His name is Thomas. He and Paul are really gut friends."

Rachel absorbed each detail as Mary described the Amish marriage services. It wasn't romantic, but more like a church service. A service that took hours with a lot of work, preparing two meals for everyone in attendance, and a honeymoon that consisted of visiting other families.

"What will happen if someone finds out about us?"

"Paul hasn't joined the church yet, so he wouldn't be shunned. But I'm not sure how my family will react to his decision. But I've never seen him this happy. And it's because of you. Nothing would make me happier than to become your sister-in-law."

Rachel wanted to reach across the table and grab Mary's hand. "Would it be easier for me to join the Amish church?" Mary's astonished expression caused Rachel to lean back in her seat. "I shouldn't have said anything."

"Nein, I'm just surprised. Have you talked to him about that?"

"Not—"

After several raps on the door, Paul walked in. "Are you girls having a good time?"

"Jah, Rachel bakes the best cookies. She's going to make a wunderbaar gut—baker." They burst into laughter and walked through the front door.

Paul leaned over and whispered into Rachel's ear before he followed Mary to her buggy. "Hullo."

Warmth spread through her midsection at the thought of becoming his wife. "Why are you back so early? I wasn't expecting to see you."

"We only worked half a day."

As soon as Mary drove away, Paul moved in the space next to her. The wisp of his breath on her cheek was the only warning she received before he pressed his lips to hers. "I missed you."

They drove to Hershey to have dinner. Out of town again. She wanted to talk to him about telling his family tonight but decided to wait until the server brought their food.

"I wish I could go to church with you," she told him.

"Really?" He searched her face. "I wish I could go with you."

That wasn't what she expected him to say. The idea of him sitting next to her in church, brought a stronger rush of longing for a normal relationship where they *could* tell everyone.

It was as if he sensed her uncertainty and wrapped his arms around her. "I want to tell the whole world how much I love you. I promise to tell them when the time is right."

It would be safer to change the subject instead of dwelling on the impossible. "You don't care for my friend Jordan, do you?"

"I have no problem with him."

"I would love for you to get to know each other." She twirled a French fry through ketchup.

"That's not a good idea, *hatzli*."

She pressed her lips into a thin line. "Why not? I love you, and he's a good friend."

"You don't see it, do you?"

"What?"

"I'm sorry. I don't mean to tease you." He squeezed her fingers and something through her middle quivered at the hidden treasure contained in his glance, even though she had no idea what any of it meant. "I'm glad for you that your friend's here."

She pulled her hand away and gritted her teeth, keeping her smile at bay. "You shouldn't keep things from me."

"It's not for me to say, but I like this." His sweeping smile brightened his eyes. "You're even more beautiful when you're *umgerent*." He chuckled. "Upset."

"I'm not upset."

"And I'm not keeping things from you." He took her hand back. "You want some dessert?"

She couldn't stay mad at him, not with that heart-stopping smile. "You go ahead. Maybe I'll just take a bite of yours."

Paul squeezed Rachel's hand, then let it go. He had to be extremely careful with her. The attraction he felt toward her was stronger than he could handle sometimes. So he pulled away and satisfied himself with watching her savor their slice of chocolate crème pie.

She should be eating his aunt's pie, at his aunt's table. Fighting the ache in his chest, he pushed the plate toward her, offering her the last piece. He longed to be a normal man who could take her home to meet his family, introduce her as his girlfriend, as the girl he wanted to marry. She had given up so much. He wasn't being fair to her, but what could he do?

She licked the fork, and at the sigh that escaped him, she flicked her gaze up to meet his.

Letting her go would kill him.

＊ 34 ＊

Summer turned into fall, and Paul still hadn't told his family. How they kept it a secret in such a small town, Rachel couldn't fathom. She thought more about becoming Amish every day. Giving up her dream of being a cosmetologist would be the hardest part. No more makeup. Hair styles. She'd have to trade in all her favorite outfits for calico dresses and white aprons. Could she go through with it? Yes. For him she would do anything.

Rachel adjusted her height at the kitchen window to see Paul better when his buggy pulled into her yard.

She couldn't drag herself from the glass pane, so busy admiring the way Paul's hair brushed the tip of his collar, the way his hat always rested just above his eyebrows.

A soft knock pulled Rachel backward on her heels. She hurried to open the door and found Paul standing next to Mary. "Come in."

Mary's gaze darted between them until it finally came to rest on Rachel. "Ride with me to the farm today. I want to introduce you to my mamm."

Rachel expected concern, however Paul's eyes twinkled with hopefulness. Did he believe her meeting his family would make a difference?

His warm hand slid into her cool one. "That's a gut idea."

Rachel turned and offered a slight nod to Mary. "I would love to. Let me grab my jacket and tell Mom. I'll be right back."

Paul followed her down the hall.

She turned and faced him. "Are you sure? If you rather I didn't ..."

"Ach." He squeezed her hand. "I want you to meet my family. They will love you." His enthusiasm eased some of her anxiety. "The only thing is ... I won't be able to stay. I haven't had a minute alone with you in a week and now she's taking you away. I have to order some supplies. So, I'll drop you off, go into town and pick you up later." He released his fingers and wrapped his arms tight around her waist. "Can I give you a proper gut bye?"

It was amazing how those few little words created a flurry of butterfly wars. "Yes."

He leaned in and pressed his lips against hers, then lifted her chin and she met his gaze. The heated look in his eyes proved he wanted to be with her as much as she wanted to be with him. "We'll spend some time together later, jah?"

His smile hurled those butterflies into a brand new battle.

Only a few minutes later, Rachel followed Mary through Paul's front door and anxiety thick as slow-pouring molasses swelled in her chest. *This is a bad idea. They will see right through me.*

Mary urged her forward. "Come on, you're going to be fine."

"Are you reading my mind?"

"Nein. But I know your heart." At Mary's nudging, Rachel forced a believable smile. Mary grabbed her hand and pulled her forward. "Mamm, I brought Rachel Adams for a visit."

"Ach, Mary, it's about time. That's all I've been hearing about. Bring her here and let me meet her."

That trickle of unease melded into warmth under her aunt's full, compassionate smile.

The smell of cinnamon and sugar filled the large, plain kitchen. Flour covered the short woman's black apron.

She reached out and took Rachel's hands. "I'm Leah Fischer. It's gut to finally meet you, Rachel."

"Thank you. You too." Rachel's eyes darted around the kitchen and through the living room. Paul's home.

"Won't you and Mary join me for a piece of shoofly pie? It's fresh out of the oven." She took one quick breath. "Have you tried the pie yet?"

"Yes, ma'am."

"Jah, well, you haven't tried mine."

"Mamm!" Mary placed both hands on her hips. "Mind your gut manners in front of our guest."

Rachel giggled at the Amish ladies. "I would love to try your shoofly pie. I'm sure yours is delicious. All the other goodies you've sent to our house have been."

"I knew I would like this friend of yours."

"I've been hoping to meet you so I could tell you thank you. My mom always enjoys your company."

The kitchen door opened and an older Amish man entered. He hung his hat on the hook and pulled at his beard. "Hullo, I'm Abram Fischer."

Rachel wanted to look away, anywhere but directly into his eyes, but he kept his gaze steady on hers. "I'm Rachel Adams. It's nice to meet you."

A halfhearted grunt released from the tall man.

Mrs. Fischer had moved toward him in those few awkward moments and reached up on her tiptoes and pecked him on the cheek. "Welcome home, Abram. This is the nice young lady Mary's been telling us all about. The same Englischers Paul's been spending so much time working for."

Abram Fischer's gaze didn't falter. "Ain't so?"

She cleared the lump in her throat. "Yes, sir. Paul's been a huge help to my mom." *And me.* The blazing started at her neck and raced up her cheeks, scorching every millimeter in between.

He finally looked away with not even the slightest hint of a smile behind his bushy beard. A hundred pound weight seemed to settle right in her gut. He hated her.

"Mamm, I forgot to tell you. I want to teach Rachel to quilt. Could she come over after school some afternoons to work on it?"

"We would love to have her, wouldn't we, Abram?"

A rough cough left his throat. "Jah."

Rachel eased her eyes toward Mr. Fischer and relaxed when a burly smile filled his cheeks.

Mr. Fischer turned and left the same way he came in, and the tightness through her middle seemed to physically unwind.

"Learning to quilt is hard work, but can be so rewarding." While Mrs. Fischer explained some minor details, Rachel was making plans. If she joined the church, they could tell everyone, and maybe somehow his aunt and uncle would accept her like Mary had.

Rachel's gaze searched Mary and Mrs. Fischer's long, plain dresses. Wearing that dress could trigger Paul seeing her not only as his girlfriend, but his future wife.

❧

At the Central Market the following Saturday, Paul started to walk toward Rachel, but stopped. It was impossible to do that here. His feelings over the last months had deepened and it wouldn't be easy to pretend he didn't care for her. He'd hoped to find a way to talk to his uncle, to bring things out in the open. Especially after Rachel's visit to the farm last weekend. His family had loved her, just as he knew they would.

Paul ached to move closer and the muscles in his arms tightened when he saw Eric Matthews intended to talk to her. Rachel had a right to talk to anyone she wanted, yet he couldn't even approach her in public. It would be too hard not to reach out to take her hand, to pull her against him, to kiss her.

Best to walk away before he did something he'd regret. He turned and slammed into Anna. "Ach! I'm so sorry, Anna."

She wrapped her arms around his waist in an awkward hug. "Paul."

"What are you–?" He twisted out of her grip, but she fell right back into him. The last thing he wanted was Rachel witnessing this scene. He searched the area where Rachel had just been standing, and took a deep, grateful breath. She had moved away. But Eric was moving toward them.

With Anna's arms still hooked around his neck, Paul caught Eric's eye in a plea for help. Paul then led her out of the building and toward his buggy.

It wouldn't be proper to leave Anna stranded here. Not in her condition. He had to do something. "Ach, Anna, have you been drinking?"

"N-o-o-o." Her whine echoed through his ear, the alcohol on her breath reeking the air between them.

Eric reached Paul's buggy, his eyes narrowed.

Anna tried to stand straight, but Paul worried she would wither like a limp flower all the way to the pavement, so he tried steadying her again. That was a mistake, because she planted a kiss right on his lips. Paul staggered backward, wiping his mouth with the back of his hand. "What are you doing?"

"You're mine, silly."

Shock stole Paul's breath.

Eric latched onto Anna's arm and maneuvered her toward his car. "I'll take her home." Anna complied, her steps clumsy. "I'll be waiting ... at the ... singing. Don't forget."

With an apologetic grimace, Eric helped Anna into his car and closed the door.

Slowly, Paul's common sense prevailed even though he was still a bit rattled. "She's drunk! The last thing she needs is for her family to see her like this."

"They're not home. I'll make sure she gets sobered up before they come back." Eric glanced toward the car, before turning back to him. "She's been doing some crazy stuff lately with some of the guys that aren't so nice. She's trying to get your attention ... but I know your attention lies elsewhere. I understand. And don't worry, I won't tell anyone. But you need to settle this with Anna." His tone contained an undeniable warning.

Settle what with Anna?

Eric drove away with Anna, leaving Paul dumbfounded. Eric knew?

$\maltese$ 35 $\maltese$

When Paul sat next to Rachel in the loft later that evening, she scooted closer and spread a blanket across their legs. "It's getting so cold." She leaned into him, and he inhaled the sweet scent of her coconut shampoo. Nuzzled against his neck, her hot breath sent warning signals through him. He wanted to take her in his arms, hold her forever, so when she kissed him, he couldn't resist.

He ventured away from her lips, tasted her ear, and ran down the length of her neck. His hands glided across her back and down to her waist.

Then something inside him snapped and he pulled back. "Rachel, we have to stop."

"Stop what?" She reached for his lips again.

He stood and she fell away all at the same time. He couldn't look at her, couldn't touch her again or he would give into her.

"Please don't leave." She lowered her chin but held to his arm. "I'm sorry."

"No, Rachel, I'm sorry." He kissed the top of her head then whispered fiercely in her ear. "It's my fault. Not yours." Paul pulled away and searched the pain in her eyes. "What's wrong?" It would be better to leave. This had gone way beyond what it should have.

"I have something important to ask you." Desperation filled her voice, her eyes glistening with unshed tears. "Will you take me to the prom?"

Paul sat straighter, her question churning in his mind. "What?"

Taking both of his hands, she looked up at him, her eyes pleading. She blinked and a tear escaped from her lashes. "The senior prom. I want you to take me to my prom."

His shoulders slumped. What was he supposed to say? He only knew what he wished he could say. *Yes, I would love to.* "You know that's impossible."

"I know." She straightened, her hands slipping away from him. "Never mind. It was stupid to even think ..."

"Nein, it's not stupid." What was he supposed to say? "I want to, but it's complicated. You know that."

Suddenly she was behind him, pressing against him, resting her head on his back. "I didn't really want to go anyway." Her tone determined as if defying the whole idea.

It wasn't fair. She shouldn't miss her prom because of him. Jordan could take her. He would. All she had to do was ask, and he'd jump at the chance. No, he would never suggest that.

"I just won't go."

He turned and covered her arms with his. "You should go."

"It's just a stupid dance."

That wasn't true. If it hadn't mattered, she wouldn't have asked him. He was angry. At himself. She didn't deserve this. And he wouldn't allow it any longer. "I'll take you."

A broken sob erupted from her throat, and she reached for him. "You will? You would do that for me?"

"I would do anything for you." It was the truth, only he still hadn't told his family. He couldn't hold her right now, no matter how much he wanted to. His strength had weakened. Wrapping his hands around her shoulders, he pulled her forward gently and kissed her forehead. "I'll see you tomorrow." He climbed down the ladder before he could change his mind.

On Sunday morning, when Anna's family arrived, she headed straight toward Paul holding a present. "Wiegeht's. I made this for you, Paul."

Paul opened it to find a beautiful blue and black scarf.

"Danki, Anna."

He hadn't seen Anna since that day at the market. It was as if she remembered none of it. He couldn't put this off any longer. During lunch, Anna stared at him with so much concentration, she never noticed when Aunt Leah spoke to her.

"Anna?"

"Jah." The word came out soft, too soft ... much too inviting.

"My aunt asked you a question."

"Ach, I'm sorry." Her tone suddenly transformed. "I was thinking about something."

The rest of the conversation around the table fell on his deaf ears. Somehow he had to confront Anna about the scene she'd made at the market, and the rumors she was spreading about him. Her eagerness to get his attention had gone too far. He didn't want to hurt her, but she needed to hear the truth.

He wanted to leave, not be stranded here. Anna's family had settled in, and it would be a while before they left. It would be rude to leave first but then Thomas and Mary prepared to set out for a buggy ride, and he worried he'd never find an excuse.

Anna rushed toward him and clung to his arm. "Would you mind taking me home, Paul. I'm feeling a little lightheaded."

"Should I get your Daed and Mamm?"

"Nein. No need to worry them. If I could just get home and lie down, I should feel better."

It would give him a good opportunity to talk to her about her behavior. It wouldn't be easy. He hated confrontation, but this was important. "Jah. I'll be glad to drive you home."

"Danki." Her calm voice didn't match the excitement in her eyes and barely veiled the hidden suggestion of her request.

He helped her into the buggy, though everything in him screamed a warning. *This is wrong—so wrong.*

Anna situated herself in the middle, leaving him on the very edge and their legs touched as he took his seat. "Do you mind sliding over? I don't have enough room."

She scooted only an inch. "I have a fresh shoo-fly pie made just this morning. I thought you could stay awhile and we could share a piece."

"I thought you wanted to lie down."

"I'm feeling much better now."

"With no parents home, that would be improper. Besides ... "

"Oh, Paul. Do you have to be so honest all the time?" Her entire body swiveled so that now she faced him fully. "I wanted to spend some time alone together."

"This attention you give me ... it needs to stop." He struggled to keep his words gentle but it was difficult. "If you were to give this kind of attention to the wrong person, it could lead to serious consequences."

"You don't have to worry about that. I'm not interested in anyone else. Only you." She extended her hand between them and rested it on his knee.

Grimacing, he grabbed her arm and dropped her hand back onto her lap. He waited until he was parked in her driveway before he continued. "I'm worried you're acting in a disrespectful way, for not only you, but your family as well."

"What're you talking about?"

"Getting drunk. Pushing yourself on me. If you were to do the same thing to someone else, they could easily take advantage of you."

She took a long exaggerated breath. "I love that you're so protective over me."

"I can't court you, Anna." He took his time, striving to be gentle with her feelings. "My heart is already devoted ... somewhere else."

Miraculously healed from her dizziness, she jumped from the buggy, fire sparking in her eyes. "Nein, Paul Fischer. You will not to do this to me. I have waited three years for you." She propped both hands on her hips. "And I'm not going to let that Englischer girl, Rachel Adams, take you away from me."

His pulse jolted like a streak of lightning.

❧ 36 ❧

Late Sunday afternoon, after the services, after his confrontation with Anna, Paul followed Rachel to the waterfall. They sat on the same moss-covered rocks, and he whittled the bark from a stick with his pocket knife. His conversation with Anna didn't go as planned, and now he worried he'd made a mistake talking to her. But right now he needed to concentrate on Rachel. Something seemed different.

"It's already so cold here. I'm sure it's still really warm in Pensacola."

Paul paled at the uncertain tone in her voice. It sounded empty. He'd never known her to be so quiet, so downcast. Those were her first words since he'd picked her up.

"Are you missing Florida?"

She leaned against his knee, leaving in its trail a mix of hope and uncertainty. Her expression was unreadable, and something in her eyes had changed.

"Is something wrong?"

"I was just thinking." Her attitude was detached, void of any emotion. "You don't have to take me to the prom. I don't want you to get into trouble."

He would tell his family. Tonight.

Why had he waited so long? He should've already told them. So deep in thought, he almost didn't notice when Rachel stood and walked toward the water. With one step in, she stretched a leg out as far as she could, her arms flailing for balance and stepped onto a rock a couple of yards out. Pulling both feet together, she clasped her hands with triumph.

"What're you doing?" He rushed toward the edge.

"Come *with* me." She turned, a playful smile finally curving her lips upward. "My dad and I used to do this all the time."

"Those rocks are slippery, and the water's ice cold. *Bass uff, as du net fallscht.* Take care you don't fall."

"I love it when you speak your Pennsylvania Dutch to me." She sent a teasing grin his way, stretched out, and moved to the next rock. Water rushed up onto her feet, soaking her shoes. "You're right. It is freezing."

"Please come back. It's too dangerous."

"Okay. I'm coming." She extended her leg, but lost her balance on the slimy moss, and with a sharp intake of breath, she slipped into the water.

"Rachel?" Paul hurtled across two rocks, captured her hand, and lifted her up into his arms in one quick motion.

"Whoa, it's so cold."

Paul steadied himself with each stride across the rocks, carrying her to dry ground. Her drenched garments soaked through his shirt instantly. He reached the bank and set her down and dropped to his knees by her side. Rubbing her arms, her face, her hair, alarm spiked through him when she closed her eyes. "Rachel, are you hurt?"

"It's cold-d-d."

"I know, *liebchen.* You're soaked. I need to get you home."

"I'm so s-s-sorry."

The whisper of her voice, stilled him. "You should be. You almost scared the life out of me." He wrapped the blanket around her. "You're shaking." Her teeth chattered, her lips shivering. He had to get her home. "We have to go."

"Nooo, I'm okaaay." Her body shuddered uncontrollably, rocking his with each motion. "I don't want to ruin our day."

"Nein, you haven't ruined anything. We just have to go."

"Waaait, I have a change of c-c-clothes in my bag, in the b-b-buggy."

"You brought clothes with you?"

"I always d-d-do." She paused as her body gave into a violent shudder. "It's a s-s-softball h-h-habit."

"Take these off then and cover yourself with the blanket. I'll get them from the buggy."

Paul searched in the front, in the back, and under the seats for her oversized bag she always carried, but it wasn't there. It would take too long to drive to her house.

When he returned, Rachel lay wrapped inside the other blanket, curled up in a small span of sunshine. She looked a little warmer and that made him feel better. "I couldn't find your bag."

Rachel sat up when he rounded the corner. "Oh n-n-no. I must've left it on my bed."

Then he noticed her wet clothes lying on the rocks a few feet from her. "Are you all right? Are you warmer."

"A little better." Her lips trembled as she stood, the blanket slipping from her shoulder.

He wrapped his arms around her, securing the thin material back in place. Coolness emitted from her body, and every curve that had been etched in his memory, was now pressing against him. He had to go. "I need to get you something dry to wear. My uncle's house is closer on foot. I'll get Mary. She'll find you something to wear."

He didn't want to leave her, but had no choice. It would be better for her to stay in one place, in the sun, than to ride in the open air of the buggy with only that lightweight blanket.

He raced across the field and reached the front door out of breath. "Mary, do you have something Rachel can borrow. To wear?"

"To wear?" A shadow fell across Mary's face, and she glanced behind her. Paul hadn't noticed Thomas standing in the kitchen.

"What's wrong?" Thomas and Mary asked simultaneously.

"We were down by the creek. She slipped on a rock and fell in. Her clothes are soaked and we only had a light blanket."

"*Was in der welt?*" Mary spoke the question more to herself, glanced at Thomas, then hurried upstairs.

Thomas stopped him with a look. He seemed to be considering the situation. "You're courting an Englischer?"

Paul didn't find the disapproval in Thomas' eyes he'd been expecting. It was more intrigue. Maybe it would be easier than he thought to tell his friends and family. Paul released a steady, gratifying breath. "Jah. I am."

Mary returned with a sack. "*Schnell,* Paul. She must be freezing. We have to hurry."

Thomas would have many questions. Questions he was finally willing to answer. Right now though, Rachel needed him and that outweighed everything else.

Paul sprinted back across the field, Mary following. "She's near the waterfall. You go and help her into the dry things. I'll wait here, by the buggy."

The crinkling of dry leaves caught his attention before he reached his wagon. *What was that?* He searched through the trees, but saw nothing. Then Anna stepped out into the clearing, holding a bright, rectangular object. Very similar to that little phone Rachel always carried with her.

Anna's eyes were fuming, and he froze.

A vine of agony coiled through his chest, strangling the air from his lungs. "Anna? What are you doing out here?"

"What's wrong, Paul. You look *naerfich*." So intent was he on that thing she held in her hand, he missed when she eased closer, pressing against him. Hard. "So, you want to accuse me of falling all over you, yet you bring your Englischer aldi to the woods and coerce her into undressing."

Panic leaked into his veins. "It isn't what you think. It was an accident. She fell into the water."

"This looks nothing like an accident." Anna brought the phone to life, shoved two pictures in his face, and he stopped breathing. Rachel trying to cover herself with the blanket, but failing. Rachel and him wrapped in an embrace with only the cover of that blanket. What had he done?

"Act your age, Anna. You're a little old to be a blabbermouth." Paul's stomach cramped, because he knew that was her exact motives. And there was nothing he could do to change it. But still he had to try. "You'll be in trouble yourself showing pictures you took with a phone. You know that's against our rules."

"You have no right lecturing me about our rules."

"I already told you, it isn't what it looks like. And it's none of your business. You and I are not courting, Anna."

"Jah, it's my business now. *You* are my business, Paul. If you would've just courted me like you should've done in the first place, none of this would be happening. And your precious little Englischer wouldn't get hurt."

"You're not doing anything to her."

"You're right, I won't have to. Because *you* will break up with her. And if you don't, I'll show this to everyone in your family and to everyone in our community. What will they think about your little aldi then? What will they think of you?" She brushed her fingers down the length of his arms, quickly, seductively, before he could snatch away. He scanned her face, remembering each word as his gut turned to stone. "I'll be looking forward to riding home with you on Sunday." And then she was gone, leaving him trapped in a raging fire without a trace of water.

Mary finally came back, Rachel by her side. When he saw Rachel dressed in Amish clothing, it felt as if someone snatched his heart right out of his chest. Every ounce of his attention was suddenly focused on how he was going to get out of this, how he was going to protect Rachel.

As soon as Mary headed across the field, Rachel darted toward him like a rabbit fleeing it's enemy and grabbed his hand. The bitter cold, shocking against the warmth of his fingers. "Thomas knows?"

Paul couldn't deny the truth. A truth that he'd been happy about. "Jah."

"He didn't know about me and now he'll ..."

"Don't worry. It'll be all right." He spoke the words, but the reassurance didn't reach his heart. He was worried. More worried than he'd ever been. But it had nothing to do with Thomas. Right now nothing mattered more than keeping Rachel's reputation from being tarnished by Anna's twisted lies.

He steeled his mind against the certainty of what needed to be done and grasped Rachel around the waist. With his help, she climbed into the buggy. "Thank you." She immediately pulled her feet under her legs. "I'm so sorry, Paul."

His fingers trembled as he reached for the reins. "I just want to get you home and warm."

"I ruined our afternoon." Silent tears swirled down her cheek, but her voice remained steady.

"You haven't ruined anything." He had. He should've been honest with his family from the beginning.

They reached her house, and once inside, she took his arm, stopping him from taking another step. "Do you love me?" She reached for his face, her finger brushing over his brow, his cheek, and coming to a halt on his lips.

"You know I do." His lungs rejected the fresh air. He was incapable of taking a full breath.

"I just want to love you." Rachel's breath released in a soft pant between whimpers. "No matter what."

He seized her, crushed her against his chest, and merged his mouth with hers.

How was he going to let her go?

❈ 37 ❈

Rachel changed into her pajamas and climbed into bed still feeling a chill. She snuggled under the covers, her pulse racing, remembering that kiss. It almost felt like goodbye.

Why had she asked him to take her to prom? It was selfish. She knew his answer. And she knew why. She wanted to go, but was it worth hurting him?

And now Thomas knew about her. Paul's reaction when she reached the buggy spoke deeper than any of his words. He was devastated. There was no denying it. She cried harsh tears into her thick pillow. It wasn't fair. None of this was.

What if he decided it would be easier to date an Amish girl? An Amish girl wouldn't put demands on him. An Amish girl wouldn't have to go to a prom. He wouldn't have to keep an Amish girlfriend a secret.

She needed to tell him she was ready to give up everything to join his Amish church with him.

Mary already accepted her, and her family treated Rachel with love whenever she visited. Rachel wanted to be a part of their family. She was falling in love with all of them. They would accept her and Paul as a couple eventually. They just had to. Maybe they would admire her for giving up everything to join them, all because she loved one of their own so much. She had to make his aunt and uncle believe that. She had to make Paul believe it.

Rachel lingered by her locker Monday morning, thinking how hard it would be not to see Paul until the weekend, when she noticed Kelli standing beside her.

Startled, she glanced up. How long had Kelli been there? And how long had Rachel been staring aimlessly inside her locker. "Hey."

Kelli didn't respond, but leaned against the locker, gloom emanating from her expression.

"What's wrong? You look like you've lost your best friend."

Kelli grabbed her hand. "Did you spend the weekend with Paul?"

"Yes." Not daring to think the worse, she inhaled hard, bracing herself for whatever was coming next. "Why? What is it?"

"You were with him all day Sunday?"

"After church. Later in the afternoon." Then a shadow fell over Kelli's face and foreboding crept up Rachel's spine, panic suddenly racing through her veins.

"I don't want to tell you this, but you should know."

Something happened ... something was wrong. Had someone else found out? Air was slowly sucked from her lungs and she could no longer speak.

"Paul gave Anna a ride home in his buggy.

"What? What do you mean? When?" She exhaled. It had to have been a long time ago, way before they started dating. The same ride he had told her about.

"Sunday afternoon. I saw them together."

"You're sure it wasn't Mary?"

"It was Anna's farm. And when I saw him, I waited. He stayed in her yard for several minutes before he left. I know how Anna is, and I didn't want you to hear it from her or anyone else."

The world seemed to start spinning, her feet no longer steady. No. It had to be a mistake. He wouldn't. Would he? It had to be only a simple ride home. There had to be some explanation. But why hadn't he told her?

"I'm sure it's nothing. But I thought you should know. I'm sorry."

Rachel faced Kelli gluing on a smile. "No. Don't be sorry. Thank you for telling me. I'm sure it was no big deal."

"I've got to get to class. I'll see you at lunch." Kelli walked away as Rachel stared after her.

I need to go home. No. There was no need to go home. Paul was working in Hershey and she wouldn't see him until this weekend. How was she going to wait that long to hear the truth?

Rachel slammed her locker. She carried the sick feeling in the pit of her stomach the rest of the day. Why hadn't he told her? *Stop this! I have nothing to worry about.* He wouldn't do anything behind her back, but he had said nothing about it.

Out of all the Amish girls in Lancaster County, why did it have to be Anna?

This was Rachel's fault. She had put too much pressure on him.

What was she supposed to do? Ask him or just pretend she didn't know and wait for him to tell her. But what if he never did?

Paul was standing by his wagon in her yard when she pulled into the driveway after school. Rachel's pulse stuttered. Why was he here?

Pressing her palms against her stomach, she took a deep breath. After climbing from the car, she treaded toward him, but Paul wasn't looking in her direction.

She licked her dry lips and prayed the shakiness in her middle didn't ease out with her words. "Hey there, handsome."

Still, he didn't look at her. "Hullo, how was school?"

His expression looked wrong, tired. *This is bad, very bad.*

"I'm so surprised to see you. I thought you'd still be in Hershey, working?" She fought against the nervous butterflies.

"I left Caleb in charge for a while. I needed to see you." He finally glanced at her, his brow crinkled, and she could've sworn there was a light sheen in his eyes. "Can we talk?"

"Of course." She had to tell him. They wouldn't even have to wait until she graduated. She could join the Amish church, and they wouldn't have to hide their relationship anymore. This was too much strain on him—on both of them. She followed him, her insides empty.

No matter how she tried, Rachel couldn't push the image of Paul and Anna sitting side-by-side on his buggy seat from her mind. Was Anna the reason he acted so distant?

His face was worn, like he'd aged years overnight. "Let's go inside the barn."

"Okay." She took a step, hoping he'd take her hand. When he didn't, she took his.

Everything would be okay, they were together and could get past this. It was only a minor bump in the road. This was what she'd wanted, to talk to him. To learn the truth. But a voice in her head kept saying over and over ... *something's wrong, very wrong.*

Rachel headed toward the ladder, but Paul tightened his grip on her hand, stopping her. He had never acted this way.

"Rachel, I'm leaving. I'm moving to another Amish community, in another state." His words fell in a low tone. "I have to leave my uncle's house."

"I've been thinking about this for a while, and I've decided to join the Amish church with you." She rushed on, leaving him no chance to argue. "I'll wait until I graduate if that's what you want, but we don't have to, I don't ..."

"Did you hear what I said? I'm moving. And you have cosmetology school to think about. It's what you've always wanted, the experimenting, the freedom. You shouldn't be talking this way."

"I don't care about my hair, or my freedom, if that freedom doesn't include you. And I'm not going to college." She crossed her arms. "I don't need to if I'm going to join the Amish church."

"I would never let you do that."

"It's not up to you." Something deep in her gut clenched. "It's my choice."

"You would've never considered this if it hadn't been for me. Rachel, you don't belong with me. You belong here with your mom. She needs you."

"I need you." She grabbed his hands. "I love you. I want to be with you." She shook her head trying to wipe free the painful images emerging. Losing him, living without him. "We tried keeping it secret, but it didn't work. Your family can't hurt me." She swallowed hard. He waited, with no indication of impatience. "You're the only one that can hurt me."

"I've *been* hurting you, and I can't do that anymore. That's why I have to let you go." He looked at the ground, his eyes heavy with pain. "We just can't be together anymore." He took a deep breath, and then moved slowly toward her.

"Is this about Thomas finding out? Or is it Anna?"

For one brief moment, his gaze softened, but then it hardened again, and she wasn't convinced it had really happened. "It has nothing to do with anybody. I'm just no good for you."

"You don't want me anymore because I'm not Amish. I'm not good enough?" Rachel was surprised how calm her voice sounded—how numb she felt.

"I don't want you to be anything but what you are. It'll be easier for you to forget about me and go on with your life. I shouldn't have let it go this far."

"Don't say that. We can make this work. I love you. You love me." She said the words, but she wasn't so sure how he felt anymore. She took a deep breath. "I'll finish school first. It's only a few more months. We can do whatever you think best."

His eyes held a warm look for the first time since he'd arrived. "I have to go. Gut bye, Rachel."

"Wait, please." She reached for him, but he grasped her wrists, stopping her before she could cling to him.

He leaned forward and kissed her forehead. "Take care of yourself." He strode past her, leaving her in a dazed silence. The barn door slammed behind him, sending a sharp tingling pain racing across her skin.

No, he couldn't really be telling her goodbye.

His buggy pulled from the yard, and the farther away the sound, the emptier she felt, the more panicked she became.

A light rain fell from the sky and the wind twirled around her in an unnatural way. Droplets stuck to her hair, her face.

He was gone.

She raced inside.

Mom was standing in the living room entrance. "Rachel?" She

turned toward her mom uneasily. "I heard Paul leave. He didn't stay long."

The sound of his name released the pain ripping through her. Breathless, Rachel shook her head, desperate to escape the ache swelling in her chest. "He's leaving." Mom started to say something else, but she cut her off. "I can't talk about this right now."

Rachel hurried upstairs, locking the door behind her. She sank to the floor, her knees scrubbing against the carpet. She slipped into a restless sleep, only to awaken to shrieking screams. Her screams. Rain beat against the windows, the sky growing darker with each second. She sat straight up, gripping her arms around her waist. The pain that had only sprayed small doses of mist at her earlier, now drenched her with agonizing, unrelenting grief.

Throat tender, she swallowed. It hadn't been a dream.

❦ 38 ❦

Days ran together as raw emotions of overwhelming sorrow pulsated through her veins. Rebellious consciousness clutched her most nights, but then there were some moments of unhindered rest. It was more than sleep, it was deeper, it was paradise. Moments when Paul's presence hovered, his breath like a warm breeze against her skin. If with only one peek she could see his face, with one touch ease the tremor in her fingers, with one kiss satisfy her thirst.

Rain beating against the window, Rachel woke, stifling a cry into her damp pillow, the same way she did every morning, early in the darkest hours, before the sun began to rise. She swiped away the long strands, wetness lingering on her cheeks. He had been the one man made for her. But in only one day, within a few devastating moments, that dream had been shattered.

There were no words of reassurance, no pledges of his unending love. Only goodbye.

With each day, the chances of ever seeing him again grew slimmer. School wasn't for a few hours, so she slipped on her running shorts and headed outside and down her path.

Running had always cleared her mind, had always been a balm. She needed desperately for something, anything to soothe away the unending sadness suffocating her. Sweat gathered and clung to her skin with each mile. But the grueling attempt to drive him from her mind only heightened her memories with each step. His face was clearer, his voice in her head sharper. So she kept running, mile after mile, every single day, before school and after school. She pushed herself harder each day, clinging to the escape frantically, desperately.

The long, unforgiving days stretched into weeks, months. Could her friends, her classmates tell a part of her had been ripped out?

Going through the motions of school became a consolation, an outlet where she could be involved in something of significance, regardless of whether it mattered. But some days were worse than others, when pretending was too hard. And today was one of those days.

I can't do this.

She rushed down the hall, the bathroom seemed miles away. When she finally reached it, the sinks were lined with girls fixing their makeup. She slipped into a stall and held her chest, willing away the moans, reaching beyond the surface.

After they all left, Rachel inched her way toward the mirror and wiped the fresh tears running down her cheeks. She no longer recognized the person staring back at her.

In the cafeteria, everyone talked around her, but she couldn't concentrate on any one conversation. Her tray of food sat untouched. Finally, the bell rang and as she was leaving, a flier in the cafeteria caught her attention.

Softball tryouts—Friday

Softball. The thought drifted through Rachel's mind and gave her a moment of relief, but the relief dissolved just as quickly.

Climbing into her car, the sound of cheerful voices and laughter echoed all around her. Everyone acted as if the world still went on just as it always had. She drove away angry. Hers would never be the same again.

Every day on her way home, she searched the faces of each person as Amish buggies passed by, only to be disappointed time and time again.

She drove toward Paul's house, like she did every day. And every day was the same. When nearing his house she clamped the steering wheel and shifted, unable to get comfortable. She imagined him waiting for her, seeing her car, and running out to meet her. She swallowed hard as she pulled past the trees that blocked the view of his family's farm. If only she could stop and talk to Mary.

Rachel pulled over and pressed her fists against her eyes until she could breathe without sobbing. The sting of emptiness threatened to pull her under, and she gasped for air.

She turned the car around, driving blindly, still struggling for air. The car veered to the middle of the road. A horn blared, seizing her full attention. Her adrenaline spiked as she straightened and maneuvered the car back to her side in one solid motion. What had she been thinking driving in that condition? She should've waited. She knew better.

Her arms, her hands, her legs trembled during the short drive back to her house. She ran to her room and locked the door behind her. She lunged onto her bed and pushed her face into her pillow, muffling the sounds of her sobs.

Turning over, she stared at the ceiling. Images of Paul flashed vividly. Him hanging a shutter, walking across the yard, sitting next to her in the loft. No matter where she turned, no matter where she looked, he was there. The curves lifting his cheeks when he smiled. The earthy, clean, fresh wood smell that clung to him. She could almost hear the sound of his hammer beating on something downstairs.

After dinner, Mom wrung a washcloth over the kitchen sink and spread it across the side. Something Rachel usually didn't notice. But tonight Mom had been quieter than usual. And then Mom turned to face her. "I'm selling the house."

Rachel had started walking away, but stopped in her tracks. "What? What're you talking about?"

"I need to get you away from here. We're moving to the city."

Get me away from here. Rachel bit the inside of her lip, hard, the taste of blood trickling onto her tongue. Her thoughts raced. "Where?"

"I don't know yet. But definitely in another state."

"You want to leave Pennsylvania? But I'm graduating in a few months."

"I'm not planning to do anything until after you graduate. I wouldn't do that to you." She grabbed her cup from the counter. "But you'll be going off to college in the fall."

"I'll be coming home." Rachel lifted her eyebrows, forcing a lighter expression onto her face. "A lot."

Mom scrutinized her reaction. "You'll be in Florida. You won't be able to come home every weekend."

Her gaze fell to the wood floor beneath her, admiring the dark stain *he* had polished himself. Another reminder of his presence. They were everywhere. "I'm not going to Pensacola State."

Mom set her coffee on the table and settled into the chair. "What?"

Rachel cleared her throat. "I changed my mind."

"But you've wanted to go there your whole life. You and Samantha. All your friends are in Florida."

"You're the one who made me come here. Now you're going to force me to leave." Her tone, her attitude was much sharper than she'd intended.

"I had no choice. It was the best thing for both of us," her mom snapped back. "It's almost as if the accident has happened all over again. You do nothing but homework and run."

"I'm getting ready for softball." The lie was easy, but necessary. She couldn't leave. What if he came back?

"Softball?" Mom's brow crinkled. "You haven't played since ..."

"I know. Tryouts are tomorrow."

"You're trying out?"

"I have to. This will be my last chance to play."

Mom broke the connection of their locked gaze, not giving away even a tiny hint of her looming response. "You still need to get away. Why don't we go home for a few days?"

Rachel should've been happy. That's what she'd wanted, until everything changed. Now, she couldn't imagine returning to Florida. "Home. When?"

"During spring break."

"Okay, I'll let Sam know we're coming." The animation in her tone surprised even her. Plastering on a smile, she hugged her mom.

"Honey, you're not the only person who has ever gone through something like this."

"I know that." But in reality it hadn't felt that way. It was impossible to think anyone else had ever suffered this way.

"I'm worried about you." With a sad smile, Mom switched quickly to another line of attack. "He's not coming back, Rachel. It's time to move on."

She inhaled, slowly, carefully. "I will. I am. I've got homework." She took the steps two at a time only reaching her room and closing the door milliseconds before the harsh sobs erupted.

After a full hour of feeling sorry for herself, Rachel finished a math assignment and walked downstairs. Mom sat on the couch, reading a book, the news on television playing softly in the background.

Rachel couldn't bear to stay in her room any longer, or to sit in the room across from her mom. Not right now. "I'm going to the loft for a few minutes."

"Okay. But don't stay out there too late. I want you in before I go to bed."

"Yes, ma'am."

Rachel hadn't been in the barn since he left. She took one slow step after another as she climbed the ladder. She lit the wick and the lantern illuminated the loft. She remembered his reason for leaving it on the small wooden table. If only he would stop by now, but that would never happen. He was gone.

Rachel pulled down the plaque he'd made and ran her hand over the beautiful carvings. Her finger caught in a groove on the back and she turned it over. An inscription stared back at her. She walked to the table and held it over the light.

Rachel—I will always love you. Paul.

She collapsed against the wall, her tears falling again endlessly, without relief.

I have to get out of here.

By the time the sun rose over the horizon, she knew she had to do something different, something meaningful. She couldn't keep doing this to herself.

She wouldn't.

Rachel leaned against the wall next to Kelli's locker. "Are you trying out for softball today?"

"Yeah, are you?"

"I think so."

"Really? That's great, Rachel." Kelli's eyes shimmered as she wrapped both arms around her. She pulled away still grasping to Rachel's arms. "We'll have so much fun. I've missed you so much."

"Yeah, me too. I'm excited." Thoughts of her daddy and *him* molded into one, and she turned from Kelli's gaze. "Meet you at the field."

As the season started, and her team played back-to-back games, she stepped right back onto the field as if she'd never left. Things were looking better, each day she felt stronger. Even though her thoughts continued to revolve around him, the pain was ... bearable.

Weeks later, on a Friday afternoon, Jordan was standing by her car in the school parking lot. "Hey."

"Hey, what're you doing here? His expression was filled with pity, like he was waiting for her to break at any moment, but then it changed, and he pulled her into a hug. Rachel stiffened but relaxed after a few seconds. Why had she ignored him? It didn't matter that he didn't agree with her relationship with ... *him*. Jordan had always been one of her truest friends. She needed him. But this wouldn't be easy. She'd gotten so used to tuning everything out, to being alone in her misery.

He looked at her carefully. "I figured this was the only way to see you."

"I'm sorry, Jordan. I've been so busy. Softball practice, games, and so much homework."

"Can we hang out for a while? I miss you."

"I would love to. What do you want to do?"

His eyes brightened. "Well, I have an idea, but I thought we could grab some dinner first."

"Okay." The enthusiastic voice she tried to muster fell flat. She texted her mom trying to fill the void when she could think of nothing to say.

He took her to a restaurant, away from the Amish community, just as Paul had done so many times. She pushed the stabbing thought from her mind. "Thank you ... for coming."

"You don't have to thank me." He took her arm and led her to a booth in the corner.

The waitress took their orders and as soon as she left them alone, Rachel leaned forward. "When do I find out what we're doing next?"

"Be patient." He winked. "You never did have any."

"Ha. You're one to talk."

He crossed his arms.

"I know I haven't been the best friend lately." He came with no questions, even though she had taken none of his calls and refused to see him the few times he'd stopped by.

"We've been friends since we were kids." His tone deepened. "I'll always be here for you."

If only she could return to that time and stay there forever. Mom had been right. Losing Paul was almost like losing her dad all over again. Like the grief was only in hiding, waiting for the perfect moment to reappear, to throw her back into that lowly place of hopelessness.

"I'm taking you to the fair."

A real smile filled her lips for the first time since he came. "Really? How did you even know they had one here? Isn't it an odd time of year for a fair?"

"It's not a real fair, but something similar. On the way into Paradise I saw a few signs." He reached across the table and grabbed her hand. With a gentle squeeze, he released it. "We've never missed one, until last year. I miss those times."

"Me too."

When they reached the parking lot, the Farris wheel lights brightened the entire lot. Rachel wrapped her arms across her waist as Jordan guided her through the gate and forward onto the dirt path. She inhaled the combined aromas of popcorn, cotton candy, and funnel cake, bringing back many memories.

"Should I get wristbands so we can ride everything?"

"Absolutely. Let's rock this carnival out."

His grip on her waist tightened. "That's my girl."

She could do this, if she kept her focus on the distant past and off things that could never be.

Jordan pulled her forward. "Look, they have our favorite ride."

Rachel stepped on her tiptoes. "The twirling thing that rocks back and forth as it spins? What's it called?" She closed her eyes, trying to remember. "The Tilt-A-Whirl."

"You didn't forget."

She met his gaze. "How could I? We've ridden it a million times."

Once seated on the familiar ride, she fastened her seatbelt. It started in slow motion, then sped up with each spin. Her smile widened until she was laughing out loud, until her jaws were hurting. But every single moment was an act. None of it felt real.

Dizziness swept over her and the lightheadedness overwhelmed her until she thought she would pass out.

Jordan took her hand. "Are you all right?"

She studied the way his eyes narrowed with concern. She pulled her hand away from his. It wasn't the calloused hand or large fingers she wanted to feel gripping hers. "I'm fine. Maybe we should've started with a ride that had a little less spinning." With a plastered-on smile, she strode forward. The last thing she wanted was to hurt him. But right now she needed distance. "Let's try the carousel."

They spent the next few hours riding everything at least twice. She tried blocking out her pain, to pretend she was back in Florida, back before things got so bad.

Jordan bought them a candied apple, and then won her a bear in a basketball game.

The walk back through the gate and into the parking lot came way too fast. "Thank you for this. For everything."

On the drive home Jordan took her hand. This time, the warm gentleness surprised her, it felt natural. He'd always been like a brother.

Rachel lost herself in memories on the ride back to Paradise. She was back in Florida, waiting for Jordan to come home from college. They always spent at least one day at the beach, always had dinner at Sonny's BBQ, and always watched one movie while he was in town. She allowed the memories to flow from one to the other until a horse and buggy drove by and her thoughts came crashing back to the present.

Above all else, she was determined to stay in Paradise. But was she making the right choice?

❦ 39 ❦

Desperate for a diversion, Rachel drove down the narrow streets of Paradise and stopped at the Central Market. The scents of grilled sausage and onions nauseated her. She scanned the quilts and wooden plaques near the front door. Then her mistake slammed against her chest. Too many Amish moved through the building, her eyes searching each one. She moved closer to the front and her gaze landed on the one person she never expected to see.

Jason.

The lump in her throat thickened. She took a step back and turned in one solid motion eager to escape without being seen.

"Rachel?"

She stopped mid-stride. "Mary?" Rachel's hand flew to her chest as she tried to hide the panic coursing through her. "It's so good to see you."

Mary came toward her and looped Rachel's arm through hers. "Do you want to walk outside?"

More than happy to flee the open expanse of the market where Jason could spot her easily, Rachel followed Mary through the double doors. "I've missed you."

"Jah, me too. It's been so long." A strange look crossed Mary's face as if she were fighting against her own reaction. "I'm sorry, Rachel."

"How is your family?" She wouldn't bring Paul up. Rachel couldn't bear to hear he had moved on with his life. With Anna.

"Mamm and Daed are gut." Mary led her toward the grassy meadow where the horses grazed. "I have an uncle that isn't doing well. They're not expecting him to make it through the weekend."

"Oh, Mary, I'm so sorry."

"He's suffered for months. He will be happy and healthy when he goes to be with our Father in heaven."

Rachel had always believed that, but hearing Mary say it suddenly shaped a new meaning into the depths of her heart. *He will wipe every tear from their eyes. There will be no more death or mourning or crying or pain* ... Her daddy wasn't mourning or crying. He was no longer in pain. Just the thought of Daddy standing by Jesus, singing praises to Him in his baritone voice, brought a lighthearted smile to her lips.

Mary touched her shoulder. "How are you?"

How could she answer that truthfully? "I'm staying busy. My friend Jordan ..." She thought of yesterday and shook her head. "He's been a good friend."

"Ach, I tried to tell Paul." Mary rubbed the horse's mane. "He wouldn't listen."

Hearing his name in her accent, so similar to his, created a burning sensation through her midsection. Her pulse thumped violently through her chest. Shivers swept through Rachel, and she leaned against the fencepost, pressing her arms against her stomach.

"Thomas and I married. We're staying in the same house until the one we've wanted becomes available."

"I'm so happy for you. How is Thomas?"

"Wunderbaar gut. We're expecting a bobblin in November," she whispered.

"Oh, Mary, that's so exciting." Rachel's tears burned her eyes. She felt truly happy for Mary but sad at the same time. She'd hoped to be Mary's sister-in-law someday.

"You should come by the house. I know Mamm and Daed would

love to see you." Mary met her gaze, eyes filled with grief. "Paul isn't here. He won't come back."

Rachel shifted in her own personal earthquake. How hard it would be to go to that house again! "I'm leaving to spend the week in Florida."

"How exciting for you to get to visit your friends! Please stop by the house when you get back." Mary embraced her. "I better find my family. Thomas is silly when it comes to me these days." Rubbing a circle around her belly, she beamed. "He says I'm fragile."

Rachel watched Mary walk away, hating to let her go. Mary was her last real connection to him.

❧ 40 ❧

Paul's uncle was getting worse. Mary wrote, begging him to come for a few days. She assured him Rachel wouldn't be in town for the week. There'd be no risk of a chance meeting.

He could visit his family, his uncle, and then return to Hershey where he'd been staying.

Paul drove his buggy into Paradise from the opposite direction, avoiding Rachel's house even though everything in him wanted to veer his horse in her direction. Months had passed since he'd been to Paradise. There were too many reminders of Rachel here.

He walked to the barn needing some time to himself. Filling Nelly's trough, he stared into the splashing water. Knowing Rachel was in Florida, hundreds of miles away, didn't make it easier.

The barn door screeched as Aunt Leah entered. "Paul, I need to talk to you about something, and I just want you to hear me out before you say anything."

He turned off the hose and propped his arm on the fence.

She moved toward the stall and fed Nelly an apple. "Mary told me about Rachel, about your feelings for her."

His heart slammed around in his chest. How could Mary do that to him? Would Aunt Leah ask him to never return?

"I knew you were keeping something from us. And I should've already talked to you about this." She lifted her hands, then let them fall. "I just kept hoping it would go away."

He should've been honest with his family from the beginning.

"Don't be upset with Mary." Why would he have a right to be upset? Paul kept quiet and waited, confused. He made circles in the dirt with his boot. "I forced it from her. Ach, you two are so close, I knew you must have talked to her. And then she told me about Anna spreading rumors and how pushy she's been. Paul, you were so young when your parents died. I had no reason to tell you. I wanted you to be happy here, happy living our lifestyle. You were thriving. Some young men and women want to leave, but you never did. Not that I know of anyway. Not until Rachel."

What did his parents have to do with this? "I don't understand."

"Paul, your mom and dad weren't Amish, but Englischers, just as I was when I met your uncle."

His grip tightened on the railing. "What?"

"I met your uncle when I was nineteen then I fell in love with him."

The truth bore into his soul. He wasn't who he'd always believed. His aunt was an Englischer. And his aunt and uncle were still together. And happy. "I'm not Amish?"

"Not by birth. You were born into an Englisch family, just like your mama and me. You've been like a son to us. A piece of my sister who I loved so dearly and grieved so desperately." She grabbed a handkerchief and wiped her eyes.

"Why are you telling me this now?"

"I lost you anyway. You left us and will probably never come back. Mary told me you wouldn't let our reaction to your relationship hurt Rachel. I understand better than you know, because I was that girl. Your uncle has always been so hard on you. I know he's the main reason. His father had nothing to do with him for years after we married. I admire you so much for loving Rachel enough not to put her through that."

"So ... so, what're you saying?"

"You don't have to make a choice. You can be with her and still be a part of our family. I know the turmoil you must've been feeling for so long. And I'm sorry I didn't tell you sooner. Of course, your uncle knows and persuaded me to tell you the truth. You've always been a strong, hard worker. He's so proud of you. The reason he pushes you so hard is because he sees your potential. He knows you have what it takes to succeed."

He could've married Rachel without losing his family. They would've still loved him. They would've loved her.

"Rachel is a wunderbaar gut girl. You should go to her."

His mind spun in a whirlwind of what could be. What could've been.

"I'll leave you to your thoughts, but please think about what I've said. I hate for you to leave again, but no one can make that decision but you." She left through the barn door, looking back once before letting the door close.

He settled on the bench. How had he lived all these years and not put that together? He was only four when his parents died, but still he should've remembered. The memories of his mom and dad were so vague.

And Rachel. How he wanted to talk to her! The reason he left came flooding back. Anna threatening to destroy Rachel's reputation with those pictures. He had no choice but to agree to let Rachel go. Somehow, Anna had believed that if Rachel were out of the picture, he'd naturally fall back on her. How wrong she'd been! Instead, he'd left —to spare Rachel's reputation, instead of taking up for her. Then he remembered the part of Mary's letter, the part he wished he'd never read, the part explaining about Rachel and Jordan. How she'd found happiness with him.

He should've never left and now it was too late. He should've stayed and fought for her—for them.

Paul wouldn't be able to sleep until he drove by Rachel's house. He couldn't stop thinking about her, about how much he'd hurt her.

Rachel wouldn't be there. Not yet. But then he noticed lights as his buggy approached the farmhouse. Had they come home early? The lantern burned in the loft. It felt as if all his breath bottled up in his chest.

He stopped Nelly near the edge of the tall pines, giving him the perfect view of her house. It would take all his strength to keep going. He should tell her the truth. She deserved that much.

Paul wanted more than anything to see Rachel's face one more time. Hadn't he left his favorite chisel? Any reason would do. He sent Nelly forward and came to a stop directly in front of her house, ready to turn in, when a dagger ripped through his chest. The porch light glowed on Rachel and Jordan standing in the yard, in an embrace. It was true. They were together. Paul could hear her laughter. It was a full, carefree laugh. One that ended Paul's doubt. She wasn't pining for him. She'd found happiness with Jordan, a normal life, one without the complications he'd caused. Exactly what he'd wanted for her.

With heavy limbs, he snapped the reins and pushed Nelly on.

Back home, he hurried upstairs, avoiding everyone. Throwing his shirt across the room, he stared into the darkness as he leaned against the door. The image of Rachel in Jordan's arms tortured his every thought. What had he done?

He'd given up the only girl he'd ever loved.

❧ 41 ❧

Jordan had pulled into Rachel's driveway long after the sun hid behind the trees. When he climbed from the truck, she had met him in the yard. She had been sitting in the loft soaking in the cool breeze from the open window, her mind tortured with thoughts of summer, softball, planting vegetables. And a garden snake sneaking up on her and a certain Amish man rescuing her.

When Jordan had pulled her into a long hug, she didn't resist.

"How's my favorite girl?"

"Better now." Jordan had a way of making her forget. At least for a while.

Jordan searched her face. "What did you do today?"

"Went to the Central Market."

"By yourself?" His overprotective attitude was reasonable. They'd grown up together and Jordan had always treated her like a younger sister. But today it annoyed her, prompting too many painful memories, especially after her chance meeting with Mary.

"Yes, by myself." She moved a few paces from him. "I saw Mary and talked to her awhile."

He shrugged. "Is that supposed to be one of those Amish people?" His scathing tone injured her wounded heart even deeper.

"She's not just an Amish person. She's one of my best friends." She hadn't meant to be harsh, but Jordan was pushing her. Away. She didn't want that, but he was getting real close to leaving her no choice.

"I didn't mean anything by it." He took her hand. "Maybe we should talk about something else."

Stretching her lips into a forced smile, Rachel concluded it would be best to steer clear of all Amish conversation for more than that reason alone. "Yeah, you're right."

He turned and faced her fully. "I know this is a little backwards for me to ask you, but I want to take you to your senior prom."

She absorbed each word, reeling with the question that had changed everything. "I'm not going to prom."

He grabbed her shoulders and turned her to face him. "What?"

Rachel's heart thudded in her chest. That had been one of her last conversations with Paul. One she still regretted. "I'm not going."

"When are you going to move on?" His tone deepened. "It's your senior year. There's no reason to miss your prom on account of that Amish scum ..." Jordan stopped.

That last statement threw a chunk of burning coals into her blazing temper. Leaning against his truck behind her, she wrapped both arms tight against her stomach and turned before she said something she'd regret.

"Rachel, I'm so sorry." Jordan tried to take her arm, but she jerked away. "I shouldn't have said that."

"Just go." Emotion clogged her throat and silent tears streamed along her cheeks as she stared out across the yard, her anger swelling, her heart yanked in two.

Jordan moved into the space next to her. "I'm sorry."

Rachel made every effort to overlook the snide remark Jordan made but she couldn't. Her heart sided with Paul.

It always would.

The next morning, Paul had barely sat at the breakfast table before he captured everyone's attention. "I'm leaving Pennsylvania. And I'm planning to try the Englisch life." He glanced at his uncle first. What would he think?

Searching each of their faces, his gaze stilled on Mary's. Tears filled her eyes. "Oh, Paul, I don't want you to leave again. Can't you do that here?"

"I'll come and visit someday, I promise. But I have to go and I'm leaving tomorrow." It would be a long time before he would be able to keep that promise, but Mary would understand.

"Ach, you can be Englisch here just as easy as anywhere else," Aunt Leah added.

Uncle Abram cleared his throat. "Paul, you're already settled in your business. You have plenty of work. And everyone's constantly asking for you here."

Paul leaned back and took a deep breath. "We were awarded a new project on the east coast, and Caleb Lapp has agreed to go with me."

"When?"

"We're leaving at first light."

Uncle Abram crossed his arms. "If that's what you need to do, we'll stand behind you. You'll always be welcome in my home."

Mary pushed herself up from the table, though Thomas grabbed her arm trying to stop her. "Won't you even try?" Shaking her head, Mary left the room without another word. Paul met Thomas's understanding gaze.

If only it were that easy to go to Rachel and make everything right again. But he couldn't. He had to start over again, somewhere new. It would only complicate things for Rachel if he showed up now. He had hurt her enough.

Rachel fidgeted all the way to the Fischer's house, but she had promised Mary she'd come for a visit. Two weeks had already passed. She couldn't put it off any longer. Pulling onto the familiar path, Rachel parked the car. She held her elbows tight against her sides as she walked toward the front door.

Mary met her in the driveway, and they shared a brief hug.

"How's your uncle?"

"We buried him last week. It was a nice ceremony."

Rachel followed Mary up the porch steps, her heart heavy for her friend.

"I'm so glad you came. Would you like to visit out here on the porch? It's a beautiful morning."

"That sounds wonderful."

"Come in first, and I'll fix us a glass of tea. Mamm and Daed will want to see you."

How much did they know?

"I thought you'd have come sooner. You came back earlier last week, ain't so?"

"We didn't go." Rachel answered, her throat constricting.

Her heart skipped a beat as they walked inside and the steam of boiling collards filled the space over the stove, the scent strong.

"Rachel Adams." Mary's mother wrapped an arm around Rachel's shoulder. "How wunderbaar gut to see you."

A smile reached through Rachel's tightened lips and filled her mouth. "You too." Their hug was interrupted by the sound of the back door.

Leah walked toward her husband. "Abram, look who came for a visit."

"Gut day, young lady. It's gut to see you again."

Mary linked her arm through Rachel's. "We're going to visit on the porch. Let me know when you need my help."

Rachel opened the front door, her fingers trembling. They acted no different. She exhaled as she sat on the swing. He never told them anything.

Mary pushed her foot against the wooden planks. "You know they'll want you to stay for dinner."

"I don't want to intrude."

"Mamm will set a place for you whether you stay or not." Mary patted Rachel's hand. "I understand if you feel uncomfortable."

"I'll think about it."

Mary laughed. "Gut enough. Guess what? I'm hoping to buy a quilt shop in town."

"A quilt shop?"

"I'm waiting until the bobblin comes. Thomas doesn't want me on my feet all day."

Rachel wrapped her arms around her friend. "Oh, I'm so happy for you."

"So you never went to Florida?"

"No, instead, I'm going on a youth missions trip next weekend."

"That sounds fun. When Paul came ..." Mary stopped.

The news took Rachel's breath. They both looked at each other at the same time. Mary hadn't meant to tell her. "He was here? For the funeral?"

"I wasn't going to say anything."

"Is he staying?" Rachel looked toward the barn. He might still be here?

"No, and he won't be coming back." Her voice was certain.

The lump forming in Rachel's throat plummeted and bottomed out in the pit of her stomach. She'd missed her only opportunity to see him.

"I told him you'd be in Florida. That's the only reason he agreed to come." Pity filled her eyes.

There was that buggy in the middle of the road, stopped in front of her house. It was him? He had stopped. "That was him?" She'd been with Jordan. "He was there." He must have seen them. Together. "I have to go."

Mary called after her. "I'm so sorry, I didn't mean to upset you, I..."

"It's not your fault." Without looking back, she hurried to her car a yelp escaping her throat.

She couldn't get the image of his buggy sitting there from her mind. She drove slowly out of Mary's driveway onto the road. Why hadn't she known it was him? She would've chased after him.

It had been months since he left, yet the gravity of pain felt as if he'd only left yesterday.

Her mom stood at the sink washing dishes when Rachel walked inside. She grabbed the towel, drying her hands as she walked quickly toward Rachel. "Are you okay? What happened?"

"It's nothing. I'll be in my room." She climbed the stairs, clinging to the railing. When she reached her room, she opened her Bible, holding it to her chest. She pulled it away, the paper crinkling as she searched through the scriptures. It had been months since she'd turned to Jesus. Why? He was the only one who could bring her comfort. Finding a verse, she prayed it to the Lord.

Turn to me and be gracious to me, for I am lonely and afflicted. Relieve the troubles of my heart and free me from my anguish. Psalm 25:16-17

Working as an Englischer proved to be more difficult than Paul had imagined. They'd been working in the city for weeks, yet he couldn't get used to the difference. His Amish heritage still clung to him, as if permanently stamped on his skin.

Paul rolled the too tight shirt sleeves up. How long would it take to get used to jeans and ball caps.

Caleb climbed from the ladder laughing. "Buddy, we're not in Amish country. And it wouldn't hurt to lose some of the Pennsylvania Dutch." Caleb moved to stand in front of him. "You need to do something to get your mind off that girl. At least you're the one who broke her heart and not the other way around."

Paul stared into the busy street. It had been months, but still he thought of Rachel every hour of every day.

Like Caleb. Paul had been so insensitive. Caleb was crushed when his Englischer wife left him and took up with another Englischer. An ex-boyfriend.

"Why don't you at least tell her what you've found out? It could change everything."

"Ach, nein. She's with Jordan."

"You don't know that for sure. They were gut friends." Why would Caleb of all people encourage him to reach out to her? "You're not Amish. You should go to her. She deserves to hear the truth. From you." Caleb slapped Paul's shoulder. "If not, you need to move on, man."

He should tell Rachel about his parents and his decision to try the

Englisch lifestyle. What if she found out from someone else? He wanted to go to her. More than he'd ever wanted anything in his entire life.

Caleb returned to the ladder. "Why don't we check out that Englischer church on the corner?"

Church? Paul hadn't been to a service in months. What would it be like to attend an Englischer's church? He suddenly couldn't wait to find out. "Jah. Let's do it."

Sunday morning, Caleb drove them down the narrow street and weaved through the cars in the parking lot. "There's no empty spaces. That must be a gut sign."

"Jah. Do this many people usually attend an Englischer church?"

"Depends on several things. The preaching, activities offered, and style of worship."

Only one thing circled his thoughts. He would experience the same type of worship service as Rachel.

Why hadn't he thought of this before? It would be like having a piece of her.

They stepped inside the large sanctuary, and Caleb led them down the middle aisle separated by wooden pews on both sides. Paul and Caleb took a seat near the middle. Stained glass forming a picture of Jesus holding a child spun rays of different colors through the room.

"This would be a good place to help you decide how to settle your past."

Paul listened as the congregation sang the contemporary songs the Englischers played on the radio. Some of the same songs he'd overheard Rachel singing when she thought no one was listening. The memories were still fresh as if he'd heard her sweet voice yesterday.

No one knew the relief, if only for a very brief moment, at his glimpse of hope. A small smile broke out across his face—a single smile to God in thanks.

❦   42   ❦

Ocean City, Maryland, felt nothing like Florida. Rows of houses filled each street, set only yards from each other. But getting away from Pennsylvania, even for a little while, was exactly what Rachel needed.

The small beach house sat on a cul-de-sac. A wooden porch led them inside. They entered through the living room area, and an older couple greeted them with hugs.

"You all must be so tired from your drive." The woman's singsong voice rang through the small room with affection. "Get your things put away and come and join us in the kitchen. We have sandwiches prepared."

Rachel followed Kelli into the last bedroom on the right and unloaded her things on the first bed. Kelli and the other girl's conversations were filled with lighthearted laughter. Drifting back in time, she remembered feeling that same way.

Rachel and her dad on the softball field, her mom in the stands wearing matching T-shirts, cheering for their team. The sound of a bat cracking as the ball soared to center field. The umpires yelling strike, the smells of popcorn, peanuts, and cotton candy.

I need you, Daddy. You should be here, my senior year watching me play high school softball. I'm still good. It's all because of you. Everything you've ever taught me, every stance, every drill, every trick to psych out the batter. I still work on my pitching mechanics every single day. Can you see me? Can you see the pain I'm hiding from the rest of the world?

Why did you take him from me, God? What can I do? When will I ever feel normal again?

Rachel slipped from the room long after Kelli and headed toward the kitchen.

The lady busied her hands placing turkey, ham, and cheese on slices of bread. "I'm so glad your group is here."

"Thank you for inviting us into your home." Rachel moved to the edge of the counter. "Is there anything I can do to help?"

"If you'll grab the mayo and mustard from the refrigerator, we'll be set."

Rachel rummaged through the fridge. She set the items by the sink and the familiar breeze from the ocean swept in through the open window, catching a wisp of her hair. The sky burst with a mix of orange and red, painting the blue sky.

As the others filtered into the room, they took seats around the long table, the girls talking in hushed tones.

Kelli moved in the space in front of her. "Are you all right?"

"I'm fine."

Maybe she'd feel better tomorrow. She could always hope for that. And couldn't wait to feel the sand between her toes again.

The next morning, Rachel stepped onto the sand and took off in a jog, headphones in her ear, her favorite Toby Mac song playing. The ocean breeze whipped against her face. The wave's white foam slowly faded as another one rushed in behind it.

Rachel missed running on the soft sand before the heat of day. There weren't many people out this morning, only a few fishing. Beach chairs sinking in the sand, rods stretched out beyond the shallow shore.

She picked up her speed, the beat to the song echoing her footsteps. Seagulls flew above, searching for breakfast.

And then her thoughts shifted.

The perfect picture of Paul sitting in front of her house, right there within her reach, haunted her thoughts. Why had he stopped ... if he didn't still care? Dreams emerged every night since—dreams of him coming back. They seemed so real. He was there. Only she'd missed her chance. She slowed to an unhurried jog. Closing her eyes for a brief moment, a slow smile filled her lips. He had come back for her.

And for the first time in months she felt hope all the way to her bones.

The sounds from the puppet stage reached Paul's ears and he listened as he worked. A crowd filed in around the performers and children listened to each story of Jesus. One smaller child clung to her mother peering over her shoulder. The mother laughed, encouraging the child to watch the performance. Paul enjoyed the distraction.

Familiar chords of music streamed from the speakers. Paul dropped his hammer as the voice followed through the microphone, the voice he would know anywhere. Paul jerked to a halt and looked at the blue cloth of the stage. A dangerous knot filled his stomach. Two girls and one guy sat outside directly behind the stage.

Could the person with this voice be standing just inside the blue screen only yards from him? The words of the song drove deep into his soul. *It's not her. It can't be.*

He wanted to rip away the curtain to reveal the singer of a voice so familiar, one he would long for the rest of his life—the one who owned his heart. But he couldn't. It would scare them and destroy what they were trying to do.

He never acknowledged that he'd overheard Rachel singing. She never told him she enjoyed it.

Why hadn't she? He embarrassed her so easily. The color filled her cheeks, right now in his very vivid memory of her. Anticipation brought him to a halt when she exited the partition and then moved in his direction. It looked just like her, but there had to be some mistake. Was this possible?

His muscles ached to move in her direction. "Caleb, I'll be right back." He walked away, not waiting for a response. He couldn't let her out of his sight, not even for a moment, until he was sure.

The young woman didn't face him, but sat sideways with her eyes closed. Her hair looked the exact color of Rachel's, her face the same as the one burned in his memory. Waving her arm through the air, she shooed a seagull away. When she smiled there was something different about it. Her smile had always been striking. It could bring warmth to even the most coldhearted person.

But now, there was a sadness hidden beneath as if something had permanently damaged her. Grabbing the wooden stair railing, he realized that he was the one responsible.

He had only made it halfway to her when she stood, walked toward the back of the stage, and disappeared behind the cloth. Only a curtain separated them.

Moments later, her voice came through the microphone again. It was really her. How could this be?

God, what does this mean? Why would you bring her here now? Please show me what You want me to do.

He had no choice ... he had to go to her. He had to at least tell her what happened, what he'd found out.

And then Jordan moved from beneath the curtain.

After Rachel sang "The Revelation Song," they packed to leave, and she followed Kelli and Jordan toward the sandy stairway. "Let's make sure to get some pictures together before we leave." It was time to start adding to her collection again. This was her senior year. If she didn't, one day she'd regret it.

Kelli ran toward a photo booth. "Look, we can get some now?"

Rachel and Kelli walked inside, pulling the curtain behind them and made silly faces as the camera clicked every few seconds.

After Jordan took a few by himself, Rachel entered and took a few. When Jordan stepped out and Kelli took her turn, he moved in the space next to Rachel and grabbed her hand. "I want to take some with you."

Rachel bit her lip, uneasiness creeping up her spine. Jordan was almost acting as if ... No. He wouldn't think that and she nodded. "Of course."

Kelli stepped from the booth. "Sorry, didn't mean to interrupt."

Jordan released Rachel's hand and placed his own on the small of her back. "We'll be right back."

After taking a set, Rachel left Jordan inside. "Stay here, I want some of you and Kelli."

Kelli entered the booth while Rachel waited for the strips of pictures. Glancing at the building right in front of her, she admired the raw beginnings of a store the construction workers were building. As her solo pictures came through the slot, they slipped from her fingers.

❧ 43 ❧

Aconstruction worker stared at Rachel—a man wearing a ball cap and jeans, but with a face like Paul's. Their gaze met for one lingering second and then he turned rapidly and so did she. Chills raced across her arms and tiny hairs stood at attention. After a moment, she searched the area again, but he had disappeared. Of course it wasn't him. That man wasn't Amish.

Kelli's booming laugh caught Rachel in a crestfallen mood as they stepped from the booth. "He's crazy. Wait." Kelli grabbed her arm and whispered, "What's wrong?"

"Nothing." Rachel pressed a thin smile on her lips. *That was so weird.* "I just have a wild imagination." She glanced over her shoulder as she followed Jordan and Kelli down the boardwalk, itching for one more look.

The image of his buggy sitting in the road, the possibility of him watching her, wanting to see her. Urgency pumped through her veins as she half walked, half stumbled along the boardwalk, no longer able to inhale a full breath. It was as if God set a light bulb off in her brain. He hadn't taken Paul from her. He was alive, breathing, his heart beating, the same as hers, somewhere. And no matter how much she ached, she knew now what she had to do. What she should've done months ago.

She had to go to him. But first she had to find him.

❧

Paul kept his eyes on Rachel as she disappeared down the boardwalk. Why had he allowed Jordan's presence to stop him from approaching her? He pulled the pictures out he'd placed in his pocket earlier. He admired every inch of her face, four different frames of her sweet smile staring back at him. It was like a gift from Heaven. He slipped them back into his pocket.

Caleb walked up behind him. "What's going on?"

"Rachel's here." Paul stared into the distant waves, clashing with the sky. "She looked right at me."

"What? She's here?" Caleb searched the area. "You're sure it was her?"

"She was with her friends from Paradise." Taking a step forward, he lowered his arms to his sides, staring into the space where she'd been only a few minutes ago. "She was with Jordan."

"Oh, man." Caleb moved in the space next to him. "Did you talk to her?"

"She was holding his hand."

"That doesn't matter. I understand that you're trying to protect her but you love her too much. She deserves to hear the truth. From you." Caleb slapped him on the shoulder. "I hope things work out for you, man."

I love her too much? Maybe Caleb was right. He had only cared about protecting her and not hurting her worse. It shouldn't matter that Jordan was here, especially since Paul wasn't certain Rachel had moved on with him. But he was too late. She was already gone.

Dreams of being near her filled his mind the rest of the afternoon. Sitting back on the bed after work, he stared at her pictures. Beautiful, loving, precious ... the girl he wanted to cherish for the rest of his life.

Caleb banged on Paul's door as he passed. "Time to go."

Crossing the street from the parking lot, they entered the church through the front. Hundreds of members already filled the wooden pews.

Searching for a seat, Caleb motioned toward the back. "There's one."

A couple slid down to make room. Paul sat on the end, searching the crowd. Time in God's presence was exactly what he needed.

Caleb elbowed him in the side. "We got here just in time, the drama's already starting."

A girl wearing all black twirled her way onto the stage as music filled the auditorium. Grabbing a hold of the pew, he steadied himself. Kelli? She knelt down facing away as another girl danced in gracefully after her. Before the introduction of the orchestrated music ended, two more girls made their way next to the others, and they all bowed away from the audience, revealing bold letters printed in white on their black shirts. Just as Paul read the words, someone from the opposite side slowly made her way toward the other girls.

His body, without restraint, rose. *Rachel.* Words flowed from her mouth, a stunning configuration of her voice to the melody. Slowly, he sank into his seat as one of the kneeling girls stood, moved behind Rachel, and mimicked her motions. Paul was unaware at first of the exact actions of the other girl or her purpose, unable to take his eyes from Rachel.

Then a young man dressed as Jesus walked toward the front, and Rachel reached for him. Over and over. As the song built in volume, Rachel stood. It took his breath away when she dropped her black robe to the floor revealing a white dress that sparkled like diamonds. She then turned and ripped away each girl's black shirt revealing a white top underneath. Their downcast expressions transformed into joy as they danced around the stage, each girl dragging a thick strand of purple cloth and created a cross.

Paul stood clapping, his hands stinging against his own strength. Others joined in applause as he kept his eyes locked on Rachel.

Caleb pushed against him. "Go to her."

Paul searched over the crowd as people dispersed, hindering his view of the stage. "You knew she would be here."

"Not exactly. I just thought there was a really gut chance."

Paul slapped Caleb on the shoulder then hurried toward the front. He had to find her. Tonight.

"What are you doing here?"

Paul started at the familiar voice, spoken with familiarity, filled with contempt. "Jordan. Hullo." Paul's gaze swept over his face quickly, then he resumed his search for Rachel. He had to catch her before she left. With another quick glance at Jordan, he answered, "I'm working."

Jordan crossed his arms. "In Ocean City? Really? I thought you were staying in Hershey."

"Jah, I am. Going home in the morgen." How did Jordan know he'd been staying in Hershey? Right now it didn't matter. "I need to find Rachel. Can you take me to her?"

Jordan's expression hardened and his jaw stiffened. "I can't do that," Jordan hissed, the sound shrieking in Paul's ear even though vast noises saturated the auditorium.

Paul turned steely eyes on Jordan. No one would stop him from seeing Rachel. He took several steps forward, when Jordan grabbed his arm.

"She isn't there. She already left."

Paul snatched his arm free. "I have to find her."

"Wait. You need to hear this." Jordan's eyes were filled with accusation, his fists clenching and unclenching. "When you left, she was devastated for months. Believe me, that's the last thing I want to tell you, but you need to know the truth. She's happy now. Finally, after months of doing nothing but crying over you, she realized you weren't worth it. You can't show up now, just when she's figured out she doesn't need you. You almost destroyed her."

Paul stared at him blankly, the last five months flashing before his eyes. He'd hurt her even more than he realized.

"If you really care about her, you'll leave her alone. I can't watch her go through that pain again. I won't. She's happy ... with me."

When Jordan walked away, Paul stared at the space where he'd watched her perform earlier, the space that was now empty. People hovered all around him, some lingering, some leaving. Rachel was happy now. The thought should've brought him comfort. But it didn't. It brought gut-wrenching pain. Sweat warmed his scalp, thinking of all he'd lost.

There was nothing he could say.

It was his doing. He'd left her, alone, to move on. She had suffered because of him. He couldn't bring her more pain.

No matter how much he wanted her.

$$\text{❦ } 44 \text{ ❦}$$

Rachel stopped at Mary's the day they arrived home. It was hard coming back to this yard, to this house, knowing Paul wasn't here. But she had to know the truth.

It took a moment for her eyes to adjust against the brightness. Mary stood on the front steps, her long skirt swishing against the gentle breeze. Her sleeves were rolled up and flour dusted her black apron. Rachel had mourned over the idea of never becoming the wife of her Amish man. She had envisioned wearing the white kapp, the calico dresses, and laced-up boots. A lifetime with Paul was worth more than all her material things.

"Hullo, Rachel. How was your mission's trip?"

She'd felt the presence of Jesus like never before. "It was exactly what I needed."

"It's so wunderbaar-gut to hear that."

"I need to talk to you."

"Jah. Of course." She closed the front door. "We will have privacy out here."

"Can you please tell me how to find Paul? Where he moved to? Anything?"

Mary looked suddenly distracted, and her gaze lingered somewhere in the pasture behind them. "I ... I don't know where he is."

"Oh." Her voice sounded wrong, like it was somewhere outside of her.

"He wanted ... needed some time to himself to sort things out."

"I was just thinking since—" He hadn't stopped by to see her. He'd stopped in the middle of the road and then kept going. "I was just wondering if you knew." It felt as if she was standing in sinking sand.

"I'm sorry, Rachel. I ..."

"No. I shouldn't have asked. It's silly anyway. I'm not sure what I was thinking." She wanted to tell Mary she thought she'd seen him in Maryland but that it couldn't have been, since he was wearing jeans and a ball cap. She'd already made a fool out of herself. "How're you feeling?"

"Gut. I'm so glad you stopped by." Mary glanced toward the house. "Do you want something to drink?"

"Thank you so much, but I better get going." It wasn't a good time for visiting. She felt like crying and kicking something all at the same time. It wasn't Mary's fault. It was her own. She should've been stronger. "We have a championship softball game tomorrow, and I'm really tired from the trip."

"For certain sure. That's so exciting. Let me know how you do."

"Absolutely. I'll be back to visit soon. Take care of you and that baby."

"Jah. Don't worry. Thomas will see to that."

The mourning didn't hit Rachel until she drove onto the highway away from Mary's house. She punched the steering wheel. "I won't let you do this to me anymore, Paul Fischer."

She drove for over an hour through the streets of Paradise, spontaneous tears streaming down her face, her heart still aching as an eerie feeling of someone watching her led her to the safety of her driveway. Jordan pulled in right behind her and she exhaled a deep, comforting breath.

"What are you doing here? We just spent the whole weekend together." Rachel tried to hide the leftover whimpers, but Jordan must've heard them. Inching backward, she put more distance between them and ordered her mind to something else, anything else. Her blasted impulsive emotions. She'd never had much control over them, but today they were merciless.

"Have you been crying?"

"I'm tired and really sleepy." Her answer was swift, affirmative. She couldn't admit the truth. Jordan had made it very clear he disapproved of her pining over her Amish man, and she couldn't handle his judgment. Not right now. Not with her emotions teetering on the edge of instability. It wouldn't take much to generate more bawling.

"I've had to share you with everyone all day and I'm leaving this week. I needed to see you."

He was leaving her too. Then without any warning, the mourning boiled up in her chest again. "I can't believe you're leaving already. Time has flown so fast."

Jordan grasped her hand and led her to the steps. Car lights from the road flickered across the yard. "Come back to Pensacola with me as soon as you graduate. We can go to Pensacola State. Together." His gaze fell to their hands. "Remember all the times we spent together as kids. All the memories we made there. We can have that again."

If only it were that simple. "I can't go back." Rachel tugged her hand free and pressed her fingers against her knees, fighting that gnawing feeling rising up her chest. "I have to stay in Paradise."

"Rachel ..."

"I know what you're going to say, but I can't leave." Rachel stared at the stars blinking against the black sky, listening to the never ending sound of buggies rolling by. "We did make some great memories, and I'll always have those. Remember the time I pulled my hair up on top of my head trying to look older?"

"I don't remember that."

She ran her fingers across her skirt and grinned. "Good. It was embarrassing."

"Why?"

"It was around the time I realized how cute you were." Her grin widened because focusing her attention elsewhere was finally working. She glanced at him. "I had a small crush on you."

Jordan slouched beside her, covering his chest with his hand. "You had a crush on *me*? Really?"

"Don't look so surprised. Every girl in high school did." His dazed look unsettled her, so she focused on his chin instead. A strong sensation to slide away consumed her. The way his pupils enlarged, the way his eyes devoured her. He didn't blink. "What's wrong?"

She swallowed hard as Jordan took her face in his hands, pulled her closer, and pressed his lips against hers.

What was he doing?

She yanked from his grip, lurched to her feet, and climbed the few steps. Eyes wide and lungs heaving, she stared at the top of his head for three short breaths. How could she have let this happen?

Remorse nearly knocked her feet out from under her, and she grasped the porch railing to steady herself.

He deserved better than this and it was all her fault. She had monopolized his time for months. What else was he supposed to think? She peeked at him from where she now stood behind him, several feet away.

He was staring into the distance where the field met the sky. "I know you're angry with me," Rachel whispered.

"Angry with you? Why would I be angry with you?" His harsh tone caused her to stumble back. He stood quickly and moved toward his car, but then turned and faced her. "How can you not know that I feel this way for you?" Jordan cleared his throat and kicked at the dirt. "You come here to Pennsylvania and fall in love with Buggy Boy. That was the last thing I ever expected to happen."

Blinking back tears, she felt the regret all the way to her bones.

"I had been planning to ask you out for weeks. Then the accident happened. The timing was all wrong. Then I found out you were moving. My intentions were to transfer to Penn State to be closer to you, so I could date you, like I'd always wanted to.

"When Buggy Boy left, I was relieved. I knew it would be hard, but I wanted to be there and have the chance to love you. I just didn't realize how hard it would be for you. It kills me knowing a part of your heart belongs to him."

"I didn't know." Her voice broke.

He walked up the stairs and wrapped his arms tight around her. "We're friends, Rachel. And we always will be. Even though I'm leaving in a few days, I intend to keep my promise and be there for you."

Lying in bed later that evening, Rachel prayed long and hard, unable to sleep. Then a text came through from Jordan just after midnight and those six words changed everything.

I wanted to tell you earlier, but I couldn't bring myself to say it. I saw Paul. He's been staying in Hershey. I hope everything works out and that you find all the happiness that you deserve.

Jordan had seen Paul. Had Jordan talked to him? She wanted so badly to ask him, but she couldn't. It must've been so hard for Jordan to tell her the truth. *Hershey?* He'd given her more than she could've asked for—a place to start looking.

Jordan. She needed to reply, to apologize, to thank him. But she was uncertain of what to say. Anything she said would only hurt him worse. So she settled on something different. Safer.

God blessed me with you, and I'll cherish your friendship always.

Paul was staying in Hershey? Of course he was. He wouldn't give up his job, work he'd just been awarded. Only a few cities separated them. The thought brought a swift end to her enthusiasm. He hadn't let that small span of space between them stop him from staying out of her life.

❦ 45 ❦

Anxiety filled her dreams, giving her little rest. Sunlight finally seeped through the blinds and Rachel tried to hide the puffiness around her eyes with little effect.

The long day at school gave Rachel more than enough time to think. Paul's words that last day came back to her like a blade slicing away the protective layers she'd worked so hard to create. And she fought against the remembrance of each and every rejection he'd hurled at her, until one memory slithered in that had eluded her until now.

Nothing in his expression, demeanor, or actions affirmed a desire to leave, but everything voiced sorrow. He hadn't wanted to leave?

Every worry, every doubt, every longing had to be pushed to the deepest corners of her mind until after the game. Rachel stepped onto the mound ready to warm up with the catcher. Nothing in her head but throwing strikes, hitting the ball, and winning this game.

But then after a few minutes she spotted her mom looking for a seat among the crowd. She threw a quick wave in her direction. This had to be hard for her. Dad had always been her coach. Always on the sidelines. Always there.

Thrusting those memories into the secluded corner with the

others, she winded her arm in three quick motions and slung the ball over the plate for the first pitch.

Strike.

After five innings of pitching, Rachel moved to shortstop and stretched while the new pitcher warmed up.

The first girl up to bat hit the ball to shortstop, and Rachel dove to catch it. The next two balls were line drive hits over Kelli's head between right and centerfield allowing two girls on base. The cheers of the crowd faded as the next ball was hit hard to right field, and the girl on second stole third. The outfielder caught it, but the runner tagged home, tying the game.

Turning, Rachel slapped her glove against her leg. They couldn't give this game away. The next batter hit a ground ball to Rachel. She scooped it, tagged second, and threw it to first making a double play, ending the top of the inning. *That was too close.*

Rachel stepped in the batter's box and watched a low pitch. Swinging at an inside pitch, she smacked it over the centerfielder's head and reached second before the player threw the ball in. The next batter hit a line-drive to the pitcher; leaving Rachel on second.

Kelli came up next. She smacked it down first baseline past the right fielder. Rachel slid into third. Kelli only made it to first.

The next batter struck out. Rachel wanted to scream. *Don't leave me stranded out here. I need to score.* The next ball was hit into left field. Rachel's gaze trailed the flying ball, the left fielder running. She wasn't going to get to it in time. Taking off in a full run, Rachel slid into home as the left-fielder threw the ball from the fence.

The umpire yelled above her. "She's safe."

Kelli came around to second. In the bottom of the sixth, the score was now 4-3. They could use another run and still had Kelli in scoring position on second.

Rachel gripped the fence. "Come on nineteen. Give it all you've got."

It was a hard hit to third base, but was caught. Rachel grabbed her glove and Kelli's and headed onto the field for the top of the seventh.

The first ball was hit between first and second, barely gliding past

Kelli. The second was hit to left center bringing the runner to second and the batter to first.

No outs and two runners on base. *This is not good.*

The next batter hit a line drive to Rachel. She stopped it, tagged second, and threw it to first making another double play.

Two outs and no runners on base. *Only one more out.* The batter stepped to the plate.

Strike one.

The batter stepped back into the box and swung at the second pitch.

Strike two.

Rachel's pulse quickened. They were so close. The pitcher threw the ball, the batter swung, it was a solid hit between third and short-stop. Rachel dove, sliding on the hard dirt infield and snagged the ball with only seconds to throw it to first. Pulling up on her knees, she threw the ball to first base. In the last second, the ball hit the first basemen's glove before the runner's foot tagged the bag.

"She's out," the umpire yelled.

We did it.

The crowd cheered, as Rachel got to her feet and looked for her mom, but then she jolted to a stop.

❦ 46 ❧

Rachel's view was cut off as her teammates crowded in around her, squealing their excitement. She had no idea how much time had passed before the group finally shifted. The space where he'd been standing, the man with an uncanny resemblance to Paul, was now empty. It wasn't him. That man had been wearing jeans and a ball cap. The crowd made their way from the stands, no one resembling the man she'd just seen.

"You did great, honey. I'll see you at home." Rachel searched Mom's face, her expression void of anything other than excitement over the game.

Her teammates screamed and laughed a mumbled, tunnel-like sound as Rachel followed them to the locker room. Kelli walked next to her, chatting endlessly with the others about senior prom tomorrow night. Prom. The very thing that had cost her so much.

Rachel gritted her teeth against her desire to confide in Kelli what she'd seen—what she thought she'd seen.

Unwilling to let go of the image, it replayed itself over and over until she thought she would walk back to the field and search for him.

Kelli stopped on her way to the locker room door. "Do you want to ride with me to the restaurant?"

"No, I'll meet you there." Rachel's words echoed through the room as Kelli and the others stepped outside, leaving her alone.

Rachel slumped onto the bench. More pressing matters were taking up every available space in her brain at the moment. She needed some time to get herself together. For so long she'd looked for Paul in the face of every Amish person, praying each day she'd see his face. She had no picture, only every memorized detail of him.

She lowered her glove into her bat bag and zipped it in slow motion. What could've happened to cause her brain to react in such a way that she would envision him standing there, so real she could touch him? It didn't make any sense. She'd been so caught up in the excitement, the very minute they'd won the game. It was like stumbling into a dreamlike world where Paul was there, only she couldn't reach him. And she was forbidden to share it with anyone, because no one would believe her.

In the background a leaky faucet dripped every few seconds and then suddenly a loud clang echoed through the empty room. She stood quickly.

Slinging her bag over her shoulder, Rachel rushed toward her car, the eeriness of being alone catching up to her. Not until she rounded the corner, did she see a truck parked beside her car and a man leaning against that truck. A ball cap shielded his face.

Pulse throbbing, she slowed her pace and glanced behind her. The last few cars in the parking lot were already driving away.

"Rachel?"

Her breath caught at the achingly familiar voice calling her name. For a moment she could only stare as Paul slowly lifted his ball cap, revealing more of his face. She needed a moment to recover not only from the surprise of seeing him, but at the difference. Stone-washed jeans that fit him perfectly, a T-shirt accentuating the bulging strength of his biceps, dark stubble shadowing his chin and bordering his cheekbones.

It was him. The man she'd seen leaning against the fence—staring at her.

"Paul?" His precious name ripped from her throat as she tried to convince herself, that this time, what she was seeing was real.

Pushing away from the truck, Paul closed some of the distance between them. "Hullo, Rachel." He touched her shoulder and the solid presence of his hand sifted through her jersey. The small gesture validating his existence, his touch infusing her with comfort. "You were so ..." His voice was rich with admiration. "Amazing."

It's really him. Rachel couldn't tear her gaze away. The man standing before her was the only man she'd ever loved, the man she'd longed for every day for months, the man who'd hurt her more than any other.

"What are you doing here?" It was a stupid question, but she could think of nothing else to say. Not with her pulse racing and her heart aching with each beat.

"I wanted to see you play." A slow smile filled his lips. "I've never seen anything like it. You were incredible."

"I thought I saw you, but then I didn't." She blinked and reminded herself to breathe. "I can't believe you came." Finally, she looked past him to the older blue truck. "This is yours? You're driving ... a truck?"

Her gaze drifted over the rusty hood, questions probing her brain. Why was he driving, and why was he dressed that way? What was he doing here?

"Jah." A battle raged in his eyes. "There's so much I've been wanting to tell you."

Too afraid to speak, she pressed her hands against her stomach and concentrated on breathing. She ached with the need for him to proclaim his love, but what if he didn't?

Paul stared down into her face, the impact of shock and mind-altering affection fueling his core. He yearned to burrow his fingers in Rachel's hair, pull her against his chest, and never let go. A faraway look surfaced in her expression as she trapped her lower lip between her teeth. Her pained reaction and his responsibility in her confusion weighed heavily on him. Suddenly he questioned his decision to wait here for her.

Then she smiled—that breathtaking smile that lit up her entire face. "How are you?"

He'd forgotten how that smile always made him feel. Like he was the most important person in the world. He'd forgotten how much he'd missed it. "Gut. How are you?"

She stared at him for several long moments. "I'm good." Her gaze penetrated him, layers peeling away, until the only thing revealed were her honest, raw emotions. "I'm sorry, I guess I'm in shock. I never expected to see you. You said you had something to tell me?"

"Jah."

Her phone chimed and when she glanced at it, tiny frown lines creased the soft space separating her eyebrows. "I'm supposed to meet the team for a celebration dinner. I'll just tell Kelli I can't make it."

"Nein. You should go. You should be there to celebrate with your friends."

"But, I— "

"I can stop by your house later. If that's okay." He didn't want to leave her, but maybe this was best. It would give them both time to adjust to the idea of seeing each other again. The indecision etched across her face tempted him to wrap his arms around her, but then she nodded. "Okay, then." He opened her door and she slid in, her gaze lifted up toward him. "I'll see you later."

"Bye."

He watched her drive away until she disappeared before he jumped in his truck—the perfect idea taking shape. But he had to hurry before the landscaping nursery closed.

❧ 47 ❧

Rachel stared at the menu, her eyes glazing with unshed tears every few seconds. The loud chatter surrounding her was drowned out in her own afflicting thoughts.

Kelli leaned into her. "Are you all right?"

"No." She didn't want to be here. Heaven knew the turmoil she'd just encountered only minutes ago gave her plenty of reasons to be anxious. Celebrating was the last thing on her mind.

"What's wrong?" Kelli asked in a hushed voice.

"Paul's here."

Kelli glanced around the restaurant. "Where?"

Rachel couldn't believe she was having this conversation. Paul had been at the game, watching her. She automatically recalled every play she'd made, how she reacted to each play, each pitch, how she looked standing in the batter's box. "He was at the game."

She expected a swift response, but instead Kelli covered her mouth. "Come with me." Kelli slid out of the booth and steered Rachel toward the door and outside. "Did you talk to him?"

"He was waiting by my car after the game."

Kelli squealed, but then her wide smile flipped to a frown within an instant. "You left him there. I can't believe you left him there."

"He told me to come." Rachel's lips fluttered into a laughing smile. "I'm not in the mood to celebrate."

"Of course you're not. What did he say?"

"He's going to stop by my house later." She laughed over the excited tickle seeping into her stomach, but it was a feeling she couldn't indulge. Not yet.

"Are you serious? You have to go. I'll tell the others something *really* important came up." Rachel barely had time to steady herself before Kelli slammed into her with a vigorous hug. "I'm so happy for you. Go."

Rachel's lips trembled with uncertainty. She had no idea what Paul planned to tell her—or if she even wanted to hear what he had to say.

She walked to the creek as soon as she returned home. She needed some time to herself—to process it all. Propped against a tree, she listened to the birds chirp and small animals scurry through the woods. An ache deep in her chest pulled at her and her first tears fell. This was what she'd been wanting. To see him. To talk to him.

Pulling her knees tight against her chest, she fought the sobs building in her throat. It would be impossible to stop crying once she started. The empty feeling she was accustomed to now carried more sensations than she could stand. But there was also a strange sort of peace.

A branch broke nearby and Rachel jerked back. Clouds had settled in, and her vision was limited through the thick trees.

The crunching of leaves grew stronger and she stood, but the uneasy feeling wouldn't budge. *Paul?* The sound grew closer, and her heart began to hammer.

Then Jason appeared on the other side of the bridge. "Hi, Rachel." He took slow steps toward her.

She inhaled, her chest heaving. "What are you doing out here?"

"I was going to ask you the same thing." Jason moved forward and she took an awkward step back. "I came to see you. I thought I would have trouble convincing you to meet somewhere in private, but you've made this easy for me." Jason ran his fingers across his chin. "It's much better than anything I could've come up with."

She reached for her phone, but her pocket was empty. She'd left it in the car. "How did you find me?"

"I followed you home from the restaurant."

"What do you want?"

"Really, Rachel. You already know the answer." He took a step onto the bridge, never taking his eyes from hers. "We still haven't had our date."

"Date? Yeah, I … I'm … still wearing my uniform. I should go in and change." She looked past him.

"There's no need for that. You're absolutely beautiful."

"Still, I should go in. I'm meeting someone."

"No, you're not." His smile was more a pout. "I've waited so long to have you all to myself. And you're trying to turn me down again?"

"It isn't that. I just really need to get inside before my mom starts to worry." She had no way out. She would have to cross the bridge to get back to the trail. Could she outrun him? If she screamed, it would do no good. Solitude was the reason she so often came here. Rachel tightened her ponytail, trying hard not to betray her panic.

"Your mom isn't here." He stared at her as if gauging her reaction. Then he blasted her with an even worse accusation. "I was surprised to find out your Amish boyfriend left you."

"He's coming … he'll be here any minute."

"You lie." Anger darkened his face. "You're here all alone." His voice dropped. "I made sure."

"Okay." She glanced toward the house, gasping for a breath of fresh air. Could she get him closer to her house? "Where do you want to go?"

He laughed, his eyes glowing with rage. Rachel took an involuntary step back. "We're not going anywhere. This is perfect. A very romantic place for our reunion."

The stream of water flowed in the deep trench below her. Could she make it across? With one more step, he'd reach her. She had to try and took off in the opposite direction. When she stumbled over her feet, he grabbed her and crushed her against him. "Where do you think you're going?" His fingers ran down her cheek and slowly south toward her neck.

"Please, I don't even know you," she begged. "You know nothing about me."

"I know all I need to know," he whispered against her hair. "Look at it this way. You'll never be alone again. I know how miserable you've been. I saw you yesterday as you drove away from that farm, the pain on your face. The tears in your eyes. I followed you for over an hour. You don't know the control it took to not go to you. But I waited, wanting this moment to be perfect. Now we'll never have to be apart again."

His lips crushed against hers in a cruel kiss intent on punishing. The whiskey on his breath clung to her mouth. She tried squirming from beneath him, but his grip was firm. He yanked the bottom of her shirt up, baring her belly.

She screamed as loud and as hard as she could. He turned her around and pulled harder on her shirt. Rachel squeezed her eyes shut. *God, please show me a way out.*

$$\text{\ding{98}} \quad 48 \quad \text{\ding{98}}$$

Rachel's heart raced as Jason's grip tightened.

"Let go of her," a voice bellowed from somewhere behind Rachel, a voice she'd know anywhere. The same voice she heard in her memory every day. Yet it sounded deeper, angrier.

Jason released her and Rachel plummeted to the ground. On trembling knees, she edged away inch by inch. Her breath came in short spurts. Crawling deeper into the woods, she left the voices and the sound of harsh punching behind. Briars and limbs scratched her face as she pushed through the brush.

Not paying attention to where she headed, she focused only on getting as far away as she could.

She fell face first, branches scraping her cheeks. Her tears blended with dirt and leaves as her sobs grew louder. Fear pushed her until she could hear nothing but the shuffling of her body. Her hair tangled in a web of briars, and her gelatin arms and legs gave out. Numbness settled over her in the cold dampness of the woods.

Time seemed to stand still as images swirled making her dizzy. It was hard to tell what was real and what wasn't. Paul showing up at the ball game and promising to stop by later. Paul punching Jason in the mouth and knocking him to the ground. Had it all been a dream?

The faint sound of footsteps came closer. She curled onto her side scooting farther behind the thick base of a tree. Crunching leaves and breaking branches grew louder, and Rachel wrapped her arms around her legs tighter. Movement stopped and there was complete silence.

A strong hand touched her and Rachel screamed, the shrill sound of her voice echoing through the woods.

"Rachel, it's okay. It's me." Paul lifted her from the ground. "Are you hurt?"

The sound of his voice settled across her soul like a calming lullaby. She clung to his neck as he carried her through the woods and across the bridge. When they emerged into the yard, he placed her on her feet.

Mom met them at the oak tree and embraced Rachel. "Are you all right?"

Blue lights were flashing. "Where did the police come from?"

He nudged Rachel toward her mother. "I'll take care of this." As Paul approached the officer, he glanced over his shoulder toward Rachel. "Can you give her a minute? I'll be glad to help you." Paul walked away with the officer.

Mom stroked Rachel's hair. "Come on, I'll explain."

She compelled her gaze from Paul as her mother led her onto the porch, explaining how Paul had showed up moments after she did and yelled for her to call for help as he raced into the woods. Mom's tears fell freely, her face tormented. "It was as if he knew immediately you were in danger. I hadn't even noticed the truck parked on the grass."

"Neither did I." She desperately wanted to dismiss the whole scene and pretend it had never happened, but her racing pulse wouldn't comply and her breath was even more shallow. "I should've been more careful. I knew that creep was back in town."

"You know him?"

"He came into the restaurant. There was sort of another incident."

"Why didn't you tell me?"

Talking with her mom calmed some of the rough edges around her anxiety. "I didn't want you to worry. Things were finally getting better. You weren't crying as often. I didn't want to make things worse."

Fear. Hurt. Other emotions merged, claiming her mom's features. "Rachel?"

Her whispered name broke the last morsel of strength holding her together. Rachel blinked and a sob escaped her throat. The past raced forward at a blinding pace. How could she have kept the incident with Jason from her mom?

"You should tell the police."

"Paul knows. He was there." Rachel brought her gaze back to Paul. "He's here."

"Yes, baby, I know."

Rachel stared into her mother's knowing eyes. "You knew he was here?"

"He stopped by before the game."

Rachel held her arms against her chest as they fell quiet and listened to Paul's conversation with the remaining officer.

"It would be a good idea to have her file a restraining order." The policeman's voice trailed through the silent moment.

Rachel shivered as the lingering sensation of Jason's hands on her seeped into her skin.

After a few minutes of both Paul and Rachel answering questions, the officer drove away. Paul placed his hand in the small of her back and led her to the porch, the dried mud heavy on her clothes, her arms, her legs.

Mom led them inside. "Why don't you take a shower? It'll make you feel better."

She glanced at Paul. What if he left? They hadn't had a chance to talk.

After he guided her inside, Paul squeezed her shoulder. "I'll wait."

"Do you need any help?" Mom called after her as she climbed the stairs.

"No, I'll be fine." She met Paul's weary gaze, before turning the corner toward the bathroom.

Standing under the hot steaming water, she scrubbed the grunge sticking to her, but couldn't escape the feel of Jason's fingers. Images scattered through her brain, some sharper than others. His voice. His hands. Her fear. Tears blinded her vision and huge sobs shook her frame. What if Paul hadn't come? Just then a soft rap echoed from the doorway and Rachel stilled.

"Are you all right?"

She took a full breath and shut the water off. "Yes, Mama. I'll be out in a minute."

After dressing, she sniffed and dabbed her eyes with a tissue, trying to rid the errant tears that were now flowing freely. Rachel took careful steps down the stairs.

As she entered the living room, Paul came toward her. "Do you want to rest a while?" His voice was strong, yet soft, just as she'd remembered. "I don't mind coming back tomorrow."

The earlier struggle had taken all her energy, but she fought the weariness. She couldn't risk showing her weakness, not wanting him to leave. Especially now. "No, I'm fine. Do you want to sit on the porch?"

"Whatever makes you the most comfortable."

As they stepped outside, Rachel looked beyond the trees to the sky over Paradise. Her comfort was in Jesus who'd sent Paul at the very moment she needed him. "Thank you, Paul. For being there."

He smiled as he searched her eyes, then a shadow fell over his features. "Are you sure he didn't hurt you?"

"No, I promise I'm not hurt, unless you want to count my rattled nerves." Suddenly amidst her thrill of standing with Paul, a thought occurred to her. "You hit him ... really hard."

"You saw that?"

"I did." It had been an astounding moment. Paul Fischer, an Amish man, who grew up believing things weren't settled with brute force, had knocked Jason unconscious.

And he had done it for her.

❦ 49 ❦

Paul slid a chair from across the porch and plopped down in front of her. He wanted to see every feature of her face.

The scratch marks stretching across her cheeks invited a new bout of rage and he clenched his jaw. "I can't stop thinking about that creep and what would've happened ..." He bawled his fists, thinking of that animal with his hands all over her. "I should've ..."

"No, Paul." She grabbed his hands, the warmth of her fingers shocking his anger until it slowly diminished. "You did exactly what you should've done. You were there and stopped him and that's all that matters now."

"I'm sorry, Rachel. For this. For everything."

Her gaze fell as if she were purposely avoiding him. Then she put a division between them, her hands falling away with the sudden movement. He missed their connection instantly.

She looked past him toward his truck. "What's in the back of your truck? Are you doing landscaping now, too?"

"Actually, those are for you."

"Me?" Her gaze finally met his and it was all he expected. Hope, amusement, joy.

"I was going to plant you a flower garden." He pointed to the vacant space along the porch but kept his attention on her to avoid missing her reaction. She seemed pleasantly surprised and that's all the assurance he needed. "Come see them."

The walk to his truck took too long, or maybe it only seemed that way because he was aching to take her hand.

"They're gorgeous." She studied each flower, her gaze stilling on each one until she finished, then hesitated only a moment before facing him fully. "Why are you doing this?"

His eyes clinched shut as his persistent guilt dangled over him like a black cloud. "I was hoping we could do it together."

A slight look of confusion covered Rachel's face, but even still she smiled. The temperature was dropping as the sun hid behind the trees, but it wasn't cool enough for the incessant quiver of Rachel's lower lip, the tremor of her hands, or the shudder of her upper body. Standing this close but so distant was driving him crazy, so he leaned in closer until they were only a breath apart. "Are you cold?"

"No, I don't know what's wrong with me. I just can't stop shaking."

Spontaneous tears streamed from her eyes as he gently stroked the raw streaks across her cheek. Unable to bear the space between them, he brought her to him, holding her against his chest. "I left to protect you, Rachel, but it was wrong. I was wrong. About everything." Tears fell from her lashes as she glanced up to meet his gaze. "I was forced to leave you, then asked to stay away from you."

She tried lowering her gaze again, but Paul lifted her chin. He so desperately wanted to kiss her—to taste the sweetness he dreamed of every night since he left. "Rachel, you captured my heart, but you deserved so much better than anything I could offer you. A life of pain, of never being accepted from my family, my friends." Looking at her now, he knew he had hurt her worse than any of his family ever could.

"You didn't give me a chance." Something deeper than uncertainty flickered in her eyes. And then she laughed. She was angry, but only a little. And that gave him hope. "That didn't matter to me. I just wanted you." She lowered her lashes and fresh tears dripped onto her shirt.

The thought of leaving her again felt like a knife in his side. "There wasn't an hour in each day I didn't think of you. When I visited last month, my aunt told me my parents weren't Amish. My parents were Englischers."

She pulled away and looked into his eyes. Her baffled expression slowly slipped away as the truth clarified her confusion.

"I wanted to talk to you so badly. I went to your house and saw your lantern. I was so close to pulling in your driveway, but then I saw you standing in the yard with Jordan. I knew you could find happiness with him. From the beginning, I knew how he felt for you."

"Paul ..."

"I left with no intention of ever returning. I couldn't. Knowing I could never hurt you again and knowing how it would hurt seeing you with him or anybody else. I hated myself everyday for leaving, for not standing up for you. For us. And then you were there ... in Ocean City."

Rachel's eyes brightened for the first time since he'd arrived. "It was you?" Her head tilted to the side. "I thought I was going crazy, that it was my imagination. You were looking right at me. Then I turned and you were gone." She searched his face for more answers.

He drew her close, and her body trembled against his. She stayed in his arms allowing him to hold her. Touching her was something he'd only dared dream about. It felt too good to be real.

"So, you aren't Amish? What does that mean?"

He pulled free the strands of hair sticking to her face. "It means I'm also an Englischer by birth." He thought he'd gotten through to her, but then her expression fell. "I left on my own to start a new life."

She pulled away. "What about Anna?"

"Anna was never anything more than a friend. But that wasn't good enough for her. When she threatened me, I didn't think I had any other choice but to leave."

She looked past him for a long moment. When her gaze met his again, confusion smoldered in those trusting brown eyes. "I thought you were together."

"Nein."

The confused depths of brown narrowed. "But she was the reason you left?"

Paul ran his fingers through the hair on this chin. "Only because she threatened to show the compromising pictures she took of us." Her expression was torn and she shook her head. "You were barely covered with that blanket."

"She saw us at the waterfall and took pictures?"

"She saw everything and, yes, she threatened to show everyone."

Rachel gasped. "Wow!" He could almost picture her questions being answered. One by one. "I can't believe she did that."

"I left to protect you and your reputation, but I was wrong." He kissed her forehead and whispered into her hair. "I should've stayed."

She looked up at him with her beautiful face, broken from the pain he'd caused her. "You're staying in Hershey?"

Paul shuddered as he thought of the moment he had left her behind. "I was thinking about moving back here, to Paradise."

Her eyes were wild from a mixture of excitement and fear as her gaze roamed the assortment of potted plants. "So you can help me take care of the flowers?"

"So I can take care of you." He took gentle hold of her face. "There was one more thing I wanted to ask you." If ever he wondered whether God was calling him back to Paradise, to Rachel, he no longer had any doubt. Not even one. "Do you have a date for prom?"

"What?"

The genuine surprise in her voice soothed his reservations. "Your senior prom. Tomorrow night?"

She shifted uncomfortably. "I wasn't going."

He reached into the bed of his truck toward the row of vincas and pulled out the hidden white corsage wrapped with silver ribbon. "Can I take you to your prom?"

There was no response, only a happy gasp. In a matter of seconds, she was in his arms, and he held her. Then he released her just enough to meet her gaze and tenderly pressed his lips against hers. In those treasured moments, all the love they'd kept bottled up escaped into a whirlwind of life.

$\mathscr{H}$ 50 $\mathscr{H}$

Rain fell relentlessly as Rachel and Kelli spent hours upstairs styling hair, applying make-up, and painting finger and toenails.

It wasn't until the girls presented themselves to their dates that the sun finally adorned the gray sky.

Paul Fischer, dressed in a black tux and black bowtie, stood just below, facing her, his mouth slightly agape. His gaze seemed to drink her in from the moment their eyes met and Rachel's heart fluttered so swiftly, she felt light-headed.

She took the steps toward him carefully, her knee length, black dress swaying with each stride. Her pulse was leaping all over the place. Paul was truly here, truly escorting her to senior prom.

The night was like a dream. Stringed lights dimly brightened the auditorium, creating a glimmer in Paul's eyes. He spun her from one dance to the next in a way that stole her breath and made her eager to spend countless tomorrows together.

"I didn't know you knew how to dance."

He pulled her closer, his breath warming her cheek. "I didn't either."

A laugh of unattainable joy ripped from her at the promise of answered prayers and priceless treasures. Her heart and soul were infused with peace that she would find contentment in every memory, every blessing, and every new beginning.

She no longer had to chase paradise to find happiness. Because she had found something she'd never expected to find, something only God could give her.

A place to begin, to create, to live her life to the fullest one day at a time.

THE END

ACKNOWLEDGMENTS

Dreams in my world are vivid. Thank you to everyone who encouraged, blessed, and helped make this dream a reality. Every time you ask me when will the next book will be out, it's a huge boost of confirmation. Saying thank you doesn't seem like enough.

Every single reader is so valuable. You are the reason I'm on this wild and crazy and exciting journey and you make every moment worthwhile. I wouldn't be here without you.

Thank you to my husband, Rocky, for being so supportive as I spend countless hours on the computer and for always believing in me.

My children Tyler, Zachary, and Brooklyn for loving me through it all.

My editor, April Gardner, for answering all my questions and excusing the weird way I put question marks in the wrong place, even though I know the difference between a statement and question. April, thank you for helping to make this baby shine.

My critique partners who labored over chapter after chapter. I've learned so much from each and every one of you.

And most importantly, thank you, Jesus, for without you, none of this would be possible.

ABOUT THE AUTHOR

Cindy Patterson believes in life changing fiction and happily ever afters that start with Jesus. Her passions include Jesus, her husband, and her family. She's an ordinary girl wanting to do extraordinary things for Christ. In her stories, she loves to give glimpses of how God can use brokenness and make them whole. Her favorite pastimes are spending time with her family, reading, and writing. She reads a lot, drinks too much coffee, and wishes she had more time to write. She loves to connect with her readers and you can find her at cindypattersonbks.com.

DISCUSSION QUESTIONS

1.Rachel had to leave her childhood home the summer before her senior year of high school. Do you believe her reaction to the news and her attitude along the way were as expected? What do you think you would have done in this situation?

2. Paul's relationship with his uncle was strained and Paul's decision to not work on the farm added more tension. Do you believe Paul was wrong to pursue his dream of construction work instead of helping his uncle on the farm, especially when his uncle had provided him a home for most of his life?

3. What did you think about Paul's initial reaction to Rachel? Do you believe his previous encounters with Englisher's affected his perception of her? Or was it the unexpected attraction drawing him to her that clouded his thinking?

4. Who was your favorite character(s)? Why?

5. Who was your least favorite character(s)? Why?

6. Do you believe the book's title was fitting to the story? If so, how does it relate to the contents of the story?

7. Paul's decision to protect Rachel's reputation came at a high cost. Do you agree with his decision, or do you believe he should have taken

his chances with Anna's threat? How would you have responded if you were in a similar situation?

8. Rachel wanted to trust God to heal her broken heart, but it wasn't easy giving up on what she really wanted. Has there been a time when you prayed for something, but God didn't give you the answer you were hoping for? What did you learn from it?

DIVE INTO A SNEAK PEEK OF...

Broken

BUTTERFLY

A Paradise Novel

Springbrook Press

BROKEN BUTTERFLY

Mallory Scott trusts no one. At twenty-two, she's in a battle for her life. Living in a women's shelter after finally escaping an abusive relationship, the only thing Mallory is focused on is staying safe. But when he finds her again, Mallory must flee the shelter in the middle of the night and rely on the kindness of a stranger to help her create a new life for herself in Paradise, Pennsylvania, far away from everything she knows.

Eric Matthews has what every man wants: a successful job and beautiful new girlfriend. Unfortunately, it seems he is living for everyone else but himself. But when chance leads a mysterious woman to appear in his life, his world is suddenly thrown off its axis. Mallory wants nothing to do with him, and he is determined to find out why. Attracted to the one man she thinks she can never have, Mallory battles with her heart's deepest desires. Her barriers slowly break down until jealousy flares--revealing her haunted past. As destiny remains just within reach, only time will tell if a shocking scheme will separate Mallory and Eric forever.

In this compelling inspirational romance, the past intertwines with the present as a woman searches for the truth that will finally set her free.

BROKEN BUTTERFLY~ONE

Charlotte, North Carolina

Pounding echoed through the women's shelter.

Mallory Scott froze, one hand submerged in soapy, dish water. She glanced, unable to stop herself. The door was locked, bolted shut.

Jake couldn't know she was here.

Unwilling to take the risk, she hurried down the back hallway and into the bathroom. She fumbled with the lock and closed her eyes when the latch snapped. Panic crushed her torso, making it impossible to take a full breath.

The banging stopped. Her legs gave out and she slid to the floor as the sound of an unfamiliar male voice resounded through the wall separating the bathroom and den. Pine cleaner and moldy grime saturated her lungs. Part sob, part cough escaped her throat.

The voices in the next room grew louder. "It was Mr. Thomas across the street complaining about the trash container not being moved back. "Whose week is it?"

Mallory pulled herself up onto shaky knees and flushed the empty toilet. The tense atmosphere of the two story house never changed.

The tightness in her stomach eased. It hadn't been Jake. The terror had passed, for now, but would it ever be over? How could she expect anything different? She couldn't. Not when she was doing the only thing she could. Run.

"You can finish the breakfast dishes now, Mallory." The house mother's frustrated voice echoed through the dark, paneled walls.

Mallory left the safety of the bathroom and moved toward the front door. "It's my week." It didn't matter that it wasn't, that it was actually Bonnie's turn. She'd take the blame before someone else was forced to.

She moved outside to the warmth of the morning sun. Fighting the urge to run and cover her face, she walked with steady movements. Each step was calm, composed and contradicting the fierce battle raging in her chest that didn't ease until she found her place at the kitchen sink.

Stephanie, her housemate, wiped the table. "Hey, don't let Bonnie get to you. She's been grouchy all day."

"It's okay." Mallory finished scrubbing caked-on grease from the frying pan. "I just freaked."

Bonnie couldn't help her short fuse. Watching her child suffer to the point of death at the hands of a man she chose to stay with had to haunt her every minute, her every second. How could Mallory feel anything but sympathy for the woman?

Stephanie placed a thin, cool hand on her shoulder. "You're only twenty-two. You've got your whole life ahead of you. It won't be long and you'll be out of here."

After securing the last few bread crumbs scattered across the counter with the ragged dish rag, she rinsed the cloth and set it out to dry. *At least I'm safe.*

Living in the women's shelter weighed on every ounce of sanity Mallory had left.

There had to be an escape. She had to believe that.

Paradise, Pennsylvania

Eric Matthews stepped into the kitchen and inhaled the spices of simmering sausage. He grabbed a cup of coffee from the counter. "Are you expecting guests this morning, Mother?"

She lifted a casserole from the oven and faced him, her hazel eyes deep in thought. Her dark, gray streaked curls lay perfectly across her head. "No, but that's exactly what I should do. Mr. Chamberlain's sister has moved into the mansion. I should plan a brunch." Her smile widened. "Her daughter, Victoria, moved in as well. You have to introduce yourself. A handsome young man like you would be quite the catch." She set the glass dish on the table and straightened his collar. "You should be settling down. Of course, Victoria's unmarried if she's still staying with her mother."

The grim twist of his mouth went unnoticed. Being the niece of the most prominent man in Lancaster County didn't matter to him. To his mother, status was the most important thing. His stomach churned as he thought of the man—of the meeting that could change everything.

"I'm sure I'll run into her sooner or later," he told her, though he didn't plan to play his mother's match-making games. He finished his last bite and hid a smile. If he let his lips relax the slightest bit, he'd blurt his true feelings. Standing to leave, he kept his gaze averted, avoiding the delighted stare she'd give him if she found out he was heading to the Chamberlain mansion.

Eric grabbed his briefcase, climbed into his Silverado, and adjusted the air control. He drove through the long, winding roads of Paradise, Pennsylvania. Two Amish children, standing by a barn, waved as he passed. Deep in thought, he almost missed their bright smiles.

He'd already met with Mr. Chamberlain twice, but today would determine whether he'd be awarded the children's home project. After slowing for a horse and buggy, he turned onto Stragsburg Road.

He arrived at the mansion and tucked the drawings under his arm. Climbing the steps leading to the front, he rang the bell and turned toward the driveway. Spring flowers sprinkled with early-morning dew surrounded the concrete fountain. A butterfly wove in and around the colorful rows of plants, her blue wings gleaming against the sunlight.

Sebastian opened the door. "Mr. Matthews, Mr. Chamberlain is expecting you. You're a few minutes early. Can I offer you some refreshment while you wait?"

"No, thank you." Eric rubbed a hand across his belly, the starched shirt stiff beneath his fingers. "I had a large breakfast."

"I'll let Mr. Chamberlain know you've arrived."

"Thank you." Eric took a seat on the foyer bench. He studied the stair rail cascading down from the balcony. Dark, high heeled shoes sparkled from the top of the stairway. His eyes followed the slim, curvy figure moving with slow, assured steps. Dark blue jeans separated the slender waist line and tight pink turtleneck. Long, wavy hair tumbled down both shoulders.

He stood. Was that Victoria?

Allowing a few strands of hair to drift through her fingers, she locked her gaze with his. Against her deep tan, her blue eyes sparkled like sapphires. "Hi, I'm Victoria."

The scent of coconut and flowers filled the space between them. "Nice to meet you." He took her hand, the pink, manicured nails glimmering under the sky light. "Eric Matthews."

"Well, Eric Matthews, you'll have to show me around. It's easy to get lost on these back roads." She twisted the diamond pendant hanging below her neck line. "Though thanks to you, Lancaster County suddenly looks more interesting." Victoria turned and flipped her hair over one slender shoulder as she disappeared around the corner.

His mind whirled as Mr. Chamberlain walked from his office and cleared his throat. "Mr. Matthews?"

Eric took his offered hand. "Mr. Chamberlain." He grabbed his briefcase and followed the older gentleman into his office. With the image of Victoria smoldering in his mind, Eric removed his financial projections from the folder and set them on the table. Mr. Chamberlain unrolled the prints and examined the drawings.

Grasping the desk's edge with both hands, the man leaned forward. "This is interesting. I like your concept."

"I added two rooms with the extra square footage." Pointing at the corner section of the sketch, Eric's chest swelled with thoughts of the orphans. "I designed a teenager's retreat with an outside door that leads to a gazebo." His breathing quickened. He had to make this work. Not only for him, but for them. "And here a similar place for the preteens."

"What a splendid idea! The effort you've put into these drawings is obvious, and the heart you have for the children is evident in your work." Mr. Chamberlain turned and shook his hand. "I would be delighted to partner with you on this journey."

Eric shook the man's hand with his firmest grip. "Thank you, sir."

As they left the office, he ran his hand through his hair. What if he couldn't pull this off?

Victoria approached from the hallway corridor.

"Oh good, you're still here." Mr. Chamberlain wrapped an arm around the young woman. "Eric, I'd like to introduce you to my niece, Victoria."

She leaned into her uncle, her expression somber, childlike. "We've already met."

"Wonderful."

Victoria's gaze burned through him. "I was hoping Mr. Matthews would show me around."

"That's a splendid idea."

Victoria slipped a piece of paper into Eric's palm. "Call me." She sauntered away, her thin frame swinging with each step.

His cheeks flamed as he turned to face Mr. Chamberlain. He couldn't possibly entertain the idea of calling her. Not now when so much rode on this project.

"You couldn't describe my niece as shy, now could you?" He slapped Eric on the back.

Eric gave a polite laugh. "Thank you, sir, for taking the time to meet with me. I look forward to doing business with you."

"Yes, me too, son. I see us working well together."

Mr. Chamberlain's steady and sure answer hung in the space surrounding him as Eric walked to his truck, his mind racing.

I did it.

He'd been trying to land the account for months. The four million dollar job could be the beginning to his financial security, but more than that, it was something he'd dreamed of his whole life—doing something, anything to help the orphans. And if he knew anything, it was this—Mr. Chamberlain would make sure the young people were given a future filled with love.

Turning the key in the ignition, one more thing occupied his mind as he continued onto the main road—the smell of coconut and flowers.

Mallory tightened her pony tail, careful not to touch the tender scar on her scalp. She collapsed into the sunken mattress and hoped the dreams that haunted her nights wouldn't find their way to her consciousness. Sleep knew no pity.

A rough, deep voice, one she'd never forget, growled in sharp tones a floor below. She opened her eyes, terrified she'd see his face. Her lips quivered, but she didn't cry out. Wrapping the blanket in a death grip around her fingers, she yanked it to her chest.

Stephanie burst through the bedroom door and locked it behind her. "Mallory, you have to get out of here."

Blood rushed to her head. "What do I do?" The whispered question sounded absurd. She'd practiced this scene a hundred times, but the words fell from her lips in a desperate attempt to remain calm.

"Grab what you can. We don't have much time. Jake's outside on the porch."

Mallory stood too quickly and dizziness gripped her. She blinked and focused on the clock. Two fifty am. Every muscle of her body fought against her resolve to move forward.

"Bonnie won't be able to hold him downstairs long, but we can't wait for the cops." Stephanie's voice was edged with warning.

This would be her only chance to escape. Her pulse pounded, vibrating through her head. "Where will I go? It's the middle of the night."

"We'll figure that out when I get you out of here."

Mallory grabbed her worn, black duffle bag from under the bed. She crammed it with her few items of clothing and the shoe box holding her most precious possessions. Jake's harsh tone and Bonnie's high pitched voice reverberated through the walls. Stephanie was right. She had to go now.

Mallory treaded softly across the dark room, her heart thudding with the sound of each squeak of the floorboard. She waited as Stephanie pried open the window then followed her down the fire escape into the back yard. The cool breeze jolted her senses. Tall pines lined the shelter's acre of land, enclosing it from everything but the street. The exterior light illuminated several meters and she wanted to be free from the glow threatening to expose her. Her breath came in short spurts as her bare feet met the cold, wet grass, her shoes stuffed in the bag.

The shock of Jake finding her mingled with disbelief. She swallowed the tremors climbing up her throat as she followed Stephanie toward a leafy canopy blocking the starlight.

A frightened gasp slipped from her mouth as they stepped past the first row of trees. "Wait, shouldn't we go to the street?"

Stephanie shook her head. "It's too bright. This is a shortcut. Try to stay on the trail."

Mallory could see no trail. She could see nothing. The thin nightgown clung to her clammy skin. She scrambled through the pine brush, ignoring the gelatin feel of her legs. The sensation of being trapped in a nightmare filled each step. Where were they going? She clamped her mouth shut, her unanswered question stifled.

I'll never be free.

Mallory pushed past an undersized pine tree. A branch swung back and caught her lip. The rusty taste of blood dripped on her tongue.

Finally, street lights filtered through in random streaks, brightening the casing of leaves hovering above them. Briars scraped her bare feet as she maneuvered through the last stretch of trees.

"What now?" Mallory's voice trembled.

"I know someone who can help. A lady I met at church."

A silent alarm pulsated through her. "You want to go there now?"

"She lives there." Stephanie pointed in the direction of the neighborhood.

"It's three in the morning. We can't knock on her door at this hour."

Stephanie sprinted onto the street. "She won't mind. Come on."

Mallory weighed the distance and moved forward, keeping pace with the thrashing of her pulse. She didn't expect this woman to welcome them in the middle of the night, even a church-going woman.

They ran along the grass behind a row of Leyland Cyprus separating the property.

Stephanie stopped. "There it is. Wait here." After one more glance over her shoulder, Stephanie faced her fully. "Don't worry. The police have Jake in custody by now."

Mallory looked toward the dark mass of trees. Stephanie was right. If Jake had followed, he would have caught them by now. She twisted the handle of her bag to immobilize her shaking hands. Stephanie drew closer to the house, farther from her. The crunch of dead leaves beneath Mallory's feet intensified with each step inching her forward. Sudden movement in the brush echoed through the eerie silence and a hollow feeling filled her head.

BROKEN BUTTERFLY~TWO

After a long day of ordering materials for tomorrow's breaking ground at the children's home site, Eric sat straight up, his sleep-filled eyes searching the clock. *Three a.m.* He fluffed his pillow and laid back, his arms stretched out behind his head. He returned home last night only to hear more banter about Mr. Chamberlain's sister and niece's arrival. He'd been careful not to mention that he'd met the young woman.

After flipping the lamp switch, he unfolded the small, note paper wrapped in pink lines and yellow dandelions on the table next to his bed. The number Victoria had printed in perfect handwriting beckoned an inner yearning he hadn't felt in years. Her blonde hair had shimmered in the sunbeams from the skylight above the Chamberlain's foyer, the light scent of her perfume still lingered in his memory.

How could he even consider calling the bold, beautiful woman he barely knew? But then again, what could it hurt? Loneliness had become a way of life, his job requiring long hours—his well-deserved punishment for the mistake he'd made years ago.

A nudging of gratification edged the border of his conscience. He was awarded, yesterday morning, the project that would ease the guilt he wore like a cloak around his neck day after day.

With strong assurance, he determined to call her first thing in the morning, before he could change his mind.

Moonlight spilled through his window, and he turned on his side. His confidence waned as past mistakes edged into his conscience. How could he move forward, when he couldn't find a way to forgive himself?

A few feet away, a small animal, eyes glowing in the dark, skittered by and disappeared in the burrow of a tree. The blood rushing to Mallory's head slowly dwindled back to normal, and she took a full breath.

A soft light burned through the window. She inched forward with each moment she waited. What was she doing here?

The porch light shined and the front door slipped open. A woman wrapped in a robe stepped forward. She made a motion for Stephanie to come in, but Stephanie pointed in Mallory's direction. They talked for only seconds before Stephanie beckoned Mallory to join them.

All the fight drained from Mallory, and she left the safety of the trees. Each step she took was quicker than the last. She would rather die than have Jake find her.

Mallory followed them in and the lady closed the door behind them, stirring a floral fragrance through the small space.

"Mallory, this is Nancy."

In the murky light, Nancy watched her with gentle eyes. Mallory expected stiffness, not kindness. The lady brushed her fingers through her gray-streaked hair. Tiny creases lined her cheeks as she smiled and reached for Mallory's hand. "It's nice meeting you. I have a spare bedroom you girls should feel comfortable in. Let me get you something for those scrapes."

Mallory brushed a finger across her blood-stained ankles. She hadn't felt any pain. Nancy returned minutes later with a washcloth and bandages.

"I'll help her." Stephanie took the items and hugged Nancy. "Thank you so much."

"You're welcome. Let's get you two settled in." Her comforting voice produced memories of a long, lost dream.

Nancy led the way through the kitchen and into the living room stacked with boxes. Moonlight streamed in through the windows as they entered a large bedroom with a queen bed and matching dresser set.

Nancy set extra blankets on the edge. "If there's anything else you ladies need, let me know. I'll be in the next room. You girls sleep well. There'll be plenty of time to talk in the morning."

Why had this woman willingly accepted them into her home? She hadn't asked any questions. Everyone always expected something in return. Didn't they?

Mallory stood next to the bed and clung to her bag. "What did you tell her?"

"I told her you weren't safe and needed someplace to go."

"And?" She glanced at the door. "Just like that, she's willing to let us stay here?"

Stephanie yawned as she faced her. The soft glow of the lamp cast a strange glimmer in her eyes. "She's leaving tomorrow."

Mallory recalled the boxes stacked against the wall. "You mean she's moving? Oh." At least she was safe for tonight. Her chest tightened and she grabbed the bed frame as reality set in. "Where will I go? I can't go back to the house, not now. Jake knows ..."

"She wants you to go with her."

"What do you mean?" Mallory forced her voice to a whisper. "Go with her where? She doesn't know me."

"I had already told her about you."

"You did what?" Her tone jumped a whole octave. "Why?" Mallory turned her back on Stephanie. Tears burned her eyes—tears she'd fought against for eight years.

"Trust me. You can't stay here. You have to get away for good this time. This is an answer to my prayer."

For a moment, Mallory considered arguing, but Stephanie's eerily calm tone changed her mind. Only one thing she could be sure of— prayers wouldn't work for her.

"Sit down so I can clean your ankle."

The mattress springs were silent, unlike the bed at the shelter she'd slept on for two weeks.

Stephanie squatted and her hair fell into her eyes. She pushed the bleached, stringy strands behind her ear before wiping away the dried blood. "It'll be good for you to get a fresh start. And you'll love Nancy, she's a godsend."

A godsend? God wanted nothing to do with her, not that she blamed him. Only by a miracle had she escaped, but she didn't believe in miracles. "Where's she going? Can't you come with me?"

Stephanie settled onto the bed. "I'm not sure where, but I can't leave my daughter. She's safe with my aunt, but as soon as I can save enough money, I'm going to get her and get out of here. There's nothing keeping you here. This is your chance to get away from Jake forever. You'll be safe."

The events of the night were stripped away one by one, as overwhelming emotions attached to the wall of her soul eased in an ounce of hope. The reality that she would leave tomorrow settled in as Jake's voice echoed in her memory.

You're a worthless piece of trash. You'll never find anyone to love you, because you're not worth it. But that doesn't matter because you belong to me, and you'll never be able to leave.

Mallory winced, the sting of his hand still fresh in her mind. If Jake found her this time, he would never let her go. She sensed the desperation in Stephanie's voice. Her friend knew it too.

She had to go now before it was too late.

Mallory stepped into the dark living room early the next morning, after a few hours of restless sleep. With each creak of the house, her eyelids fluttered opened. With each minute, each hour that passed, she waited for Jake to appear—to take her back.

Stephanie wrapped an arm around her shoulder. "She'll take you to a safe place."

"Get Gracie and come with us."

"It's too risky. This is your break, girl. Take it."

Mallory's stomach tightened. Was she really leaving? What would happen after they arrived? Would Nancy take her to another shelter?

She tucked her hair under a Carolina-blue ball cap. A large, black jacket hung to the knees of her five-foot-six frame. If someone saw her, she hoped they'd mistake her for a guy. Jake had eyes everywhere. She had never been able to do anything without him finding out.

Nancy and Mallory hurried to the car, leaving Stephanie standing on the front steps. Moonlight danced across the sky, casting shadows on the sidewalk.

The fresh, clean scent flowing through the car vents gave Mallory an odd sense of wonder. Dreamlike moments beguiled her, convincing her it was only her imagination, until reality found its way back. Slumped deep in the seat, she stared ahead as the sun rose above the horizon.

Nancy adjusted the volume on the radio. "I guess you're wondering where we're headed."

Mallory didn't answer. It didn't matter where they ended up. She wouldn't be any different and neither would anybody else.

At the stop light, Nancy rested her head against the seat. "I have a cousin who lives in the Lancaster area of Pennsylvania. A small town called Paradise. Have you heard of it?"

"No, ma'am." It was only a white lie. She had to be careful. Just because she had read every book she could get her hands on about the world, trying to find the perfect hiding place, the perfect place for starting over, it didn't mean she had to be honest. At least not today.

"I've lived there most of my life. It's nice and quiet. My cousin needs an extra housekeeper or two. I promised to come and help when his sister arrived." Something in her eyes changed, but then just as quickly the smile lighting them returned. "God may have planned this perfectly. This job may be just what you need."

"Job?" She bit her fingernail. "In Paradise.

"Of course, I should ask you first. I would like to offer you a job as a housekeeper, working alongside me."

"You want me to work with you?" Her voice cracked. Was this happening or had she stumbled into a make-believe world?

"I do. It will be a regular paying job. Of course, I'll be there to help you. His sister and niece moved in with him recently. Let's just say my cousin, Thomas, will need some extra help."

"Yes, Ma'am. Thank you." The idea of having a real job, a future without Jake, settled in, leaving her breathless. This could be her chance to earn enough, to save enough, to finally make her own way.

Only when they were miles down the road did Mallory allow

herself to look through the window. To her right, a young woman tended to her flower garden. The woman's brown hair hung in curly layers just like Mama's had. She blinked as memories drowned out the music.

Day after day, she had waited for her mama to come back, for her mama to find her, for her mama to love her.

The mid-morning sun hid behind dark, hovering clouds as they crossed another state.

Nancy spoke, snapping Mallory back to the present. "Are you hungry?"

Mallory's stomach plummeted as she remembered the five dollars stuffed in her pocket. The only money she had. She needed to save it. "No, ma'am."

Wherever they were going would have a soup kitchen. She wouldn't play on this woman's sympathies. Nancy had already done enough.

"I wanted to stop at this sandwich shop, if it's all right. I'm getting hungry myself."

Mallory nodded. A soft rumble filled her stomach, and she hoped Nancy left the car before it grew louder. She searched for a sign, the name of a city or county. They had been riding for hours already. How long would it take to get there? It didn't matter. Three states would separate her from Jake. The farther the better, yet the single string still tying her to North Carolina still burned through her veins, ripping her from the edge of joy she was so close to obtaining.

A few minutes later, Nancy returned with a large sack. Mallory pressed against the window to keep the smell of fresh bread and meat from making her stomach growl louder.

After climbing into the car, Nancy took a sandwich from the bag. "I grabbed you a ham and cheese sub. I hope that's okay. I should've checked with you."

She reached for the wrapped sandwich, searched her pockets, and held the money out to Nancy.

"This is on me." With a flip of her wrinkled fingers, Nancy kept her eyes averted. "Maybe one day you'll be able to buy me lunch."

Mallory had never met anyone like her. "Thank you so much."

Nancy fumbled with her purse and keys. "There's a picnic shelter in the shade. Would you care to climb out and stretch for a bit?"

That would be wonderful. "Okay."

They sat under the shade of two old Maple trees. Two small girls laughed as they climbed across the monkey bars. They jumped down then chased each other to the swing set, their blonde curls bouncing in the wind. She envied their innocence, their independence. She was here with a taste of the very freedom she'd longed to have, but the bitter taste of guilt dangled heavily in her throat.

A full smile filled Nancy's lips, her teeth flashing against the sunlight. It was a look of genuine happiness. Mallory wanted that. Was it possible this Paradise she was heading to would bring her that?

Sweat soaked through Mallory's skin as they climbed back into Nancy's car. The ground beneath her world shifted and she faded in and out of reality. For the first time in her life, she had something real to look forward to. Then just as quickly as the moment of peace settled over her it passed and the feel of crawling flesh stretched across her arms. She looked over her shoulder. Jake would never set her free.

A NOTE TO THE READER

Thank you so much for reading Chasing Paradise. I hope you enjoyed it and will tell your friends and family.

Please consider leaving a review on Amazon, Barnes & Nobles, and Goodreads. Reviews are so very helpful to Authors. Every single one of them are appreciated more than you can possibly know.

Cindy Patterson

ALSO BY CINDY PATTERSON

Broken Butterfly

Shattered Treasure

www.ingramcontent.com/pod-product-compliance
Lightning Source LLC
Chambersburg PA
CBHW021237060726
47590CB00005B/1790